Beyond Time and Distance

and

Distance

A novel by
Carmen Melnyk

Order this book online at www.trafford.com
or email orders@trafford.com

Most Trafford titles are also available at major online book retailers.

Printed in the United States of America.

ISBN: 978-1-4269-7631-5 (sc)
ISBN: 978-1-4269-7632-2 (e)

Library of Congress Control Number: 2011912370

Trafford rev. 08/19/2011

 www.trafford.com

North America & international
toll-free: 1 888 232 4444 (USA & Canada)
phone: 250 383 6864 ♦ fax: 812 355 4082

I dedicate this book to
my twin sister
for the
great love & understanding
we share despite
time and distance

The Guardians

It was a high-vaulted circular room crowned with a huge skylight making windows unnecessary. Immediately below and in the centre of the room, were seven high-backed chairs equally spaced around a low, circular marble slab. Three fireplaces kept the big room warm in the winter. The walls were hung with beautifully embroidered tapestries depicting the history of its people.

Sean, wearing a grey tunic, was slowly circling the room studying each one in turn. He had a lot to learn being the youngest and newest addition to the council. At 14 years of age, he had been asked to join the Guardians due to his exceptional skill as a healer. It was quite an honour and he was very proud to be part of this elite group.

They arrived one by one for the monthly meeting. Their different coloured tunics simply represented the sector or field that they specialized in. These were only worn at the meetings or for very special occasions otherwise they went about their daily lives in everyday clothes.

Seeing that everyone was in place, the leader dressed in a royal blue tunic, addressed the group and started the meeting. In turn, the Guardians informed the others of the activities, plans and statistics of their area. The general atmosphere got more and more grim as each account was presented with the seven ultimately looking at each other in consternation. How could things deteriorate to that extent in so little time?

The report on trade and tourism was damning. There had been a steady decline over the last two years resulting in a 20% drop in revenue from that sector. Despite all the PR and promotion describing the island as an oasis of beauty, peace and friendliness, people stayed away in droves. It was like someone was turning them away at the door.

When Derek stood up to give his monthly production report, his expression was bleak. "Production overall is also down and I predict it will continue to drop unless some drastic change occurs soon. There has been an escalating number of complaints from both employers and employees; the quality of the crafts and jewellery we produce has lessened and now the owners of the fishing trawlers are refusing to let the boats go out for most of November and December due to storms and rough seas. We had a near-mutiny and bloodshed at one of the docks just this past week. It's a good thing our friend here," he said pointing to Nolan, "was with me. While he held things under control, I managed to remove the greatest threat."

The leader of the Guardians, Dimitri, looked over at Nolan and asked, "What about your area?"

"I'm afraid I don't have good news either. There's a steady rise in reports of violent altercations amongst the people and this past July we had our first homicide in over 20 years! Things calmed down a bit after that but now there is fear and general distrust. The people of this island are good, honest and hard-working individuals yet there's a feeling of inevitability, a sort of hopelessness that is draining everyone."

Dimitri looked at him thoughtfully for a moment. "I understand. I would venture that the very essence of who we are and what we believe in is being undermined by someone or some group – like rats gnawing at a foundation. We need to find out who's at the bottom of this!"

Turning to another Guardian, he asked, "How is the search going?"

"We have had no luck in finding what we are searching for within continental Europe. I will have to go overseas as we are now concentrating on the son," he admitted regretfully as if the challenge was too daunting to face. "We missed our opportunity eighteen years ago for the father and lost her to someone else," he added shaking his head in disappointment.

"No… we haven't lost her," said Dimitri slowly, shocking all of them. "She has found her way here and is currently on the island," he disclosed cryptically, his eyes glowing softly.

They gaped at him hoping he would shed some light on this incredible bit of data but he remained close-mouthed on the subject.

They were all mulling this over when Derek, the eldest member, piped up.

"If I recall correctly, there is a little-known branch of the family on the mother's side that emigrated overseas some twenty years ago. It would give you a place to start," he offered helpfully.

"Great!" said Dimitri. "We have to move fast – there is little time and I want all of you to stay sharp. I sense that our services as Protectors will be greatly needed in the near future."

CHAPTER ONE

The Dog

It was freezing cold. A pale morning sun was slowly making its way up the horizon. Addie stood there and looked at all that whiteness in dismay. There seemed to be no end to it. It had snowed all night again! Every branch was laden with an inch or more of snow and the cars parked along the curb had a thick blanket of the white stuff on them. The houses looked like something out of Candy Cane Lane.

Everything is so still...and rather peaceful. Guess a little peace and quiet couldn't hurt after last night, she thought.

She shrugged as if to get the monkey off her back, gripped her shovel and started to clear the front walk. Lost in thought, she made a path down the middle and then automatically began to bank the snow neatly along the edge. The senseless, mechanical motions eased her mind and warmed her up.

Last night had been another one of those parties. She could vividly recall the scene: male bodies laying everywhere in a drunken stupor, smoke, thick and blue in the air with the TV blaring but no one really watching it by now. The hockey game had ended in a loss for the home team and the five of them had taken it hard needing to drown their sorrow in even more beer.

That wouldn't have been so bad except that someone had suddenly gotten the notion that she was pretty and female. Ugh! She'd barely made her escape to her room and locked the door. Thankfully, he was too drunk to do much more than bang on the door and had given up shortly after. She felt humiliated, scared but mostly hurt, emotionally and mentally. It wasn't that he had suddenly jerked her off her feet onto his lap and had started to fondle her although that did bother her. No – it was seeing her father laugh at her struggles to get free. She could still hear their lewd comments with her *father* adding some of his own. *That* hurt and she felt very much alone and vulnerable. She shook her head to clear her mind. Dwelling on it was not going to solve anything.

Taking a break from the shovelling, she turned around and took a look at the house. It was the ugliest house on the block – literally. Tall and narrow, with a small front porch adorned with a typical Canadian Tire black metal railing on each side of the standard three cement steps, the house stretched out to the back of the lot. Another section had later been added at the rear and it stood there in a disproportionate mess. Someone had had the bright, or maybe dull, idea of painting the house a dark olive green with lilac trim! *The paint must have been on sale because no one in their right mind would paint a house that color*, she mused.

To top it all, the roof sported brown shingles and through the windows you could see some reddish patterned curtains which were nothing more than bed sheets. She had made some real curtains once, she recalled, out of white sheer with a nice lace covering but her father had ordered her to take them down. In fact, he had been quite mad at her. "What do you think you're doing?" he yelled. In defence of her art work, Addie had tried to explain how it brightened the room up and let in more light. Her father had turned bright red with rage and shouted, "Exactly! Everybody can see in our house! There's no privacy! Put the other ones back right now!" He had started to rant and rave as she began to take them down. "Do you think you're some kind of princess or something? What we have is not good enough for you?! You think you're above us all. You think you're so much better than me and everybody else. Well I have news for you!" he continued getting more and more worked up. "This is MY house and as long as you're staying under my roof, missy, you do as I say. I'M THE LAW HERE!" he screamed as he stormed out of the house slamming the door.

Addie had stood there mortified, fighting tears of anger at the injustice of it all. She had only wanted to surprise her father and to make things a little better and nicer. Well! That had been shot down in flames. She had been 15 years old then. Now at 17, things had just taken a turn for the worse.

Feeling a bit cold from just standing there, she got back to work. The best part about these 'parties' was that nobody moved till about noon. This always gave her a bit of freedom which she deeply appreciated. Away from the constant criticism, away from the watchful eyes of her father who, it seemed, was only waiting for her to screw up.

At first, it hadn't been so bad. She had tried to please him and to be a dutiful, loving daughter. She had tried to make his life a little easier ever since her mother had died in a car accident when she was 12. But she made mistakes and he would get upset and yell at her. The more she tried, the more he made her feel that she could never succeed. She had made his favourite dish once only to be told that it would never be as good as her mother's. She tried to keep the house clean but in no time, it was a mess again. She just couldn't win. Slowly, inexorably, she was getting more and more resentful and bitter. It felt like she was losing herself and she didn't like that sensation.

Her solution all these years had been to get out of the house and go to the nearby park for a walk. Seeing the flowers, walking down the trails, hearing the birds sing and just feeling the sun on her thin back would lift her out of her despondence. She'd go back home with renewed energy and get into creating a nice meal or something. But now, it took more and more time to snap out of it. It was like this constant mass hovering over her, squashing her, stopping her. Thank God there was school tomorrow.

Working away, still trying to make sense of her life, she suddenly became aware of a presence nearby. Straightening up, she turned around slowly and spotted the dog. It was standing there about fifteen feet away in the middle of the path she had just made. Nothing unusual about that in itself since there was always some stray dog wandering around in the neighbourhood doing its thing. But this one was different. Addie couldn't exactly put her finger on it. Maybe it was the way the dog blended in with the snow almost like a ghost. Or just the stillness of its body or maybe the way it looked at her out of very deep blue eyes. That in itself was quite unusual as all the white dogs she had ever seen always had pale blue, washed out eyes.

"Well hello!" she said uncertainly.

The dog stared back at her, a brief flicker of one ear the only indication that he had heard her. Addie and the dog stared at each other, neither one moving, as if to size each other up. Feeling slightly unnerved by this silent dog, she shrugged her shoulders – she seemed to be doing that a lot lately – and went back to work. Deciding that the best tactic was to befriend the dog, she started talking, all the while continuing to clear the walk.

"You know, you can't just stand there. You'll have to move when it's time to do that part of the walk. By the way, where are you from? Don't you have a home? Are you just passing through and waiting for me to clear the sidewalk?" she said jokingly.

Addie stole a glance in the dog's direction and was startled to see that he had moved closer. And it wasn't just her imagination or because she had moved in his direction. No, there had clearly been some forward motion by the dog as evidenced by the melted spots on the sidewalk where he had stood earlier. This rattled her a bit as she had not been aware that he had moved.

"What's the matter with you?" she said feeling annoyed. "You can't just appear out of nowhere and creep up on people. It scares them. Plus," she added, "it's not normal to be so quiet. Most dogs will at least bark or whine or something! Did the cat get your tongue?"

She smiled briefly at her own pun but the feeling that there was something *very* different about this dog was slowly becoming more and more real to her. This wasn't just some stray mutt.

Just then, she heard a horrible crash coming from the house. She stared at it in dismay hoping against all odds that nothing more would come of it. That notion was quickly dispelled when she heard her father.

"GIRL! WHERE'S MY BREAKFAST!" he roared.

Addie stood there frozen. "Darn!" she muttered, "there goes my peace and quiet."

She turned back towards the dog, but he wasn't there! She looked around but he was nowhere in sight as if he had simply vanished.

"Just great! Now he's scared the dog away", she fumed. "And we barely got to know each other," she complained to herself.

Her disappointment was so great, tears welled in her eyes. She blinked rapidly a few times and reluctantly made her way to the house.

CHAPTER TWO

A Friend

Addie always looked forward to school. For one, she was out of the house and secondly, she loved to learn new things. The face that stared back at her was a perfect oval shape topped with the most glorious pale gold waist-length hair. She quickly tamed the wavy mass into a pony tail and tied it with a wide white ribbon. Today, she wanted to look good and had decided to wear a white blouse with the jumper that she had designed herself. She was pretty good with a sewing machine, one of the few items that hadn't been boxed and shipped to the Goodwill Store when her mother had died. She remembered watching her create marvellous shirts and dresses out of thin air practically. It was a special time when it was just the two of them. *My beautiful mother, how I miss you.*

Enough of that, she told herself. She had to focus. Today, she was giving a presentation to the Lit 30 class on whether magical creatures existed in today's day and age. Personally, she was sure they did but because of the general immorality of the cities, they would not show themselves. And if they did, it would take someone pretty pure of heart to see or recognize them. Addie put on her coat, boots and adjusted her scarf. Grabbing her books and lunch, she headed out of the door. Her spirits lifted appreciably as she walked away from the house.

She had just finished hanging her coat in her locker when she heard her best friend greet her.

"Hi Addie," Jo said. "Wow! You look great! Are you going on a date after school or what?"

Addie made a face at her and smiled.

"You know very well I never go on dates. I'm giving a presentation to my Lit 30 class today," she explained.

Jo and Addie fell into step and walked companionably to their Math class. Jo took another look at Addie. Her friend was tall and slim and walked with the unconscious grace of a princess. She had the most beautiful green eyes that sometimes sparkled with mischief and laughter. Other times, she would look at you with such depth of understanding that you wanted to blurt out your most inner thoughts and feelings.

Addie was also thinking about her friend. She really appreciated Jo's friendship which had started three years ago when The Dubois had transferred from P.E.I to Edmonton. For Jo, it hadn't been easy. She had been overwhelmed with the 2000 student body in her new High School and had been trying very hard not to show how scared she was. Addie remembered seeing her that first day she stepped in the class. Although she looked calm enough, Addie noticed that her knuckles were white with gripping her books. She had simply gotten up from her seat and walked over to her. All she said was "Hi, there's an empty seat next to me if you want." The gratitude in the newcomer's eyes had been unmistakeable.

That was the start of a simple and uncomplicated friendship. It was easy. She could just be herself when she was with Jo. Whether they were laughing over some recent mishap, teasing each other or discussing deep felt ideas, Jo never made her wrong. That's not to say they didn't have their own opinions about things but they simply agreed to disagree. They just understood each other.

The day flew by and as was customary, the two friends met outside the school and made their way to the mall. It was pleasanter in the winter to go through the mall than walk two blocks on treacherous sidewalks in freezing weather. They rarely bought anything but that didn't mean they didn't do a lot of window shopping!

The mall was unusually busy today with all the holiday shoppers. Only two weeks till Christmas. Addie had already decided on what she would get her friend but right now her concern was whether she should get something for her father. She was so deep in thought that she missed a small step and ended up on her knees, books flying out of her hands.

Before Jo could even react, a tall guy was holding out his hand to help her up. He didn't say anything. She looked up to thank him for his assistance and was struck speechless. He was the most gorgeous man she had ever seen! His very deep blue eyes, thick fringed with long dark lashes glued her to the spot as he stared into her eyes. A picture flashed into her mind of her blue-eyed dog from yesterday morning. The comparison was so presumptuous it made her smile.

He smiled back and asked in a quiet voice, "Are you all right?"

Addie was mesmerized and couldn't seem to make her vocal cords work. Unable to take her eyes away from him, she swallowed and nodded. She felt like she was drowning in a sea of blue as she continued to stare at him.

Jo broke into her trance when she asked anxiously, "What happened? Did you hurt yourself?"

"No," Addie answered, automatically looking at her friend with wide eyes. "I wasn't looking at where I was going and missed the step."

Jo didn't seem convinced and led her to a nearby bench.

"What were you thinking about so hard that you didn't see the step?" Jo demanded.

"Actually, I was trying to figure out what to get my father for Christmas. It's so frustrating to find something that will please him," replied Addie.

Just then, she realized she had never thanked the guy who had helped her up. She looked up but he was nowhere in sight.

"Where did he go?"

"Who?"

Addie waved her hand in the direction of the step and said, "The guy who helped me up. I never had a chance to thank him. And now he's gone."

She was extremely disappointed. She didn't even know his name or anything!

"Well don't worry about it. I'm sure you'll meet him again and you can thank him then. Now, let's go home."

They got up and started walking silently to the far exit. Addie was still dazed – not from falling – but from drowning in those blue eyes. She just couldn't get him out of her mind. *Guys that perfect don't exist. Where did he come from? I've never seen him before!*

Jo was also turning over a few things in her mind. *That father of hers is bad news. She rarely talks about her home life and even less about her father. But every time she has to deal with him, something bad happens. It's just not like her! I'm going to find out what's what tomorrow.*

Having reached the exit, the two friends said good-bye and went their separate ways.

CHAPTER THREE

What now?

The rest of the week passed uneventfully. It didn't snow anymore and she got top marks for her Magical Creatures presentation. She also didn't see the deep blue-eyed dog or guy again. For some reason, she tended to think of both in the same mental breath as the two events had been so close together. No matter how brief each encounter had been, Addie couldn't get them out of her mind, not that she really wanted too, she had to admit.

Addie slowly walked home from school. She was in no hurry to get there. Unlike most people, she hated weekends. Nothing good ever happened and it felt like a prison sentence. Maybe this one would be different. Jo had asked her if she wanted to go skating with her on Saturday and then come over to their house for supper afterwards. Addie was pleased but somehow she didn't think her father would let her out of the house for a whole day. She had agreed to meet Jo at the Mayfair Park open rink at 1:00 but had been noncommittal about the supper.

She was still trying to figure out a way to broach the subject with her father when she walked into the house. He was standing there waiting impatiently in the middle of the kitchen with his arms crossed tightly against his chest.

"Hi," she said.

"What took you so long?" he asked crossly not bothering to acknowledge her greeting.

Addie was surprised by his attitude. He usually didn't care what time she came in as long as his supper was ready by 6 o'clock sharp. She stood there unable to formulate an appropriate answer. She couldn't very well say, "*I walked as slow as I could 'cause I hate coming home.*" No, that would never do especially if she wanted to get his cooperation in allowing her to spend the day with Jo.

"I'm sorry," she said. "I was helping Jo with a Math problem." Which was true enough, but that had taken a whole of five minutes.

"Whatever," he replied dismissively. Then he added, "You have a lot to do so you'd better get started."

"Do what?" she asked, puzzled.

"Clean the house! And I want this place spotless!"

"Is someone coming over?" Addie asked, more and more puzzled. This was so out of character. Even when his buddies came over for their drinking parties, he had never stipulated that the house be cleaned.

"Yes," he growled through his teeth, as if this admission was very painful. "AND –," he added ominously, "I want you out of the house tomorrow! I don't want you around! In fact, you can even stay overnight at your friend's place – Jo is it?"

Addie stared at him in shock. Her mind went into hyper drive. *Great! I can go skating and have supper at Jo's. But what does this mean? Why is my father literally throwing me out of the house? And I can't just walk up to Jo and tell her she's got to put me up for the night. That would involve too many questions and explanations which I really don't have any answers to.* She continued to stand there, speechless and too confused to form any coherent thoughts. Her father jarred her out of her trance.

"Well, what are you waiting for?" he demanded. "Get started and call her now."

Addie moved automatically to the phone and dialled the number.

"Hi Addie!" Jo answered cheerfully. Call display did have its advantages. "I'm so glad you called. I was just going to phone you."

Addie still hadn't said anything and was staring unseeingly at the print on the wallpaper of the kitchen wall her mind still swirling.

"Addie?" Jo asked anxiously. "What's up?"

"Oh! Nothing's up. I was just calling about tomorrow," Addie answered smoothly coming back to present time.

"Yeah…about tomorrow – I won't be able to go skating with you. I'm so sorry."

Addie felt as if the floor had just opened up under her feet.

"Why?" she gasped.

"I have to help mom get some stuff ready. We've got some relatives coming over tomorrow night for supper and I need to make the house presentable and help with the shopping and a bunch of other things," she explained breathlessly. "They're from Spain and I've

14

never met them. Mom said they're going to give us a slide show of their country and where they live after we eat. I'm so excited!"

Jo's explanation and words barely reached Addie's stunned mind. *Something about relatives and Spain. That meant she couldn't go there for supper, never mind sleeping over.* She felt as if her world was crumbling – *Too many things going wrong... Too many problems... No where to turn to.*

"Of course, you're still invited for supper," Jo added. "In fact, Mom said to ask you if you wanted to stay overnight cause the evening might be a long one."

Addie literally felt dizzy and battered as if she was being hit at from all sides. How could someone's emotions go up and down so much and so fast in so little time? It was enough to send someone over the deep end.

"Are you sure?" she asked in a shaky voice not being fully recovered from the emotional roller coaster.

Jo, mistaking her friend's uncertainty said, "Of course! It's no bother at all and it will be fun."

"Okay and thank-you."

"Good! See you tomorrow night. Supper's at 5:30. Bye." And she hung up.

Addie stared at the phone and slowly put it back in its cradle. She looked over at her father already sprawled on the couch in front of the TV. Her eyes were slightly unfocused and she was dimly aware that her father was looking at her with a quizzical expression. She felt sick.

"What's the matter with you?" he barked. Then, not waiting for an answer to his question, he added, "Are you staying at Jo's tomorrow?"

"Yes."

Her father grunted and, settling himself deeper into the couch, proceeded to ignore her completely. Addie was glad he wasn't paying attention to her anymore. That left her free to dwell on her own problems. *What am I going to wear? I should have asked Jo if this was a formal dinner or not. Well, I can always call her tomorrow morning.*

Methodically, she picked up the various sports magazines lying around and the old newspapers. *Too bad we don't have a puppy in training – we could make use of all those Edmonton Journals.* She picked up two more magazines, one on boxing and the other on weightlifting. Looking at them critically, she decided that she had never liked violent sports or those where men thought that having huge bulging muscles was a desirable trait. *It's repulsive - just meat bodies on steroids. I don't see what's so attractive about that. And those boxers – getting hit like that over and over again with people screaming all around them when they're half out of it. It's insane.* She put those magazines in the middle of the pile so they'd be out of sight, keeping the one about the Edmonton Oilers on top. *At least, hockey is team work and it does take skill and art and strategy to win. It's too bad Wayne Gretzky was traded.*

Addie continued to work, her mind going a mile a minute. There was no coordination to her thoughts jumping from one thing to the next. When the timer on the stove went off, she took out the meat loaf she had prepared the night before. She cut out a portion, added a salad and served it to her father on a TV tray. He didn't look up but started eating as soon as she put his plate down. His eyes stayed glued to the TV as if mesmerized by the picture in front of him. *That's probably the worst invention of the century,* she thought to herself eyeing the TV with resentment. *It makes zombies out of people. Armchair critics and couch potatoes without an original thought to themselves!* Sitting down at the dinner table, she started eating not really tasting her own meal.

Looking over at her father, she saw a man in his early forties, tall and wiry with the start of a beer belly. He had dark, curly hair, dark eyes and a constant scowl on his face. She had inherited the curly hair and the height but that was as far as it went. The blond hair and the green eyes had been from her mother's side.

I'd better keep going. At this rate, it'll be midnight before I'm done. She got up from the table, put her dishes in the sink to do later and got back to work.

Tomorrow is another day...

CHAPTER FOUR

Blue Eyes

Addie woke up with mixed feelings. She had gone to bed mentally and physically exhausted. Her dreams, interspersed with blue eyes and white dogs, had been disjointed making no sense at all. She looked around her room. Her mom was smiling at her from the top of her dresser. Cheering up, she noticed the sun was just rising promising a beautiful day. The forecast last night had said it would warm up to -2C today. This was perfect weather for skating. She could feel the excitement building up within her.

She showered rapidly and after drying her hair, opted for one thick braid as she didn't want it flying around her face when she was skating.

The plan today was to first call Jo so she would know what to wear for the dinner, then go to the mall to try to find a Christmas gift for her father and pick up Jo's gift at the same time. Sears had called on Thursday and said they would hold the item for 10 days. Once the shopping was done, she'd take the bus to Mayfair Park and spend the majority of the day there. Then around 4, she'd make her way to Jo's place. Things were looking up!

Jo picked up on the first ring. "Hi!" she said. "I hope you haven't changed your mind about coming over."

"Not a chance! But I'm not sure what I should wear for dinner."

"It's very informal. Come as you are. Nobody stands on ceremony at our house. Jeans are fine."

"Great! I'll see you around four."

Things were going better and better. She got out her gym bag and packed some overnight things and a beautiful green sweater to wear at the dinner. She added her ski pants and then put her skates on top of those as she didn't want to have to carry them over her shoulder when she went to the mall. Dressing warmly, she grabbed her bag and walked out the house shutting the door quietly behind her.

Feeling totally exhilarated, she jumped over the steps and skipped out of the yard. FREEDOM!!

The mall was already quite busy when she got there. She was glad she had finally figured out what to get her father and knew just the store that would carry that. Picking up all those stray magazines last night had inspired her – a magazine rack that he could put right next to the couch. She made her purchase and then headed for Sears. Jo had been eyeing a particular slinky black gown for a month now and Addie in cahoots with Jo's mom had decided it would be the perfect gift for her friend.

With both gifts safely stored in her gym bag, she got on the bus to Mayfair Park. For some peculiar reason, Addie had butterflies in her stomach. The other passengers were unusually talkative today, the atmosphere electric with expectancy.

She got to the heated shelter, donned her ski pants and rapidly laced up her skates. With her bag safely stowed in a locker, she headed out onto the ice. The air was crisp and refreshing. There wasn't a cloud in the big blue Alberta sky. Addie loved skating. She found it relaxing, gliding along the ice, hearing her blades cut into the ice. Other skaters smiled in passing and she smiled back.

The "rink" was actually a man-made lake with a large treed island in the middle. Set in the city's river valley it was a natural oasis of calm and beauty with large expanses of snow bordered by a mixture of spruce, birch and poplar growing in their natural state.

She had done the circuit about three times when she noticed a number of people surrounding someone on the ice. As she approached, she observed a little girl, possibly of Kindergarten or Grade 1 age, crying her eyes out. After a while, Addie realized she wasn't hurt, just very upset about something. A lady was trying to find out what had happened and was she hurt, but she was inconsolable.

Addie decided to take matters in her own hands. Sitting on cold ice for any length of time wasn't such a good idea.

"Come," she said kneeling down by the little girl, "you can sit and cry on the bench just there," pointing to the one nearby.

Surprised, she hiccupped then nodded without looking up, the tears continuing to run down her cheeks. Addie helped her up. The child grabbed onto her, feet going in all directions. It was obvious she couldn't stand on her skates. It took all of Addie's skill not to fall as they made their way to the bench. How she had ever gotten that far was a mystery,

She sat the little girl on the bench and settle down next to her. Digging into her pocket, she silently handed her a tissue and waited. All the while, the little girl remained downcast staring at her skates. After a couple of minutes, she sighed deeply and looked out over the ice.

"I'm Addie. What seems to be the problem?" she said gently.

"I can't skate," the little girl whispered tremulously.

"I see. Well, maybe there's something wrong with your skates. Do you mind if I check the blades?"

The little girl lifted up one foot in response. Addie ran her finger over the blade and smiled.

"Your skates need sharpening. They're as round as a baby's bottom."

The little girl giggled and for the first time, looked up at Addie trustingly out of very deep blue eyes, thick-fringed with long black eyelashes. Addie went into shock. The color drained from her face. It was like someone had just squeezed her heart and she couldn't breathe. Her head started to spin. She was so dizzy. She put her head down between her hands and took a deep breath. *What's the matter with me! Get a grip on yourself* she chided herself. She looked up at the little girl who was staring at her with a perplexed expression.

"Are you sick?"

"No. I'm all right. I just got a – a little dizzy." *How can I tell her I just got a shock of my life? And that I must be insane? And that I'm seeing blue eyes everywhere!*

She smiled at the little girl to prove her point and said, "Let's go get your skates sharpened, okay?"

"Well, I don't know," she said sitting back solidly on the bench.

Addie raised an eyebrow questioningly. "It's just that Grand-papa said I could hurt myself, that I could get cut," she added defensively.

Addie looked at her silently thinking furiously. *How can I get her to see the advantage of sharp blades? I can't very well contradict her Grand-papa. She's got to make up her own mind on this. Hah! A little education on the subject might just do it.*

"Here – I'm going to explain and show you something."

She crossed her leg over one knee so that the blade of her skate was toward the little girl.

"I'd like you to feel the side of this blade gently then do the same on your skate."

The little girl reached out tentatively. Addie smiled patiently, encouraging her to go ahead. She felt the blade briefly with her finger then with great seriousness proceeded to feel her own blades. She repeated that a couple of times getting bolder as she went. Satisfied with her new found knowledge, she looked up inquiringly.

"The edge on the skate is what allows you to move forward and to turn. Without a sharp edge, you have no control."

Addie stood up and said, "Watch how I use the edge of the blade to push off." She went a short ways exaggerating the movement a bit while the little girl watched intently. "Now, it's your turn."

She slid off the bench and Addie briefly grabbed her hand to steady her. She moved one foot ahead but immediately started to lose her footing. With arms and feet flailing, she veered into Addie for support and they both crashed to the ice.

Green eyes met blue eyes cautiously and then they both grinned at each other.

"Okay – time to sharpen my skates!"

Laughing, they got up and made their way slowly to the shelter.

"What's your name?"

"Trinity," she answered. "I'm five."

"That's nice!" *Where's the adult in charge of this child?!* "Is someone with you today?"

"No – Grand-papa and Grand-maman dropped me off and they will pick me up at noon."

"They left you here by yourself!?"

"No-o-o, not really," she prevaricated.

"Go on."

"Well… I told them that my… that Kolyn was here already and that he would take care of me. But I don't know where he is. He said he was going skating too. And I wanted to show him that I was a big girl."

Her lips started to trembled and her eyes got kind of moist.

"Don't worry," Addie said soothingly. "I'll stay with you until we find him."

Once in the shelter, Addie helped Trinity with her skates and took them to be sharpened. She came back

23

right away saying, "It's going to take about 15 minutes. Would you like a hot chocolate while we wait?"

"Yes please, with the little marshmallows if may," she answered politely.

Addie, still wearing her skates, made her way on the rubber mats to the food kiosk. She ordered and paid for two hot chocolates, then made her way back a bit self consciously. With the added height, she was attracting a fair bit of attention.

CHAPTER FIVE

Mystery Solved

Addie stayed with Trinity teaching her how to skate. The little girl learned very quickly and had excellent balance. She was so happy and so proud to actually be able to skate. Although she still fell every now and then, she would pick herself up like a good sport and keep on trucking.

They had been on the ice about half an hour when Trinity looked at her watch.

"It's almost noon."

Addie was stunned. *She's only five and she can tell time plus... that watch didn't come from Zellers.* That's when she noticed all the little things she had missed before – the assertiveness of the child, her precociousness, the seriousness with which she listened to all instructions as if she had to get it right the first time...

Impatiently, Trinity tugged at her hand and said, "Let's go back inside, now."

Hand in hand, they made their way back to the shelter. Once there, Addie helped her with her skates and took her own off. It was nice to feel her toes again.

She was putting on her boots when Trinity suddenly jumped off the bench.

"Grand-papa, Grand-maman!" she shouted running towards them. "I can skate!"

Addie turned around to see a very well dressed couple probably in their early sixties. He was a tall, swarthy man with greying hair, dark eyes and a slightly stiff expression. She was shorter and somewhat plump but she had the same dark complexion, very black hair and dark eyes. *That's weird*, Addie thought, *they're not at all what I expected. How could that be? She is so fair...*

"Come," Trinity said pulling them along with her. "I want you to meet my friend, Addie."

Hearing her name pulled her out of her conjectures. She stood up smiling and shook hands with both while Trinity made the introductions in a most graceful and competent manner.

"Grand-papa, Grand-maman meet Addie. Addie, Mr and Mrs Sanchez."

Then Trinity picked up her skates and exclaimed, "Addie got my skates sharpened! See!" There was a startled gasp from both Sanchez.

"You shouldn't have," she said.

"It's dangerous and she could have been hurt! She could have cut herself!" he added accusatively.

Trinity gave Addie a silent "*I told you so*" look shrugging her little shoulders. His tone of voice raised Addie's shackles. She wasn't going to stand for this nonsense but she didn't want to get off on the wrong foot either and cause some distress to Trinity.

Several were watching the small group covertly but when the tall, dark-haired man walked in from the other end of the shelter, his skates casually slung over his shoulder, many turned to ogle him. He was built like a god, his muscled chest filling the navy blue turtle neck fitted over slim hips and dark jeans. He came to a dead stop as took in the small group, his deep blue gaze widening in surprise.

What are they doing here? And that's the girl from the mall! His heart did a happy little flip. *She looks frustrated about something.* Curious, but for some inexplicable reason not willing to be seen, he approached and sat down on a nearby bench close enough to hear what was being said.

"I'm truly sorry if I overstepped my bounds. I'm sure you are very concerned about her safety but Trinity couldn't skate at all with dull blades. It is much safer to have sharp edges on your skates. After all, one wouldn't want her getting a concussion from hitting her head on the ice due to dull skates."

They both stood there staring at her as if she had violated a world peace treaty or something.

"Thank-you for your concern," Mr Sanchez said stiffly. He nodded to his wife who was busy fussing over the little girl, took the skates from her hands and walked away. She quickly followed holding on to Trinity's hand.

Trinity twisted around and waved. "Bye Addie. I had fun today. Thank-you!"

Addie watched them go pensively. *Something's not right. It doesn't make sense. She doesn't look at all like her grand-parents. They are probably her guardians or something like that,* she finally decided. *But one thing I know for sure is that they are not poor!* Her stomach growled. *Guess I should eat something.*

She got herself a cheeseburger and another hot chocolate and sat down by her skates to have her lunch. She finished the burger and was staring at her hot chocolate deep in thought when someone sat down across from her and commented, "It takes integrity to stand up for what you believe."

Startled, she looked up and met a pair of very deep blue eyes smiling at her!

"You!" she blurted out. "I mean, who are you?" she amended.

"Kolyn," he said smiling at her confusion.

"Of course!" she muttered to herself. Having recovered from the shock of seeing him again she said belligerently, "Where were you all this time? Trinity said she came to meet you."

"She did?" Genuine surprise registered on his face. "I had no idea. I asked her this morning if she wanted to go skating with me and she said she preferred to stay home. The little minx!"

For a moment, neither one spoke simply looking at each other. Kolyn had broad shoulders narrowing down to a trim waist followed by long muscular legs. Black wavy hair topped his classical-shaped face but his most striking feature were those deep blue eyes accented by long dark lashes and thick eyebrows set in a wide intelligent brow. *He is so handsome and charming*, thought Addie. On his end, Kolyn was equally taken. *She is so beautiful! This is the second time we meet. Who is she? I need to know.*

He smiled at Addie and, leaning forward slightly, said earnestly, "Thank-you for taking such good care of Trinity. It is very much appreciated."

"You're welcome," she replied simply. "And I wish to thank *you* for helping me up the other day when I tripped in the mall."

"It was no trouble at all."

The moment of silence that followed was full of unspoken questions. Both seemed loathe to breaking the magic that seemed to stretch between them.

"Are you going skating again?" he asked eventually.

"Yes. I have a few hours to kill."

"Great!"

They laced up their skates and set out on the ice. They were both excellent skaters and made a striking couple gliding gracefully in unison. As they skated, the conversation flowed easily from topic to topic. They seemed to have similar opinions on the world events and people in general. At one point, Addie stopped to readjust her scarf.

"What is your full name?" Kolyn asked.

"Ariadne Renée Cargill," she said her cheeks turning even pinker. "But my friends call me Addie."

"It's a beautiful name and it suits you – Addie," he said softly.

"And yours?"

"Kolyn – spelt K-O-L-Y-N," then added the rest, "Roy of Cebrae."

"Kolyn Roy of Cebrae. That's a very royal name, your majesty," she said grinning at him impishly.

He stiffened imperceptibly and looked at her oddly for a split second then his face broke into a huge smile.

"Well, my queen, will you do me the honour of skating some more with me?" he said bowing gracefully in her direction as he held out his hand.

Laughing, she curtsied and placed her hand in his.

After a few strides, Addie said tentatively, "Trinity looks a lot like you. Is she...? What is...?" She seemed unable to frame a coherent question about the relationship.

Quickly grasping what she wanted to know, Kolyn came to a stop and turned her towards him.

"She is my daughter," he announced watching her reaction with a guarded expression.

Addie stood there nonplussed. It was one thing to *think* it but quite another to be confronted with the truth. She felt crushed, disappointed. Finally, she slipped her hand out of his and stepped back putting some distance between them. Her big green eyes stared at him accusingly.

"Then why are you spending time with me? Shouldn't you be with her mother?" She couldn't quite say the word *wife*.

Unsteady, she turned to go but her front pick dug into the ice and she lost her balance. Kolyn reacted quickly. He grabbed her arm saving her from a complete spill. She was grateful for that small mercy as she felt humiliated enough as it was.

"Addie, will you please hear me out?" he pleaded.

She stood there with her arms crossed against her chest and nodded. Her eyes reflected the loss and pain she was feeling deep inside.

He took a deep breath and started. "When Trinity was born, I was out of the country on a business trip. I wrapped up everything as fast as I could but it was still a few days before I got home." He paused, various emotions crossing his handsome face. "There was a letter. She said she had never wanted a baby and that my … lifestyle was not … good enough." He smiled ruefully and added, "She arranged with her lawyers to get a divorce and has since remarried to a Greek tycoon. She has never been in touch. I employed the Sanchez to care for my daughter when I couldn't be home but I mostly raised her myself."

"I'm sorry," Addie said. "Is that why she calls them Grand-maman and Grand-papa?"

"Yes, they've been with her since she was born."

She looked at him considering all this information and her lips formed into a reluctant smile, her big green eyes shining.

"Okay – we can keep skating," she said holding out her hand.

He grabbed it joyfully and laughed.

"You are a strange girl!"

The rest of the afternoon was spent pleasantly getting to know each other. Sometimes serious, sometimes light with banter, they talked of everything and anything. Neither one wanted the afternoon to end.

"It's nearly 3:30. I told my friend I would be at her place by 4:00," she said reluctantly.

"I understand."

They made their way silently to the shelter lost in their own thoughts both feeling regret at having to end this perfect afternoon. Having removed her skates, Addie was trying for the third time to tie them together but her hands were shaking too much. She was close to tears.

Kolyn very gently put his hand over hers and said, "Let me help."

She nodded mutely, not trusting herself to speak. He tied her skates together and set them down.

"Addie," he murmured gently lifting her chin, "Don't be sad. We will meet again. After all, we've already met twice. It's destined."

"But how?" she whispered.

"Trust me."

She collected her bag and left to catch her bus. He stood there for a while watching her, then went to find his rental car.

CHAPTER SIX

Boundaries Set

Knowing the door to be unlocked, Addie rang the doorbell just to announce her arrival and walked in. She had just put her gym bag down when Jo appeared at the top of the entrance stairs.

"Hi!" they both said in unison. Laughing, they gave each other a quick hug.

"I'm so glad you're early. How was your day?" she asked as they made their way to her room.

"Excellent! I met a most interesting little girl. She was crying her head off 'cause she couldn't skate all because she had the dullest blades on the planet. I got them sharpened for her and then she did beautifully."

"Why am I not surprised," exclaimed Jo. "You are the epitome of kindness itself."

"I couldn't help myself. She was such a doll – big blue eyes, very black hair. She said her name was Trinity. She certainly has a mind of her own."

Addie continued to describe her adventures with the little girl but was reluctant to tell about her afternoon with Kolyn. The memory of it seemed too precious and personal to even share with her best friend.

"Well, I'm going to let you freshen up and change then you can come and help out with some of the preparations."

That was fine with Addie as she wasn't one to stand by idly watching others do the work. She washed up and put on her beautiful green sweater. It was mid length with puffed sleeves up to the elbows which then fit tightly down to her wrists. The cowl collar fell in graceful folds over her chest. Addie took the braid out of her hair and brushed it till it shone, leaving it flowing loosely over her back in gentle waves. The only make-up she indulged in was a bit of mascara to her long eyelashes. Her cheeks were still pink from the afternoon's fresh air and exercise … and maybe something else. Satisfied, she stored her belongings neatly and went downstairs.

As she walked into the kitchen, Jo marvelled at her appearance.

"Wow! You are so beautiful! You look like a princess! We'll have to find you a charming prince," she kidded.

Smiling, Addie teased her in return. "Flattery will get you everywhere!"

She gave Mrs Dubois a hug and said, "It smells heavenly. Is that gingerbread cake I detect?"

"You're dead on!" Jo piped in. "Mom made it especially for you 'cause she knows it's your favourite."

"That is so thoughtful. Thank-you!" she said with a lump in her throat. Addie had learned at a very early age to be self-sufficient and this kindness overwhelmed her. Jo's mom always treated her like a very special daughter. She felt safe here.

"What would you like me to do?" she volunteered.

"Work your magic on the table. We'll need eight place settings," Jo answered.

The place was soon buzzing with activity and by the time the doorbell rang, everything was ready. Addie remained in the kitchen, adding finishing touches to the salad while The Dubois went to meet their guests. She could hear the usual hugs and handshakes and good wishes.

A couple of minutes had gone by when Jo suddenly ducked into the kitchen chuckling, "Addie - there's someone here that you might know."

Curious, Addie went into the living room with Jo following closely on her heels.

Her entrance was greeted with a high pitch squeal of delight and a small form launched herself into her arms.

"Addie!"

"Trinity?!" she said hugging the little girl.

"I'm so happy to see you! I missed you," she said twisting her arms around Addie's neck.

The Dubois were laughing but the "grand-parents" were watching the goings on disapprovingly. Meanwhile, Addie was searching for another pair of deep blue eyes. And then she saw him standing by the doorway. Across the confusion, their eyes met setting her heart beating at a mad tempo. It was as if nobody else existed. She saw him shake his head slightly as if to enjoinder her to silence. She nodded ever so slightly. He walked up to them and gently pried Trinity from around her neck.

Setting her down, he "introduced" himself. "Kolyn... and you must be *the* Addie who made such a remarkable impression on my daughter."

35

He leaned over kissing first one cheek then the next in a truly French or Spanish greeting.

"Now do you trust me?" he whispered in her ear.

Addie broke into a grin, "I'm pleased to meet you."

Supper was a lively affair with various conversations happening all at once. Trinity insisted on sitting next to Addie. Kolyn was sitting across from her with Mrs Sanchez on his right and Jo on the other side. Often their eyes met distracting her thoroughly. *I could sit and look at him all day – such beautiful eyes!*

She wasn't following the conversation too closely so she wasn't sure what suddenly caught her attention. There seemed to be some tension in the room. And then, she caught the drift of the conversation. Mr Sanchez was making his views known on the benefits of a utopian society and had everyone's attention.

"I believe that people should not have to work. A person's livelihood should be provided by the state. This would allow every one the chance to pursue their personal interests," he expounded.

Addie was shaking her head. Jo was watching her intently knowing full well what her views were on this. *This is going to get interesting*, she thought gleefully.

Just then Kolyn asked, "Addie, what do you think of a society where no one has to work?"

"I think it would be doomed to failure," she replied categorically.

"What makes you think that?" cut in Mr. Sanchez almost rudely.

Addie gave him a speculative glance and then turning back to Kolyn answered him directly.

"People *need* to work. It's what gives them purpose and a sense of belonging. If they only receive and never get a chance to contribute, you'll get a society of criminals."

This last bit was aimed at Mr Sanchez who flushed darkly from anger.

Quickly suppressing his emotions, he smiled sweetly at Addie and said, "Well, it would be hard for you to know that for sure since you're still going to school and haven't had to work yet."

It was Addie's turn to flush at the veiled insult. "*How dare he?*" she thought indignantly. Realizing that this was getting out of hand, she looked to Jo for support. Her friend smiled at her and surreptitiously lifted her thumb as if to say "*Well done!*" Addie grinned at her feeling vindicated, her good humour immediately restored.

Trinity, who had been eating quietly during this interchange, said in her clear voice, "Papa works." General merriment greeted her statement, the cordiality of the evening restored.

As promised, Kolyn set up the slide show after the meal and Mrs Sanchez started narrating the story behind each picture. Addie was sitting in a big easy chair with Trinity on her lap. At first, the little girl was watching with interest the projected pictures of her country adding comments of her own. But in no time, she fell asleep snuggled in Addie's arms.

Addie adjusted her position slightly so her arm would be supported. Then, in an automatic maternal gesture, she gently brushed Trinity's dark curls from her eyes and softly kissed the top of her head. Kolyn was watching them with an unfathomable look in his blue gaze. *Mother and daughter – so right, so perfect,* he thought but instantly deep regret and sorrow filled his eyes. *I can't. It's not safe.*

Sensing the change, Addie turned to look at him. She was struck by the desolation in his eyes. Not understanding, tears filled her beautiful green eyes. Mutely she reached out to him. He took her hand and squeezed it gently and then let go. Feeling totally bereft, Addie latched on to the little girl on her lap with both arms, trying very hard not to fall apart. She wanted to cry.

Their silent communication had not gone unnoticed. Mr Sanchez was balefully glaring in their direction through the dim light, lips tightly compressed.

When the lights were turned on, Addie kept her gaze down feeling numb. She didn't want to look at anyone just yet.

Kolyn stood up and bent down to take the sleeping child from Addie's arms. Half asleep, Trinity protested and reflexively grabbed on to her sweater.

"Looks like I might have to take you both home," he said lightly but the deep emotion in his eyes belied his tone.

Trinity was eventually transferred into his arms and preparations were made for all of them to get back to their hotel suite. At the door, Kolyn asked Mr. Sanchez if he could please take Trinity to the car. With his daughter being taken care of, he turned to face Addie.

Somehow knowing that he wanted to speak to her alone, the Dubois gracefully retired leaving them alone.

"Addie," he said taking her hands in his, "will you have brunch with me tomorrow?"

"Yes – I would love to."

"Good! I will pick you up at 11," he said happily, his deep blue eyes smiling at her.

Then, very tenderly, he wrapped his arms around her. She looked up trustingly, dazzling him with her smile. A sense of inevitability coursed through him as he lost himself in the depths of her beautiful eyes. Lowering his head, he brushed her lips questioningly. Her response was undeniable. With a soft gasp, she leaned her body into his and kissed him back hungrily. The effect was like a shot of adrenaline as a fierce emotion overcame him. Shifting his position, he crushed her against his chest and, holding the nape of her neck, kissed her passionately all reason fleeing in the face of the tumultuous explosion happening in him.

Breaking apart suddenly, they stared at each other wide-eyed, their hearts hammering in their chest. Kolyn was the first to recover and he gave her a slow, happy smile. Unbidden, Addie lay her head in the curve of his shoulder taking a deep contented sigh. It was like she had found home. He held her quietly for a little while longer, his cheek resting against her head. Knowing he had to go, he brushed the top of her golden hair with his lips and with great effort, let his arms drop.

"Tomorrow…" he promised. And he was gone.

She gently closed the door behind him realizing that she had irrevocably fallen in love with Kolyn Roy of Cebrae.

CHAPTER SEVEN

Warnings and Farewells

When Addie woke up, she noticed Jo watching her with suppressed merriment.

"Good morning, sleepy head," she said cheerfully. "Did you sleep well?"

"Like a queen."

Jo chuckled. Last night's events suddenly flooded in Addie's consciousness. Blushing, she sat up on the edge of the bed and smiled ruefully at her friend.

"Guess I've been swept off my feet!"

This time Jo laughed outright. "And by a *prince* no less!" she announced dropping her bombshell.

"WHAT?!" Addie was fully awake now. She gaped at her friend for a moment in a daze. Then the impossibility of the situation came crashing in on her. Putting her head in her hands she groaned, "What am I going to do?"

Immediately contrite, Jo crossed the room and put an arm around Addie's shoulders.

"Addie! Addie, you deserve happiness whether it's a prince or a janitor or a three-headed monster."

"But a PRINCE?!" she wailed trying to come to grips with this turn of events.

Jo took Addie's hands away from her face, forcing her to look up.

"Do you love him?" she asked seriously.

"With all my heart and soul," Addie replied fervently, her big green eyes reflecting the force of her emotion.

Jo hugged her. "Then it will be all right."

Thinking of her love for Kolyn made everything simple. There was no prince, no complications – simply a man who had stolen her heart.   Addie decided to confide in her friend and tell her about her afternoon with Kolyn.

"I need to tell you something. I... I've met Kolyn twice before last night."

"Eh? You've been holding out on me!" she kidded.

"Remember when I fell at the mall? Well that was Kolyn but I didn't know it at the time."

"I recall saying you'd probably meet him again and that you could thank him then. Did you?"

"Yes at the rink." She then proceeded to give her the highlights of their encounter. "No wonder he looked at me so strangely when I teased him about his name. I said, '*That's a very royal name, your majesty*'. He must have thought I was psychic or something."

Both girls exploded with laughter. Then Addie glanced at her watch jumping up, "Is that what time it is?! I've got to get ready!"

"You can borrow some of my clothes if you want," Jo offered anticipating her friend's needs. They were about the same size and height so that simplified matters a lot.

"Thanks. I wasn't prepared for all of this."

Since it was the dead of winter, the girls skipped over the dresses and opted for a nice white sweater over dark pants.

"Could I also borrow one of your winter coats – I only have my ski jacket with me."

Jo pulled out a beautifully tailored mid-length coat with fur trim around the collar. It fit perfectly. Taking it off, she draped it over her arm.

Feeling suddenly extremely nervous, she asked her friend, "Am I doing the right thing?"

In response, Jo hugged her silently and then said wisely, "Only you can decide that but a love like yours cannot be destroyed."

Together, they made their way downstairs. Mr and Mrs Dubois were relaxing at the kitchen table sharing some quality time when the girls entered.

Sensing some tension in Addie, Mrs Dubois inquired, "What was all that laughter upstairs?"

"Oh, that was Addie – she's psychic!" and briefly related what had happened.

Mr Dubois then astonished Addie. "You are a very perceptive young lady. And," he added seriously, "I do believe you have the Sanchez, especially Mr Sanchez, pegged correctly."

At that moment, the doorbell rang. Addie smiled at them and went to get the door. Kolyn was even more handsome this morning.

"Good morning, Addie," he said formally.

"Hi!" was all she could say.

He helped her with her coat and then, taking her face gently between his hands, kissed her softly.

"You are so beautiful," he whispered, admiration in his deep blue eyes.

Her answering smile took his breath away. He groaned and took her hand.

"Ready?"

The drive to the restaurant was short. Neither one spoke for some time. After a while, feeling more relaxed, Addie inquired, "How's Trinity today?"

"Funny you should ask. Do you know what she asked me first thing this morning upon opening her eyes?"

Addie looked at him expectantly.

"Please, can I see Addie today? I want to see her everyday!"

He had just parked the car. It sounded like *he* was saying that too!

Addie lost herself in his deep blue gaze. Her heart was beating furiously.

He looked at her thoughtfully for a moment and then giving her a mysterious smile as if he had just reached an important decision, said, "Let's go eat."

They were expected. They handed their coats at the door.

"Good morning, Sir. Your table is waiting," said the hostess.

With his warm hand gently resting on her back, they followed her to a quiet area of the dining room. His regal bearing and her unconscious grace caused many patrons to stare as they went by. Addie was glad to sit down, not being used to so much attention.

Brunch was ordered and arrived promptly. They ate, casually chatting about inconsequential things.

Once coffee was served, Kolyn gazed at Addie steadily and announced, "There's something I need to tell you…about who I really am."

Her big green eyes lit up with anticipation, having some idea of what he might tell her.

"Please understand that I have never meant to mislead you."

She nodded, giving him a half-smile.

"My full title is Kolyn Roy of Cebrae, Prince Regent of the Kingdom of Cebrae," he said officially.

Watching her intently, he was surprised by her poise and composure. He had expected a bit more … dramatics for lack of a better word.

"You took that …quite well," he said unsure.

Addie smiled, and reaching across the table, took his hand.

"Jo filled me in this morning. I hope you don't mind. I wasn't so calm then," she admitted sheepishly.

He laughed. "How much did she tell you?"

"Just that you were a prince," she related, colour rising in her cheeks.

He looked at her curiously wondering what was making her blush. Deciding to leave that for now, he continued with the demographics of his kingdom.

"We actually live on a small island off the northern coast of Spain in the Bay of Biscay. There are close to five thousand inhabitants. The island has fertile land and is pretty well self-sufficient. We do carry on trade with Spain, France and other European countries. The island is mostly supported by a fishing industry and tourism."

He paused to collect his thoughts. Addie waited patiently, feeling that there was something much more crucial yet to come. He carried on in a low voice staring at the table.

"The kingdom is ruled by a monarch – my Father... he is not well physically. I have been working closely with him for the past four years but I don't know how much time we have." Anguish in his eyes, he looked up at Addie.

"You love your father very much, don't you?" she whispered gently.

"Yes," he said simply. "But there is more. There is turmoil in our little kingdom. It is being undermined from within but we don't know who is behind it."

Addie gasped.

"What is it?"

"I – I ...," she stuttered, not quite sure how to put it.

He gave her a perplexed look and repeated, "Tell me... what is it?"

Cautiously, hoping he would understand and not think she was crazy, she started, "There may be people *very* close to your family who are covertly working against you – people in a highly trusted position."

She stopped abruptly not sure she should keep on going. She stared at him uncertainly.

Kolyn was getting worried. It was not like her to prevaricate like this. In the short while he had known her, he had found her very straightforward and candid in expressing her views.

"Addie, I promise to hear you out as you once did for me. I trust you implicitly. Now will you please tell me what's on your mind?"

"The Sanchez," she said looking at him imploringly.

"The Sanchez?!" he repeated dumbstruck. "You think they are part of this?" He shook his head disbelievingly.

Something snapped in her. She jerked her hand out of his, confused and upset. She blinked rapidly trying to quell the tears of frustration forming in her eyes. He had just said he trusted her implicitly! Anger took over.

"Would you drop off a five-year old in a strange park in the hope that she finds her father?" she lashed out. "And would you give her such dull skates she could easily have given herself a concussion falling on the ice?! And what about his views on things!"

Her indignation abruptly spent and not wanting to quarrel with him, she put her head down covering her face with her hands, tears coming down for real now. Kolyn was stunned. He stared at Addie, his mind turning over what she had just said. Addie was sobbing quietly. Coming to his senses, he moved silently to the chair next to hers and pulled her into his arms.

"Addie, I believe you," he whispered in her hair.

"You do?" she asked uncertainly lifting her tear-streaked face to look at him.

God I love her! He nodded unable to speak and handed her a tissue. She self-consciously wiped her eyes and blew her nose. Not knowing what to do, she stared at her hands. Gently, he turned her so she was facing him.

"Addie, I trust your judgement. I will keep my eyes open."

Knowing that he might make her cry again with the news of his imminent departure, he suggested, "Would you like to go for a walk?"

Addie's smile erased the concern in his beautiful eyes.

"With pleasure."

With his arm around her shoulders shielding her from the curious glances, they went to collect their coats. As a true gentleman, he helped her with her coat, gently letting her luxurious hair slip through his fingers as he eased it over her collar. *So beautiful...*

The crisp, fresh air felt good. Addie took a deep breath and felt better. Kolyn, holding her hand was walking quietly next to her. *"How am I going to tell her we're leaving?"*

Addie was under no delusion knowing he would return to his own country soon.

"When are you going back?" she asked shocking him by how aligned their thoughts were.

"We fly out tomorrow night."

"So soon...," she murmured determined not to go into the theatrics of tears again.

Seeing that she was calmer, they turned about and went back to the car. Kolyn started it letting it warm up. His deep blue eyes were soft and tender as he softly caressed her face. She unconsciously pressed her cheek against his hand.

"Addie, I need to go home for about four months but I *will* be back for you," he promised.

Then, losing all self-restraint, he crushed his lips on hers. His kiss sent searing heat through her body. She twined her arms about his neck and kissed him back with equal passion. Her response filled him with such a sense of joy, he thought his heart would explode. He had never felt so connected to someone before and it left him a little dizzy.

Breaking for a breath, they gazed at each other, love shining in their eyes.

"I love you," they whispered in unison. They kissed again feeling strangely peaceful. The future looked bright and safe in each others' arms.

CHAPTER EIGHT

Goodbyes

It was snowing heavily when she left for school the next morning. For some reason, she didn't mind. *It is clean and pure like Kolyn.* So much had happened in just two short days that it felt like a lifetime since she'd been to school.

The day passed slowly. She had a hard time concentrating. Again and again, like a mantra, she repeated in her mind: *They're leaving today. I wish I could see them one more time.* For once, school held no interest for her. She stared fixedly at her books, unseeing, the words having been supplanted by the deep blue eyes of the man she loved and of his cherished daughter.

Her father had been suspicious when she arrived yesterday wanting to know who drove her home. Addie had been thankful the limo had dark tinted windows. She doubted he would have approved of her being kissed so thoroughly before she stepped out of the car.

"That was the Dubois' guest – Mr. Cebrae. He was leaving at the same time as I and offered to drive me home," she'd answered him nonchalantly.

"Humph," he'd grunted not convinced but had let the matter drop.

Finally, the last bell rang. The two friends made their way through the mall as usual. Jo, knowing what was troubling Addie, walked silently beside her.

At the mall exit, she said, "He'll be back."

"I know. It's just hard."

Jo squeezed her hand encouragingly and left.

When Addie got home, her father was already there. She changed and went out again to shovel the walks. She was almost done when the limo pulled up. Addie stood there transfixed as she watched both Kolyn and Trinity emerge from the car. She noticed that the little girl had been crying. She bent down and Trinity threw herself in her arms with a sob. She looked up inquiringly at Kolyn.

"She desperately wanted to see you again," he explained.

Nodding in understanding, Addie said, "I love you Trinity and I will not forget you."

"I love you too, Addie. I wish you were coming with us," she said wistfully.

E-mail! The solution came out of nowhere.

"Do you have a piece of paper and pen on you?" she asked Kolyn.

Smiling, he handed her the articles and she quickly wrote down her e-mail address. Then folding it up in a little strip, she put it in Trinity's hand closing hers over it.

"You can write to me and I will write back. Kolyn will show you how. But," she warned, "this is our secret. Keep this paper safe and don't tell anyone about it, not even Grand-papa or Grand-maman. Do you understand?"

The child looked at her trustingly, clutching the slip of paper in her little hand. She smiled and said, "Our secret."

Addie stood up and handed the pen back to Kolyn. He put it in his pocket and pulled her into his arms.

"My love," he whispered tenderly. "I will be back for you." And he kissed her hard, desperately trying to convey all his love in this one farewell kiss. Taking Trinity's hand, he made his way to the car.

She watched them go, trying to hold at bay the emptiness that was threatening to engulf her, holding on to the memory of his promise and last kiss with all her might. Her heart that had been beating so furiously just a moment ago was now slowly dying in direct ratio to the disappearing taillights.

Eyes bright with unshed tears, she finished clearing the sidewalk like an automaton and went in. She had barely hung up her coat when her father crossed the room and slapped her hard across her cold cheek. Shock and pain registered on her face.

"Wh —?" she began.

"For lying to me, you slut!" he said coldly. "And from now on, you are not allowed to go anywhere but school – not at Jo's, not anywhere! Now get out of my sight!"

Her cheek hurt. She made her way to her room and locked the door. Curled in a ball on her bed, the tears came down relentlessly.

CHAPTER NINE

Home

Kolyn's first order of business upon his return was to see his father. The trip home had been long but it had given him a chance to go over Addie's warnings. The more he thought about it, the more he became convinced that she had found the key to the political unrest in his country. Little signs he had previously missed became bright red flags.

He hurried down the wide hallway to the King's private quarters. The smiling faces of his ancestors looked down at him from their gilded frames whispering *"Welcome back, Kolyn."* He relaxed and took a deep breath. He was home.

Pushing the door open, he was startled to see his father sitting comfortably in a big chair by the fireplace, a warm blanket over his knees. A week ago, he had been bedridden!

"Father!" he said affectionately, embracing him.

"Welcome home, son."

They looked at each other fondly, noting the subtle changes that had taken place. There was color in his father's complexion replacing the ashen grey of illness and his grip showed a promise of return to his former vigour.

Deep blue eyes full of wisdom focussed on Kolyn. There was tranquility about his son that hadn't been there before and his eyes burned with a secret passion.

"You have found her," he concluded.

"Yes." Kolyn seemed to take on an additional glow as he allowed the memory of Addie to fill his mind and soul.

"Tell me about her."

"Addie," he said reverently, "Ariadne Renée Cargill."

The relief he felt in being able to talk to someone who would understand was indescribable. "She is beautiful – tall and slim with long, wavy hair that falls like a golden cloud over her shoulders… big green eyes wise beyond their years. She is kind, honest, loyal and courageous in the extreme. And… she loves me as much as I love her!"

"How does she feel about Trinity? Does she know?"

Kolyn chuckled, "Oh yes! But I will let Trinity fill you in on that herself."

"And you left Addie in Canada?"

"Yes," he replied with a faraway look in his eyes. "Leaving her behind has been the hardest thing I've ever had to do in all my life. I plan to go back for her in four months and bring her home to be my queen."

There was a moment of silence following this declaration as both father and son imagined a future full of joy and happiness.

"Now, tell me how things have been going with you. You seem so much better than when I left! How is that?"

It was the king's turn to chuckle. "I've been under the care of the gardener's new young apprentice, Sean."

"Is he trustworthy?" demanded Kolyn worriedly.

"I believe so. I have never felt this well in months. He brings me raw vegetables daily and brews me the most delicious teas made fresh with herbs from the garden's greenhouse. He can be trusted but now that you're all back," he added regretfully, "I suppose we should return him to his apprenticeship under the gardener."

Seeing that his father was tiring, he wished him goodnight and retired to his study. Turning on the computer, he started typing an e-mail to Addie.

> *My sweet Addie,*
>   *You are in my thoughts constantly. I cherish the moments we spent together...*

The next day, things went back to the normal routine. Mr Sanchez resumed his position as chamberlain of the castle and Mrs Sanchez continued to watch over Trinity seeing that she receive from her various tutors the proper instruction befitting a princess. Trinity was an avid learner and a fast study. She could spend hours looking at books or drawing pictures which left Mrs Sanchez with a lot of free time on her hands.

That evening, Kolyn took his daughter to see her grand-father. She curtsied prettily a few feet from his chair then ran the rest of the way. The king reached down and sat her on his lap giving her a big hug and a kiss.

"Hello, my little princess."

"Hello, grand-father. I missed you," she said hugging him back.

"Did you enjoy your trip, little one?"

That was Trinity's cue. She launched herself into a detailed description of her encounter with Addie.

"I have a new friend! Her name is Addie," she said excitedly. "I met her at the skating rink. I couldn't skate and was crying and she said I could cry on the bench. She made me feel the blade on her skate and then on mine. She said my skates were as round as a baby's bottom," smiling again at the memory.

She continued to relate the events filling in details that even Kolyn wasn't aware of. His eyes tightened as the intention behind the behaviour of the Sanchez' became clear to him.

"Addie gave me her ___," she broke off abruptly looking anxiously at her father.

"It's okay to tell your grand-father."

The latter raised an eyebrow in query. Kolyn signalled that he would explain later.

"She gave me her e-mail address," she whispered confidentially. "I'm not supposed to tell anyone about it. She said it's our secret – You won't tell, will you?" she implored.

The king was more and more puzzled. *Seems like my son is in on it too! Wonder what's going on?*

"Of course not! I will keep your secret," he promised giving her a hug.

Beaming, Trinity jumped off his knees and started to dance, chanting, "I love Addie, I love Addie. She will be my new mommy!"

Kolyn was thunderstruck. Although that was certainly his intention, he had not discussed it with his daughter. *Looks like we're all in agreement*, he thought joyfully. Smiling, he swung her into his arms causing her to emit a sharp cry of surprise followed by a delighted giggle.

"Come, you little minx. You can draw pictures in my study while I discuss some things with the king."

Having settled his daughter at his desk with paper and crayons, he made his way back to his father's chambers. He was sitting there, pensive. Kolyn thought he looked more tired than yesterday.

"So what is all this secrecy about?" demanded the king.

"Before I left, I wanted to let Addie know who I really was and a little bit about the kingdom. I wanted her to understand why I couldn't have her at my side just yet so I told her the kingdom was under political turmoil... She had the strangest reaction. At first she wouldn't tell me what she was thinking which is not at all like her. She is very strong-willed and not afraid to stand up for what she believes."

Kolyn then revealed his and Addie's suspicions regarding the Sanchez'.

"That's preposterous!" exploded the king. "They've been trusted and loyal servants for over five years now."

"I know. That was my exact reaction, too. I'm afraid I didn't believe her at first either."

"You have known her a whole of what — two days... and you believe her?" he said unable to accept that his son would jump to such conclusions from someone he had just met.

"Yes," he replied honestly. "Addie does not lie and would not have suggested it was the Sanchez without cause. During dinner at the Dubois', he was going on about a utopian society and his views were decidedly antipathetic to everything we believe in, the codes we adhere to."

Although Kolyn gave the king more data on the situation, he remained adamant. Seeing that things were at a stalemate, he bid his father goodnight and went to collect his daughter.

He found her curled up in his chair fast asleep. On the desk was a fairly accurate rendition of her and Addie skating together. On an impulse, he scanned it and e-mailed it to Addie.

CHAPTER TEN

Sean

Spring was in the air. Warm winds wafted over the island waking up the spring blooms, bringing with them a myriad of songbirds. The inhabitants of the small kingdom laughed and smiled, going about their business.

But in the castle, it was a different story. The king's deteriorating health was a constant worry to Kolyn. It seemed like sheer will-power was the only thing keeping him alive. The doctors and specialists from the mainland had shaken their heads and said nothing could be done about it.

So it was that Kolyn was handling more and more of the kingdom's affairs. He often came home late, exhausted but he never failed to visit his daughter even though she had been asleep for hours already.

When Kolyn entered her bedroom, he knew something was wrong. Trinity was tossing and turning, moaning in her sleep. A paper was lying on the floor by her bed. Curious, he picked it up.

She had drawn a picture of herself holding Addie's hand on the one side and his on the other. Their blue eyes and her green eyes were prominent features on the smiling faces. A big yellow sun shone on them and a small white rabbit was chewing on a carrot.

Holding the picture with trembling hands, he was overcome with a desolation so deep he had to sit down. Fingering the paper, he noticed it was bumpy as if it had rained on it. Shocked, he realized what it was – *Tears! Trinity's tears!* His heart twisted in agony. He felt as if his head would explode with the pain. He couldn't breathe, his lungs hurt from being squeezed. *Why am I punishing myself and all those I love? Where did I go wrong? Trinity... Addie... My love...*

With great effort, he opened his eyes and looked at the room. *No! I will make this right!* he vowed to himself. Kissing his daughter softly, he whispered, "I will go get Addie." As if he had said magic words, the little girl sighed deeply and relaxed, a peaceful expression on her face.

Meanwhile, in their own quarters, the Sanchez' were venting their frustration at not having their plans move faster.

"The king is still alive but I dare not change anything. He should have been dead by now," snarled Mr Sanchez.

"And Trinity is obsessed with that girl. *Every day*, she draws a picture of them all together," moaned Mrs Sanchez.

They sat there feeling sorry for themselves when, all of a sudden, Mr Sanchez looked up at his wife with a diabolical gleam in his eyes.

"I have an idea. You know that niece of yours who recently broke off her engagement – What's her name again?"

"Marietta?"

"That's it – well she could come and 'recover' here…" he said, laying out his plan. The two of them spent another hour refining it.

"We should also send a warning to that *girl's* father," he said derogatorily, an evil smile on his face.

They slept well that night and the next day put their plan in action. First thing in the morning, Mrs Sanchez called her niece and invited her to the castle subtly informing her that the young Prince was looking for a suitable wife. So it was arranged that she would fly out that afternoon from the mainland.

Then, as Trinity's regular tutor was *unfortunately* indisposed, Mrs Sanchez graciously took over the morning session. After doing some reading, Trinity wanted to draw a picture of her family.

"Come here, sweetheart," said Mrs Sanchez in a cajoling tone.

She sat the little girl on her lap and said, "Why do you keep drawing pictures of her? I think she has forgotten about you. I don't think she really loves you. She is not coming here and you never hear from her."

"That's not true!" Trinity denied hotly. "Addie loves me and she said in her e-mail that she was coming soon!"

Suddenly realizing she had just divulged their secret, she stiffly slid off Mrs Sanchez' lap and ran out of the door, choking back her sobs. She kept running wanting to put as much distance as possible from where she had broken her word. Finally, ending up in the garden, she crawled amidst some flowers and hid there sobbing.

Sean, the young gardener's apprentice, had watched her flight but then she disappeared from sight. Curious, he walked silently following the same path she had taken. He heard her sobs before he actually spotted her. Sitting up with her knees right against her chest, her little arms holding them tight, she was shaking with uncontrollable grief. He approached silent as a cat and crouched in front of her.

"What do we have here? A new flower?" he asked softly.

Trinity lifted her tear-streaked face toward the voice. Soft dove-grey eyes peered at her. They looked at each other silently. Struck by the despair in her deep blue eyes, his heart went out to her.

"I wonder if this is a magical garden where the flowers talk," he continued as if talking to himself.

"I'm not a flower," she denied in a shaky voice.

"She talks! This must be a magical garden! I'm blessed!" he exclaimed putting his hand over his heart and dramatically throwing his head back as he rolled his eyes. Trinity couldn't help but smile at his antics. *He's funny*, she thought.

"Would you like to see some other flowers with blue eyes?" he asked extending his hand towards her. "But I don't think *they* can talk," he added shaking his head sadly.

Won over by this charming boy, Trinity put her small hand in his and he gently pulled her to her feet. Keeping her hand in his, he steered her to the patch of pansies. The pretty flowers with their little faces cheered her up considerably.

Sean stayed with her for about an hour pointing out a flower here, a beautiful leaf there till he felt the little girl had her emotions firmly under control. Sitting her on a bench, he gave her a freshly dug carrot from the greenhouse to munch on.

"I'm Sean. What is your name?" he asked although he wasn't without knowing that she was the little princess.

"Trinity," she replied.

"Do you want to tell me why you were so upset?"

She paused for the longest time. He thought she wasn't going to answer when she started talking.

"I promised Addie I wouldn't tell anyone. And … and I just told Mrs Sanchez," she said twisting her hands together.

"Who is Addie?"

"She's my friend. She lives in Canada but Papa is going to bring her here and she will be my mommy."

"And she made you promise not to tell something?"

"Yes, she said it wasn't safe – that it was our secret."

Sean mulled this over. *They must have met around Christmas time – when I had to take care of the king. That means …she's met the Sanchez! I'm beginning to like this girl – she must have a rare insight into people's motives.*

"Trinity, how did it come about that you told Mrs Sanchez?" he asked curiously.

"She said that Addie doesn't love me and that she wasn't coming here. I told her that was not true because —" she broke off abruptly putting her hand over her mouth.

"That's okay – you don't have to tell me," he reassured her. *I was right! The Sanchez are trouble,* his earlier suspicions now confirmed.

"Do you want to go back to the castle now?"

"No, I want to stay with you."

She was still with Sean when Kolyn finally found them late in the afternoon.

"Papa," said Trinity hugging him. "Sean showed me some pretty flowers with blue eyes just like mine!"

Kolyn raised an eyebrow in his direction. At a glance he noted the boy's proud bearing and his steady, peaceful look as he faced the prince. There was a calm assuredness about the youth that made one relax in his presence.

"Sir, I'm the gardener's apprentice and I took care of His Majesty, the King during your absence last winter."

Comprehension suddenly dawned in the prince's deep blue eyes.

"My father did very well under your ministrations, thank-you. He mentioned the special teas you made him. They seemed to have done wonders for his health at the time."

Sean glanced in Trinity's direction unsure if he should voice his concerns now or not. Kolyn, sensing his hesitation to speak in front of his daughter, eyed him speculatively. The straightforward, honest look of the boy reassured him.

"Come to my office at 7:00 tonight," he ordered.

Sean nodded his assent and took his leave of the Prince and little princess, knowing that this would be a pivotal meeting not only for him but for the whole kingdom.

CHAPTER ELEVEN

Betrayed

Addie felt unusually cheerful walking home from school today. It was the end of March and spring had officially arrived.

Soon, I will be with my beloved Kolyn!

She heard two magpies sitting in a nearby spruce tree scolding each other and some Chickadees calling out their special song. She whistled *chick-a-dee-dee-dee* and they answered back. Laughing out of sheer joy, she skipped over a small puddle of water and, holding her backpack at arms length, twirled around and around till she was dizzy. Hanging on to a tree till she got her bearings back, she then continued on home.

Her father was sitting on the couch watching some sports program apparently oblivious to her arrival. She dropped her bag in her room and headed to the kitchen for a glass of water.

Leaning contentedly against the counter, her eyes focussed on the table. A large fancy envelope with a royal crest on it was lying there in plain view. It was addressed to her father. Alarm bells went off and her heart started beating at a mad rate. Putting down her glass of water with shaky hands, she picked up the letter next to the envelope. *It was written on the official stationery of the Kingdom of Cebrae!* She started reading…

> *Dear Mr. Cargill,*
>
> *I deeply regret to be the one to have to inform you of a grave matter concerning the welfare of the Kingdom of Cebrae.*
>
> *It has been discovered that your daughter has been carrying on a secret correspondence with the Prince of Cebrae for the past few months.*
>
> *I am sure you understand that this cannot continue. The Prince will be marrying a lady befitting his rank in the near future and we cannot afford a scandal to tarnish the Royal family's name.*
>
> *As this is a delicate situation, I trust you will handle it with utmost expediency as you see fit.*
>
> *With respect,*
> *Mr. Sanchez*
> *Chamberlain to the King of Cebrae*

Addie's legs wouldn't support her and she crumpled in the nearest chair as a crushing pain squeezed her heart. She didn't know what to think. Her heart was refusing to believe he didn't love her while her mind was busy justifying his actions. *As a prince, he has to follow…* The letter fell out of her nerveless hands, fluttering to the table. She felt strangely numb as if she was having an out-of-body experience. Her father was now standing across the table from her. She had no idea how he had gotten there. His lips were moving but she couldn't hear anything. She looked at him curiously.

All of a sudden, he banged his fist on the table demanding, "What do you have to say for yourself?"

Jolted out of her state, she tried to form a coherent answer.

"It's not true... a lie... I...," she said staring at him in confusion.

He leaned across the table, getting his face within inches of hers and said in a deadly voice, "Do you deny you've been carrying on a secret correspondence with the prince?"

"Yes – I mean, not really!" she answered totally bewildered.

And then her father exploded! He grabbed her wrist, twisting it painfully. Unable to help herself, she circled the table in an effort to ease the pain putting herself within easy reach of her father's wrath. Struggling frantically to free herself, she kicked out at him in her panic. He let out a roar of pain and started hitting her with his fists. He didn't care where his punches fell. Shoulders... neck... head... all the while screaming invectives at her and saying, "You're just like your mother!"

With a strength and desperation she didn't know she had, Addie fought back. Losing their balance, they crashed to the floor. Searing pain shot up her arm and, mercifully, she blacked-out.

Having the upper hand astride the still form of his daughter, he lifted his arm to deliver a crushing blow to her face when, out of nowhere, a strong force field froze him in position. Annoyed, he struggle against it. Then it came – wave after wave of excruciating pain assaulted him mentally, shocking him over and over. It seemed to go on forever. He couldn't think... he couldn't remember... Without warning, the force field was abruptly withdrawn causing him to crumple into a ball, falling away from the girl's body.

The motion jarred Addie into consciousness. She tried to sit up and inadvertently put her weight on her injured arm. Nearly passing out again, she managed to roll over onto her stomach and crawl to her room.

I've got to get out of here... I've got to get out of here... I've got to ...

The mental refrain helped her to focus. Like in a bad dream, she got her gym bag out stuffing a few essentials and a change of clothes into it. Sick and dizzy, she looked around her room slowly, knowing she was never coming back. Walking over to her dresser, she picked up two frames – her mother's smiling face and the picture Trinity had made of them skating together – and added them to what was now all of her worldly possessions.

She gripped her bag with her good hand and left the room. Stepping around her father's form still curled in a ball, she collected her coat and left the house, never looking back.

She walked painfully, her arm throbbing, not sure where she was going. Just going ... away ... somewhere far... Unconsciously, her feet took her to the park that had been a constant source of succour for her in the past. She felt numb, her mind blank. She walked by the phone booth that had always stood there and stopped, staring at it stupidly.

"*Call Jo!*" a voice whispered in her head.

As if hypnotized, Addie dug out the needed change from her coat pocket and punched in Jo's number.

"Hello? ...Hello?" Jo was ready to hang up when she heard Addie's voice.

"Jo – I'm hurt… Come…get me." Her voice was weak and seemed to come from far away.

"Addie, where are you?" she cried out suddenly panicked.

"Park…" and the line went dead. Addie, no longer able to stand, fell to her knees. She crawled out of the booth and was violently sick. Feeling marginally better, she made her way to a large elm and curled up at its feet.

"Kolyn…," she whispered in desperation. Shivering, she huddle in a ball her coat offering little protection. "I'm so cold." And the tears came slowly coursing down her cheeks.

A big white dog with deep blue eyes suddenly materialized at her side. She felt herself being enveloped in a bubble of warmth and time ceased to exist.

CHAPTER TWELVE

Long Distance

The castle was a beehive of activity. Preparations were already underway for the annual spring Fête set for mid-May. The Cebraeans were laughing and smiling as they went about their various duties.

Kolyn was also in an excellent mood as he made his way to the dining room. After his meeting with Sean a few days ago, it had been arranged that Mr Sanchez would leave forthwith to be his ambassador in some fabricated trade talks in Italy which were expected to take about a week. His Italian contact and friend owed him a big favour and would play along. Sean was to replace him as the King's personal attendant during his absence seeing that he was already somewhat familiar with the required duties.

It had only been four days, yet there was a marked improvement in the King's health and general well-being. Kolyn was not a violent man but he felt a certain satisfaction in laying the trap for Sanchez. *I'm going to nail his hide,* he thought gleefully.

He walked into the dining room smiling widely. Marietta was already there dressed in a low-cut slinky gown that fit her like a glove. She was a tall and very beautiful woman with jet black hair and full lips. Having mastered the art of social chit chat, she kept Kolyn entertained with her descriptions of the social life in Madrid. She was an outrageous flirt and coquette but no matter how hard she tried, Kolyn seemed unaffected. The latter was polite and wisely kept out of her reach. She left him cold, his mind and soul already overflowing with love for his beautiful blond princess.

Tonight, however, he was more charming than ever, smiling and laughing frequently to her chatter. *Tonight*... she thought smugly.

After dinner, Kolyn retired to his study. Waiting for about half an hour, Marietta went to find Trinity. She knew that the little girl spent some time with her father every night before going to bed. She found her drawing another picture – same theme as always she observed, her lips tightening with jealousy.

"Trinity," she said sweetly, "your father would like to see you earlier tonight."

Trinity, who was always happy to spend time with her father, took her hand willingly and together they made their way to the study.

"Hello sweetheart!" Kolyn said as he made his way around the desk.

Marietta, who was slightly in front, fell into his arms exclaiming, "Oh, Kolyn!" and proceeded to kiss him passionately.

Trinity stood rooted there, horror in her deep blue eyes. With a strangled gasp, she turned about and fled the office.

Wrenching himself out of Marietta's stranglehold, he cried out after his daughter's fleeing form, "Trinity!"

His eyes black with rage, he turned to the woman and said in a tightly controlled voice, "Get out of this castle –NOW! And don't ever set foot on this island again!" Not waiting to see if she was leaving or not, he hurried down the hall after his daughter.

He found her in her room, lying on her back staring at the ceiling, dry-eyed. Kneeling by her bed, he pleaded, "Trinity, please listen to me. I don't love her and never have. I sent her away. She's never coming back."

Trinity remained unresponsive. Kolyn continued in a low voice filled with longing, "I love Addie – she is my only love. I will never love anyone else except for you, my beautiful daughter."

The little girl started to cry and threw her arms around her father's neck. Gathering her in his arms, he kissed her and held her till she calmed down.

"I promise you that I will go soon to get Addie so she can be with us forever."

Nodding, she said, "I miss her so much sometimes it hurts."

"I know," he whispered in a choked voice.

Kolyn made sure his daughter was feeling better and having settled her comfortably in bed, left to make sure his order had been executed. Unable to face that woman without doing her harm, he summoned Security. He quickly informed him on the need to escort Ms Marietta Lopez out of the castle and to ensure she left the island.

Left to his own, Kolyn sat down in a big chair by the fireplace, staring at the dancing flames. He felt exhausted. Resting his head on the back of the chair, he let his mind wander back to the promise he had made to his daughter. *I will see you soon, my love...only a few more things to clean up. You were so right! The Sanchez' will be tried for treason...*

Kolyn had no idea how long he sat there when he caught a slight movement out of the corner of his eye coming from the doorway of the study. The hair rising on the back of his neck, he saw Trinity's small form standing there rigidly in her white nightdress, her big blue eyes wide and ...unfocussed. Her dark curls contrasted sharply with the deathly paleness of her face.

With a startled cry, he launched himself out of his chair and ran to his daughter grabbing her in his arms. She was frozen. He wrapped her in a warm blanket and sat down by the fireplace with his daughter in his arms.

"Trinity! Trinity, what's wrong? What happened?" he asked worriedly.

"She's gone," Trinity answered in a flat voice devoid of all emotion.

"Yes..." Kolyn said puzzled, "I sent her away."

"No," contradicted his daughter, "not her."

"Who's gone, then?" he demanded, totally confused.

"Addie – I can't find her anywhere!"

Shocked, he lifted her chin so he could look into her eyes and asked a bit sharply, "What do you mean?"

"It's all my fault! I told Mrs Sanchez that Addie sent me an e-mail!" she confessed, her big blue eyes brimming with tears. "Now she's gone... I can't find her!" and started to cry with deep body wrenching sobs.

Fury in his heart against the evilness of those responsible for all this pain, he held his daughter tightly against his chest, rocking her gently. *What have they done!?...How come Trinity can't find her? What does this mean? Where's Addie? She should be...*

Fighting a rising hysteria, he put Trinity in the chair and dialled Addie's home – *Ring... ring... ring... ring... ring...* The pressure in his head was unbearable. He hung up and dug out the Dubois' number. With trembling hands, he dialled again and waited...*ring... ring... ring...*

"Please pick up," he begged silently.

"Hello?" answered Mrs Dubois.

"It's Kolyn ..."

There was a startled gasp at the other end. "How did you...," she began.

The room went black and his ears filled with an awful roar. He felt like a drowning man. Gripping the desk as hard as he could, he somehow managed to stay upright.

"Trinity knew. What happened?" he asked in a faraway tone, feeling detached from his body.

"She was hurt but she is safe now. She is sleeping upstairs. Jo is with her."

Mrs Dubois filled him in with what sketchy data she had upon which he announced that he was flying in tomorrow and hung up. This time, he summoned Sean who arrived somewhat bleary-eyed. For some reason this young man had become a trusted friend.

"I apologize for waking you up at this time. I must go to Canada immediately."

It was his turn to fill in Sean and then, putting his hands on the young boy's shoulders, he said seriously, "I trust you. I need you to watch over Trinity while I

73

am gone. I do not want her left in the castle alone under the care of Mrs Sanchez. Take her to your own home if you have to but keep her safe for me."

"Sir, I will keep her safe. I would give my life for her," he promised.

Waking up his daughter who had somehow cried herself to sleep, Kolyn informed her that Addie was at Jo's house omitting the rest of the details and then asked her if she would be willing to stay with Sean while he went to Canada to get her.

With an understanding far beyond her age, she said, "I will stay with Sean while you take care of Addie."

Smiling wisely, she took Sean's hand. Father and Guardian stared at her in amazement.

Chapter Thirteen

Protected

Kolyn entered the bedroom quietly where Addie was sleeping. His heart twisted when he saw her beautiful face so bruised and battered. Her left arm lay across her stomach, the wrist in a bandage. Very gently, he caressed her cheek, tears forming in his eyes. Shame and remorse at not being there to protect her burned his mind.

Just then, Addie opened her eyes and saw him. Tremendous joy and love poured out of her eyes as she reached toward him only to let her arm drop, the light in her eyes extinguished. *He's marrying someone befitting his rank...*

"Addie, my love...," he started to say but she turned away silently. Distraught, not knowing what to do, he whispered, "I love you!"

He stood there uncertainly for a moment and as silently as before walked out of the room.

Jo met him halfway up the stairs. Taking one look at his ravaged expression, she led him to the kitchen and sat him down. She poured him a cup of coffee, settled herself in the chair across from him and waited. Minutes went by before Kolyn finally looked up at her with anguished eyes.

"Tell me what happened."

"I'm not sure what happened exactly except that she called me from a phone booth and we found her in the park. I think her father beat her. Her wrist is badly sprained but not broken. Dad and I will be going over there today to get her belongings."

"I'm going too!" he declared.

Jo shook her head, not sure that was such a good idea. Picking up on her train of thought, he said, "I'll behave – I just want to know what happened."

"Okay, we could use an extra hand," she agreed smiling.

Half an hour later, equipped with boxes and empty suitcases that she had somehow rounded up from their basement, they drove to Addie's former home. The door was unlocked so they just walked in. Mr Cargill got up from the couch when they entered.

He looked at them vacantly, smiled and said pleasantly, "Would you like some coffee or tea?"

Not waiting for their answer, he tottered over to the kitchen counter and set the water boiling.

All three stared at him in bewilderment. Mr Dubois made a circular motion by his head, nodding in the direction of Mr Cargill. Not wanting to stay in this crazy house any longer than necessary, Jo headed toward Addie's room, her father close behind.

Kolyn stood there looking around the room curiously when his eye caught something familiar on the kitchen table – *his royal crest* on a piece of paper! Picking up the stationery with unsteady hands, he silently read the deadly missive with mounting rage.

"I'M GOING TO KILL HIM!" he roared brandishing the letter like a sword.

Alarmed, Jo and Mr Dubois rushed out of Addie's room intent on preventing the intended homicide. Mr Cargill was cowering in the corner of the kitchen but Kolyn was nowhere near him.

"Kolyn, what is it?" inquired Mr Dubois anxiously.

"THIS!" he exploded handing the letter over so he could read it.

Jo, reading over his shoulder, said softly, "That explains everything," earning herself some curious stares. "We'll talk later. Let's get this done and get out of here."

Everyone was in total agreement and with all three pitching in, made short order of Addie's few belongings.

When they got home, Addie was curled up in a big chair by the fireplace, sipping warm tomato soup.

"Hey, sleepy head," Jo greeted her with a friendly hug. "Glad to see you're up. How are you doing?"

"Better – I got hungry, so that's a good sign, right?"

"You bet! We got all your stuff from your room."

"Great!" she said closing the subject. Then, as if in afterthought, asked, "Did you get my bag from the park?"

"Yes, last night."

"Thank-you."

Kolyn, hovering in the background, was extremely concerned. This short conversation seemed to have taken a lot out of her. *She seems so subdued... and she won't look at me.* Not wanting to add to her stress, he made his way to the kitchen and collapsed in the nearest chair holding his head in his hands.

"She is a tough girl – she will be alright," said Mrs Dubois patting his shoulder sympathetically.

"Thank-you for all you've done for her," he said gratefully.

"She is like a daughter to me," she said fiercely, "and I won't let anyone else hurt her!"

Catching her drift, Kolyn looked at her seriously and vouched, "I will never hurt her – I love her with all my heart. I wish to make her my wife ...if she'll have me."

Mrs Dubois laughed. "You two star-crossed lovers! Of course, she'll have you – she loves you too! She only needs a little bit of time right now."

Feeling extremely reassured, Kolyn hugged her and went to find Addie. *There's time enough to sort out all this mess. Now I just need to talk to her.* He walked into the living room and sat in a chair facing hers. For the longest time they just looked at each other. Gazing in those deep blue eyes, Addie smiled as she remembered something. Kolyn smiled back raising an eyebrow.

"The first time we met, you reminded me of a dog I had seen the previous day," she said startling him.

"A dog?!" he repeated not sure if this was good or bad.

"A big white dog with deep blue eyes – just like yours!" she clarified.

Kolyn was dumbfounded. *She has seen one of our Guardians!*

"And," she continued, "I saw him again when I was hurt in the park. He kept me from freezing to death."

Too stunned to speak, he stared at her. *They are also protecting her!* The relief he felt was so great, tears formed in his eyes.

Alarmed, Addie asked anxiously, "Kolyn, what's wrong? Don't you believe me?" *Does he think I lost my mind?*

"I do!" Suddenly feeling like laughing and dancing, he took her face tenderly between his hands and kissed her. Joy written all over his face, he said, "Addie, my love, we are meant to be together. Tomorrow, when you are stronger, I will help you get over this traumatic experience and then I will tell you some more things about Cebrae."

This time when he kissed her, she abandoned herself to his lips, love shining in her eyes.

CHAPTER FOURTEEN

Cebrae

Addie was stiff and sore the next day. She had just managed to get herself in a sitting position on the edge of the bed when Jo entered the room, a plastic bag and tape in hand.

"Good morning. I thought you might want to take a hot shower this morning so I got these to cover your arm."

"You must have read my mind – I'm so stiff today. I didn't know I had so many body parts!" she said getting to her feet with effort.

Jo looked at Addie critically while she fitted the plastic bag over the bandage.

"There you go, my rainbow-coloured friend," she teased gently. "When you're done, breakfast and Kolyn are waiting for you."

Blushing, Addie hurried to take her shower. The warm water relaxed her tense, aching muscles and after a while she decided to wash her hair. Feeling clean for the first time in days, she dried herself as best she could and got dressed. Her long, thick hair hung wetly down her back. Grabbing a brush, she headed downstairs.

Embarrassed, she handed the brush to Jo but then Kolyn stood up reaching toward it. "May I?"

Blushing furiously, Addie sat there stiffly deploring her lack of independence. However, under Kolyn's gentle ministrations, she soon relaxed finding that she quite enjoyed this ...this sensuous feeling. His hands caressing her hair from crown to tip evoked strange butterfly sensations in the pit of her stomach.

"Sometimes, I brush Trinity's hair."

"How's our little girl?" she asked unconsciously linking them all together.

"She's fine. I spoke to her this morning. She can't wait to see you again."

Then in a curiously strange voice, he added, "You two have a very special bond." Lost in the horror of that night, he continued in a faraway tone, "She came to my study the night you were hurt totally distraught and said 'She's gone – I can't *find* her.' That's how I knew something had happened." His voice broke with emotion.

Wordlessly, Addie stood up and wrapped her good arm around Kolyn wanting to ease his pain and sorrow. He held her possessively against his chest, his throat tight and kissed the top of her head very tenderly.

"I don't know what I would have done if I had lost you, my love."

The Dubois stood there mesmerized by the poignancy of the scene unfolding before them. Then, reality asserting itself, Jo exclaimed, "I'm starved – let's eat!"

After their late breakfast, Addie and Kolyn made their way hand in hand to the nearby park. It was an unusually warm day, the sun beating down on them. They walked silently each lost in their own thoughts. Having reached a secluded park bench, Kolyn made sure she was seated comfortably and settling himself down next to her said, "Tell me what happened the night you were hurt."

"I was in a really good mood and when I got home I saw the letter. My father grabbed my wrist and then we fought. I left the house and called Jo. They came and got me," she answered sketchily.

"What does the letter say?" he asked softly.

Bit by bit, he pulled the details of that horrid night – her shock on reading the letter, her pain, her panic, her struggle with her father, her flight, her despair. Addie went over the events several times in a detached sort of tone but Kolyn could sense that there was something else troubling her.

"Has your father ever hit you before this?"

"The day you left," she admitted and as the memory came crashing back in full force she broke down in body wrenching sobs, the floodgates wide open.

Kolyn sat there quietly, letting her grief run its course. After some time, he quietly handed her a tissue.

Addie looked up and gave him a shaky smile. "I thought my heart would break. When my father slapped me, I was surprised I could still feel anything."

Looking around at her surroundings, she was amazed at how bright the trees and grass seemed to be. It was like she had just been given a new lease on life. Smiling, she jumped up and, stretching out her good arm, spun on herself once.

She stopped in front of Kolyn and said seriously, "I feel much better. Thank-you for listening." Her beautiful green eyes were warm and soft.

Grinning from ear to ear, he pulled her onto his lap and gently kissed her bruised face. *My Addie is back!*

"Let's walk and I will tell you about our magical island."

Side by side, they followed the winding trails of the park, Addie listening intently as Kolyn began.

"The isle of Cebrae was first discovered about 2000 years ago by some very powerful magi seeking refuge from the insanities of their government. Organizing themselves, they formed a secret council of seven which came to be known as The Guardians to the initiate. Their goal was to form a society free from the barbarities of man toward his own kind. It was decided that the island would be ruled by a benevolent monarchy and so the tradition began. Upon the first King's coronation, The Guardians, as a symbol of their support and protection, presented him with a big white dog with deep blue eyes."

Addie gasped turning her beautiful green eyes to look at Kolyn in wonder. The import of what he had just divulged was not lost on her.

"That's right. They have been protecting you," he said somewhat possessively. "The dogs are simply a form The Guardians assume in extreme emergencies and are rarely seen by the general populace but *never* before by someone outside the realm of the kingdom."

Stunned, Addie stopped dead in her tracks. *"Why me?"* she wondered silently.

"I don't know…," Kolyn said slowly in answer to her unspoken question.

There was a moment of silence as he held her in his arms, then very tenderly he caressed her face, his deep blue eyes shining with passion.

"I don't know," he repeated, "but now that I have you with me, I don't plan to ever leave you again. Addie… will you stay with me forever? Will you be my beloved wife?"

Addie felt as if her soul had just taken flight, soaring to unimaginable heights, her heart expanding to the limits of the universe. With all her love shining in her beautiful green eyes, she gave him the only possible answer – a simple "Yes!"

Mindful of her injured wrist, Kolyn kissed her passionately, releasing all of the pent up emotions of the past few months. The power of their love consumed them as they gave up body and soul to each other.

CHAPTER FIFTEEN

The Truth

Jo, sitting in a big chair with her legs curled under her, was attempting to read a book in an effort to pass the time until Addie and Kolyn returned but she was so distracted thinking of them that the words just danced around on the page. Disgusted, she got up and wandered aimlessly around the house. *What's taking them so long? I hope everything is fine.* She picked up the hairbrush that had been left lying in the kitchen and made her way upstairs to put it back in its rightful place.

She had just reached the top of the stairs, when she heard the door open. Flinging the brush onto the bed, she ran downstairs taking them two by two. She was just in time to see Kolyn give Addie a long kiss.

"Ooh…," she murmured coming to an abrupt stop.

Breaking apart, they turned as one to look at her. She was struck speechless by the tremendous happiness and peace emanating from them. Then Addie, breaking her link with Kolyn, smiled mysteriously and gave her a big hug.

"Jo, how would you like to be my bridesmaid?"

It only took her a split second to put two and two together.

"Addie – I'm so happy for you! Congratulations!" she said crushing her friend in a bear hug.

"Ow!" admonished Addie, rubbing her wrist.

"Sorry." But her exuberance knew no bounds. "Mom, Dad! Addie and Kolyn are getting married," she yelled running into the kitchen.

Kolyn watched her indulgently, loving her free, uninhibited spirit. *I'm glad Addie has such a good friend. It's unfortunate they will be separated soon. But... that can change...* he decided already formulating a plan in his head. A secret smile on his lips, he took Addie's hand and led her to the living room.

That night, they celebrated. After the girls had gone to bed, Kolyn stayed up for a long time talking to Mr and Mrs Dubois… They booked their flight for the next day. Kolyn was anxious to return to the kingdom as soon as possible. There were a few loose ends that needed to be taken care of.

They arrived to the Isle of Cebrae late in the evening. Addie went straight to the room that had been prepared for her, exhausted. Despite that, she marvelled at the beauty and warmth of the castle but mostly at the kindness with which she was treated by the staff that were there to welcome them. Feeling totally secure, she fell into a deep healing sleep.

Kolyn, the infamous letter in his breast pocket, made his way to his father's quarters. *There is something I can do tonight. The sooner these vipers are off this island, the better I will feel.* Pushing the door open, he saw Sean sitting with his father head bent over a chess board. *Good they are both here.* His father, a tea in hand, appeared quite healthy and relaxed.

"Father," said Kolyn giving him a hug and turning to Sean shook his hand raising an eyebrow in query. Shaking his head imperceptibly, Sean said, "Welcome back, Sir!"

With the preliminaries and the small talk over, Kolyn announced, "I have brought Addie back with me." Pausing, trying to figure out how best to put this, he finally blurted, "She was savagely beaten by her father as a result of a letter sent from this castle."

Sitting up straight, the King demanded, "Do you have proof of this?"

Silently, Kolyn pulled out the letter and handed it to his father. The King put his tea on the table and started reading, his eyes narrowing to slits as he got to the signature. He looked at his son for the longest time.

"Tell me what happened."

Kolyn started at the beginning, telling of Trinity's distress, his frantic efforts to locate her, Addie's fight with her father, her escape to the park and the call to Jo.

"If it hadn't been for the protection of *our* Guardians, she'd be DEAD!" he declared forcefully.

"Our Guardians protected her!" The King's mouth was hanging slightly open in his surprise.

"Yes, but the strangest part is that her father seems to have gone a bit daft. He's not all there anymore."

Sean stiffened and Kolyn shot him a suspicious glance. *He knew ...but not that part!* His father reached for his tea and took a long slow sip.

"What else is there?" he asked expecting the worse.

"Father, how is your health?"

"I'm fine. I won't keel over by whatever you have to say. In fact, since Sean has been plying me with his excellent teas, I feel quite well."

Kolyn nodded at Sean, giving him the floor. The King didn't miss the silent interchange and looked expectantly at the young man.

"Sir, you were being poisoned slowly," Sean announced gravely.

This time, the King blanched visibly the truth staring him in the face. He struggled with his emotions.

"He will be hung for TREASON!" he declared loudly. "But what about Mrs Sanchez?"

"She is just as guilty working to alienate my daughter from Addie and myself." He then filled him in on the niece and their plotting.

"Then it's decided. I will have them arrested first thing tomorrow morning and they will be punished for their crimes against the Kingdom of Cebrae. Now leave me," he ordered.

Back in his study, Kolyn looked at Sean kindly.

"You are a Guardian," he stated respectfully, sure of his knowledge.

Sean nodded and said, "At your service, my Prince."

"Thank-you for watching over the King and my little princess. You have done well."

They each went their way, Kolyn at peace with himself. An irresistible urge to see Addie one more time today guided his footsteps. She was fast asleep, her golden hair spilling across the pillow. He kissed her softly and whispered, "I love you."

Her lips curled into a tender smile. Groaning with desire, he pulled himself away from the bed and headed to his quarters. In no time, he was fast asleep dreaming of beautiful green eyes.

CHAPTER SIXTEEN

Reunited

Sean took Trinity's hand as they made their way to the castle from his parent's house. This had been the normal routine for the past few days.

"Are you going to show me some more bugs today?" she asked enthusiastically.

"We'll see… maybe later…," he replied evasively, "but first, breakfast for the little princess."

He knew Kolyn was already there waiting for his daughter and he was looking forward to seeing her reaction. The love between the prince and his daughter was really something special to see. *I can't wait to meet Addie! The bond between those three is very powerful…*

Entering the breakfast room, Trinity spotted her father immediately.

"Papa!" running to him as fast as she could. He scooped her up and hugged her tightly.

"Hello sweetheart," he said lovingly, "how have you been?"

"Fine! I spent a lot of time in the garden with Sean. He knows ALL the bugs and he gave me some pretty flowers for… my… room …," she trailed off looking around as if searching for someone. Her deep blue eyes clouded over in disappointment as she asked in a small voice, "Where's Addie? You said you were going to get her!"

"Relax pumpkin," Kolyn said reassuringly. Making his eyes big and round, he whispered conspiratorially, "She's sleeping."

The relief that exuded from his daughter was almost tangible but it was the glow surrounding Kolyn that arrested Sean's attention. It seemed to expand out from him and fill the room. He suddenly felt warm and peaceful. *Wow! I don't think even the Guardians have seen this before. I'm really looking forward to seeing them together.*

"Please, Papa, may I see her, please?" Trinity begged.

"Of course!" he said taking her hand and leading her down the hall to Addie's room. "You will need to be gentle with her because she was hurt and her arm is in a bandage."

When they entered the room, Addie was still sleeping.

"You can sit in this big chair and wait till she wakes up, okay?" he whispered.

Trinity nodded. He picked her up, sat her in the chair and made his way out of the room. He was sure his daughter would not have the patience to sit there and wait but rather would take matters in her own hands. Having no intention of missing this reunion, he backtracked silently staying out of sight and was just in time to see Trinity slide off the chair and walk over to Addie.

Getting her mouth close to her ear, she whispered, "Wake up!"

Addie was either a very light sleeper or she was ready to wake up but when she heard Trinity's imperial command, her eyes opened. Big blue eyes were peering at her anxiously. Slightly disoriented, she quickly glanced around the room – *Right! I'm in the castle!* Sitting up rapidly, she extended her good arm toward the anxious child. "Trinity!" she croaked, her voice thick with emotion.

Needing no further encouragement, the latter scrambled onto the bed and wound her arms tightly around Addie's neck. With her one arm, Addie hugged her back, kissing her hair, her cheeks, her nose…

"My beautiful little girl! How I missed you!"

"Me too!" said Trinity fervently. "Are you going to stay with us forever now?"

"Yes, forever…," and hugged her again.

Kolyn, feeling his heart would explode if he didn't do something about it, entered the room. Sitting on the edge of the bed, he took both of them in his arms, kissing each in turn. They held each other, two dark heads and a golden one, forming an unbreakable triangle.

Sean, who had been despatched by the King to deliver an urgent message, was waiting for the Prince at the end of the hall. He noticed a strange glow coming from the room, pulsing, expanding and reaching out into the castle…

"Whoa! …I've got to let the Council know…" Thrilled beyond belief, he got up to do just that, forgetting for the moment the message he was supposed to relay. Just then, Kolyn and Trinity came out of the room reminding

him of his duty. *They are so happy!* He couldn't help but stare at them, a bit wistful of their happiness.

Perceiving his state of mind, Kolyn said, "One day you too will find great happiness."

"Strange as this may sound, I believe you, Sir," Sean said grinning.

Then he handed the sealed despatch to Kolyn saying, "The King needs to see you right away. The birds have flown the coop."

Born to command, Kolyn strode down the hall to the King's quarters after having rung for a maid to care for Trinity's breakfast and another to inform Addie that he would meet her later in the garden.

Chapter Seventeen

Alliances

Kolyn found Addie in the garden. She was walking slowly, her long hair fluttering in the breeze as if it had a life of its own. He watched her bend down to pick a daisy and then the petals started coming off one by one. Smiling, knowing exactly what she was saying to herself, he crept up stealthily and caught her in his arms. She let out a startled yelp.

"He loves her!" he said finishing off for her.

"Kolyn!" she said arching her neck and resting her head onto his shoulder.

"He loves her very much," he repeated nuzzling her neck.

Giggling, Addie twisted in his arms to face him. "And I love you, my handsome Prince," she countered locking her arms around his neck.

He kissed her hard, his hand tangled in her hair at the nape. "You are so beautiful, my lovely Addie and ... so desirable!" he whispered, pressing her closer against him. A warm sensation travelled through his body as he gazed into her beautiful green eyes. Reluctantly, he released her and taking her hand, said, "Come, I need to brief you on some new developments."

The way he said that made her feel totally included in his life and some of her uncertainty as to what her role would consist of in this relationship went by the wayside.

"The Sanchez have escaped and are nowhere to be found on the island."

"I'm not surprised. I bet they left as soon as they found out we were coming back," she declared.

Shocked, Kolyn stared at her in amazement. Her shrewd guess was dead on as they had been seen leaving within the hour after he had informed his personal staff of his and Addie's arrival.

"How did you know?"

"Because their kind are cowards at best. When things get hot, they run."

He nodded absentmindedly, his mind off on a different tangent. He realized that he had sorely undervalued Addie's role in their union, now and for the future.

"Addie," he said in a contrite voice putting his hands on her shoulders, "I have underestimated you – I have not given you the credit you deserve and I apologize."

Searching into her eyes for some understanding, he continued, "I realize now that I don't want just a beautiful wife who will make me proud but rather an equal partner. Someone with whom I can share all my thoughts and problems and joys; someone who will help me through the rough spots and celebrate my accomplishments; someone who will help me rule wisely and justly. My sweet Addie, will you be that beloved, trusted partner?"

Addie gazed seriously into Kolyn's deep blue eyes, and said softly, "Kolyn, I want to share your life – ALL of it!"

Slow smiles spread on their faces, their love for each other expanding in an ever widening sphere surrounding them, protecting them. Exhilarated, Kolyn hugged Addie to his chest and swung her around and around in absolute joy. Laughing like school children, they danced around on the garden path.

"Tonight, we are having a special dinner with my father and some close friends to celebrate our engagement and the deliverance of the Kingdom of Cebrae from suppression," he announced proudly.

Like a frightened filly, Addie went rigid, eyes wide with concern. *I don't have anything to wear! And this ugly thing...*, she despaired mentally.

Sensing her fear and uncertainty, Kolyn pulled her into his arms and said, "Do not worry, my love. I will be at your side plus...you have a way of enchanting everyone you meet, so there!"

But he was starting to understand her better and better and knew that this wasn't what she was really concerned about. With a mischievous glint in his eye, he said, "There is a surprise waiting for you in your room – I think you should check it out while I go take care of a few things." Kissing her nose lightly, he left her gaping after him.

Addie walked back to the castle, secure in her love and the new understanding they had just reached. *I've never been so happy*, she reflected her eyes glowing. When she reached her room, she almost turned around thinking she had made a mistake. It was bustling with activity and the bed was covered with beautiful gowns! Overwhelmed, she stood there with tears of gratitude in her eyes.

Trinity, who had been waiting impatiently for her to return, saved the day.

"Addie! We're having a party for you!" she said enthusiastically. "And you will be the prettiest girl there!"

Smiling at her exuberance, Addie couldn't help but relax. The rest of the afternoon was spent pleasantly with the maid and seamstress equally falling under her spell. After much deliberation, she opted for a dark green creation with long sleeves and a high neck. There were still a few stubborn bruises on her lower neck and shoulders which she didn't care to advertise. The long sleeves would hide the unsightly bandage and artfully applied make-up covered all traces of the recent beating. Carmelita, now her personal maid, had convinced Addie to leave her long hair flowing freely down her back but had still woven in various small braids decorated with sprigs of Baby's Breath.

"My lady, you are beautiful!" she exclaimed candidly.

Smiling, Addie took one last look at herself in the tall mirror and was amazed at the difference a beautiful gown and a little care with her hair could do.

"Thank-you, Carmelita, you are a magician!"

The latter flushed with pride and then reminded Addie, "Your Prince is waiting to see you in his study."

There was still half an hour before dinner as she made her way to meet Kolyn. Feeling extremely nervous, her stomach in knots, she was sure she wouldn't be able to eat anything. She knocked lightly and entered leaving the heavy door to close behind her by itself.

Kolyn stood transfixed by her beauty, unable to breathe, his heart hammering in his chest. *She is a goddess!* Finally, he extended a hand toward her advancing like someone in a dream. She took a step forward hesitantly and in an instant he had her in his strong arms kissing her passionately. The rest of the world disappeared as their love exploded once again.

"My sweet Addie, how I love you!" he whispered against her lips.

"And I can't even spend an afternoon without wishing I was in your arms," she admitted hopelessly.

Laughing, Kolyn said, "I will have to give you a little token for those long afternoons."

Taking Addie's hand, he slipped a beautiful ring on her finger. It was most unusual – made of white gold it held two triangles placed tip to tip with a large blue white diamond in the centre. It reminded Addie of a butterfly.

"Thank-you, it is so beautiful!" she said choked with emotion.

Leading Addie to a chair by the fireplace, he knelt down beside her, holding her hand tenderly. "The triangle is the strongest geometric shape known to man and it's able to withstand a tremendous amount of pressure without crumbling, twisting or anything. And the diamond, being the hardest naturally occurring substance on this planet, is rare and precious." Love in his beautiful eyes, he continued, "This ring symbolizes us, Addie. We are each a triangle and the diamond in the centre represents our binding love reflected in all of its brilliance. I am entrusting this ring to you my beautiful, sweet Addie and I am appointing you Guardian of our love."

"I will always cherish this gift from you and I will safeguard our love," she promised.

Slowly, they stood up and with a tender kiss, sealed their commitment to each other. Silently, Kolyn took her hand to lead her to the reception.

"Wait!" she said putting on the brakes. "I don't know what to do, what to say! How do I address the King, your father, the other guests...?"

"You are such a natural at this; I completely forgot you have no experience in this domain. Will you forgive my oversight?"

"Only if you teach me real fast!" she teased.

"All right, you may address the King as 'Sir' or 'Your Majesty' although I doubt very much he will go for that last one. He may even consider having you call him 'father' once he falls in love with you too."

At that, Addie's eyes clouded with sorrow getting bright and shiny with unshed tears.

Alarmed, Kolyn asked gently, "Why so sad all of a sudden?"

With a catch in her voice, Addie replied, "It's my father... the last time I saw him he was curled in a ball on the floor." The memory of that night flashed before her eyes making her dizzy. Shaking her head, she asked, "What happened to him? Why was he like that? I need to know that he is alright." She stared at Kolyn, anguish in her beautiful green eyes.

Kolyn took her in his arms, rubbing her back gently and murmured, "Your father is alright but I don't know what happened either. We will need to talk to the Guardian who was protecting you that night."

Addie smiled, comforted and trusting that she would soon have the answers she was seeking.

They made their way to the dinning room with Addie muttering to herself *Sir...Sir...Sir...* in different tones of voice. That had Kolyn chuckling as they entered the room.

The room went dead silent and eighteen pairs of eyes turned to watch as the Prince and Addie approached. Both tall, slender and graceful, they were breathtaking as a couple but it was the glow of happiness radiating from them that mesmerized all in attendance... all except little Trinity.

"Papa, Addie!" she said joyously, running to them.

Kolyn picked her up and gave her a big kiss. Her eyes shining with happiness, she turned to Addie and said laughing, "Did Papa tell you that you're the prettiest girl?"

It was Addie's turn to laugh softly and bending close to Trinity's ear said in a loud whisper, "Not yet!"

Those near enough to hear broke into smiles and chuckles, the formal atmosphere prior to their arrival evaporated under the ever expanding glow spreading into the room like a balm.

Addie felt totally relaxed with Kolyn holding her hand and Trinity the other. Together, they approached the King who was, for the first time in a long time, unable to come up with the usual greetings and platitudes generally bestowed on guests. *She is beautiful, gracious and ...powerful. She has this whole room enchanted by her mere presence!*

"Father, may I present Ariadne Renée Cargill, my fiancée."

Addie bowed slightly and the King surprised everyone by embracing her. "Welcome to the Kingdom of Cebrae and to this family, Ariadne."

Smiling, a twinkle in her eye, she said, "Thank-you, Sir, I am honoured. Please call me Addie."

The King smiled, acknowledging her request and placing her hand on his arm escorted her to the dining table. Kolyn followed behind holding Trinity's hand admiring the sensuous figure walking ahead of him. The seating arrangements were somewhat informal but the King sat at the head of the long table with Kolyn and Addie to his right, Sean and Trinity on his left. The rest of the guests took their places following some tacit agreement as to the hierarchy amongst them.

Surveying this elite company, Addie was amused at how prominent dark blue eyes seemed. Her gaze met one of a gentleman across from her and she suddenly had the feeling that she had met him before. *But that's impossible – I don't know anyone here.* He was dark-haired possibly in his mid-twenties with deep blue eyes. As she continued to look at him, she got prickles up her arms and down her back. Unbeknownst to her, Kolyn was carefully monitoring her reaction.

As she continued to puzzle over this strange feeling, a picture superimposed itself between her and this blue-eyed man – that of a big white dog! Recognition dawning in her beautiful green eyes, she flashed him a wide smile that illuminated her whole face.

Stunned, he stared at her for a brief moment and then hung his head as in …*remorse*? This unexpected reaction on his part confused her and she turned to Kolyn, deeply perplexed, her eyes full of questions.

Gently squeezing her hand, he leaned closer and whispered, "You're right. We'll meet later and talk."

Thankfully, the next course was being served distracting her sufficiently for the moment to join in the general conversation.

"How did you meet my son?" asked the King.

"We met at the skating rink, Sir," she replied but not wishing to go down that line, she artfully detoured the questioning. "Actually, I met little Trinity first at the same rink," she explained looking fondly at... *her daughter!* The magnitude of that realization left her sort of breathless.

Meanwhile, the King and Kolyn looked at each other knowingly both being masters at the art of foiling undesired questionings. *Nicely done*, thought the King admiringly. Kolyn thought he would burst with pride!

When desert was served, the King stood up to make the formal announcement of their engagement.

"My son, Kolyn Roy of Cebrae," he said looking fondly at him, "has requested our blessing in his upcoming marriage to the charming Ariadne Renée Cargill. They will be wed at the annual Fête in mid-May."

A storm of applause broke out with all the guests standing as one to acknowledge the new couple. Addie was a bundle of nerves gripping Kolyn's hand under the table. The guests having resumed their places, he stood up and helped Addie to her feet. Sensing she was ready to bolt, he whispered, "Concentrate on our ring, my love." Addie closed her eyes briefly and relaxed.

"Father, dear friends, we thank you for your good wishes. Your support and protection has been and is greatly appreciated. Addie holds my heart in her precious hands and I hers for the rest of our eternal lives."

Slowly, he turned to face Addie – their eyes locked onto each other and with great restraint he kissed her very tenderly. The force of their love was tangible and it spread to all those present raising them to a level none had ever experienced before.

They had just sat down when a small hand reached for her. Trinity had made her way to their side of the table unnoticed and she stood there silently imploring Addie to take her in her arms. Kolyn, ever perceptive, knowing that she couldn't do it because of her wrist, picked up his daughter and placed her gently on Addie's lap.

She wrapped her little arms around her neck and declared, "I love you."

"And I love you my sweet daughter," said Addie hugging her tightly.

Like this morning, a magical triangle was created when Kolyn joined them forming a visible glow around them. The Guardians were watching this phenomenon with awe exchanging various glances with each other.

With the meal over, most of the guests took their leave of the royal party again expressing their congratulations and best wishes to the happy couple and to the King for his hospitality.

"Prince Kolyn, Princess Addie," said Addie's appointed Guardian, "I wish to extend on the part of the whole Council, our congratulations and offer you our continued support and protection."

"Thank-you, Nolan," said Kolyn graciously, "it is very much appreciated and I wish to thank you personally for protecting Addie when she needed it."

Addie then floored them both. Taking both of Nolan's hands in hers, she kissed him on the cheek and said, "I wish to thank you for several reasons. First of all, for showing me what I was searching for in life that day on the sidewalk and for guiding me to Kolyn; and for keeping me warm in the park. I owe you a great debt that I hope to be able to repay someday. Thank-you!"

Nolan stood there nonplussed. *How did she figure all that out?! How is she aware of these things? How did she even recognize me earlier?* He continued to stand there unable to respond in an intelligible manner.

"I would like to know what happened to my father during the fight and why he was curled up in a ball."

Nolan stared into the depths of her eyes, realizing he had no choice but to tell the truth. *There is something about her that makes you want to confess your most guarded secrets. I don't think anyone could lie to her!*

He started in a low voice, "I arrived too late to protect you from getting hurt altogether. You were unconscious lying on the floor and your father, astride your body, was taking aim to smash your face with his fist."

Addie's legs wouldn't support her anymore. She felt weak and dizzy. Kolyn moved behind her and held her tightly against his body. She nodded to Nolan to continue, her eyes filled with pain and sorrow.

"I froze him so he couldn't move but he was still fighting inside and then... I... I lost... control. I punished him. I made him feel pain like he had never felt before. I was enraged and kept it up for too long.

Your father no longer… remembers. He… he… is like a child now. I'm so sorry," he whispered, his eyes tortured with remorse.

Silence followed; no one moved. Addie closed her eyes, her mind in turmoil unable to decide how she should feel or react. *He saved my life. My father is like a child,* the two balancing each other out. Time stopped with her indecision.

Slowly, she became aware again of her surroundings. *Kolyn is warm, he's holding me. I am with him…* Opening her eyes, she looked at the wretched Guardian in front of her and her heart went out to him. From deep inside, compassion welled in her and she knew what she had to do.

"Nolan, my Protector," she said getting his attention, "thank-you for telling me what happened. You did what you did and it cannot be changed.   I am alive thanks to you and with my beloved Kolyn. We will take care of my father. Go in peace."

Nolan reached for her hand and kissed it. The last week had been hell for him, knowing that he had misused his power.

"Thank-you, Princess," he said, his deep blue eyes clear again, "you have true greatness."

He left feeling himself again.

Kolyn silently took Addie in his arms and kissed her murmuring against her lips, "I love you so much! You are so beautiful inside and out!"

Addie pressed her body closer to his in response. Being in his arms, knowing that her love was fully returned, she put the past behind her. Holding hands, they went to bid goodnight to the King and the last few guests.

Chapter Eighteen

Preparations

Addie felt refreshed as she made her way down to join Kolyn and Trinity for breakfast. Today, her wrist wasn't hurting at all and she figured she would be able to remove the bandage within the next few days. However, there was something niggling at her consciousness like a puppy unwilling to give up the slipper he was chewing. Something she needed to do… something important… but it was eluding her, causing her brow to crease in frustration.

All worries fled when Kolyn greeted her with a warm kiss.

"Good morning, Sunshine," he said happily. "We have been languishing here awaiting your esteemed presence," he teased her.

Laughing, Addie gave Trinity a hug and took her place at the table, radiating love and contentment. Plans were made for the day including a private audience with the King and a full tour of the castle and grounds.

"Addie, what are your wishes concerning your father? I want you to know that whatever you decide, I will support your decision fully." Grateful, she responded, "I have given this some thought already. I think he would be happier staying in familiar surroundings but he cannot provide for himself in his state."

"I understand. How do you feel about full time live-in home care for him? I can call Mr Dubois for his assistance in locating a suitable companion for him."

"Thank-you, Kolyn. This is very generous of you."

"It's the least we can do to put this right. I will make the arrangements today," he assured her.

Relieved, Addie gave him a brilliant smile which took his breath away. Smiling at her tenderly, he said, "Soon, my love, we will truly be one. The wedding preparations are underway, Jo and her family will be arriving in three weeks and ...the Sanchez are no longer a problem."

As he mentioned the Sanchez, Addie's hands started to shake so violently she had to put her cup down abruptly.

"That's it!" she exclaimed a strange look in her eyes, the elusive, niggling thoughts of earlier suddenly becoming crystal clear. Her whole body went ice cold.

"What –?" he cried out gripping her hand, apprehension written all over his features.

Closing her eyes to block out the unbidden images, she heaved a shuddering sigh. Kolyn was beside himself with worry.

"Addie," he beseeched, "what is happening?"

"Later...," she murmured staring at Trinity, her body tense with dread. Wide-eyed, she pleaded, "Kolyn... is it possible to meet with all the Guardians at the same time?"

Unable to keep up with her, he stared at her some unknown terror gripping his heart. *What is happening? Why all the Guardians? It's never been done before...* Marshalling his emotions, he took a deep breath, calming himself down. Looking at Addie, he was struck by the pain and loss in her beautiful eyes. Getting up from his chair, he pulled her into his arms squeezing her against his heart, rocking her gently.

"Of course, we will meet with the Guardians," he promised.

He could feel some of the tension leave her body and wanting to fully assuage her fears, he whispered softly, "We are together now – please don't worry."

Her mind eased considerably, she kissed him tenderly and then she picked up Trinity hugging her fiercely, "My sweet daughter, I love you so much!"

Her gesture sent cold shivers down Kolyn's back. It was like she was saying good-bye while still trying to protect her from all the evils in the world. *This has something to do with Trinity...*

Later, sitting across from Addie in his study, his daughter safely in the care of her tutor, he demanded, "Now, please tell me what is causing you such anxiety."

Organizing her thoughts, she began, "Some people have twisted minds and they will go to any lengths to get what they want, uncaring of who they hurt in the process. Such will use all manner of lies and treachery carefully orchestrated to achieving their goals. They have no conscience."

Kolyn listened to her intently, not interrupting, innately sensing the truth of her words.

"The Sanchez do not want us to get married and they will do *anything* they can to stop it from happening." Tears in her beautiful eyes, she said, "They will use Trinity –."

Kolyn felt as if someone had just twisted a knife in his heart. With a strangled gasp, he tried to negate the horrible scene his mind painted for him. "No-o-o!" but he knew deep down that Addie was right. It was her turn to comfort him.

Softly caressing his face, she said, "Forewarned is forearmed."

Vowing that this time he would not fail to protect his loved ones, Kolyn declared, "Let's meet with the Guardians."

The meeting was set for one hour hence. Kolyn had contacted the leader and had simply told him that they wanted to brief the whole Council on a matter of national security. Something in the Prince's voice alerted him to the urgency of his request and all members had been summoned immediately. *I wonder if this has something to do with Princess Addie*, he mused. He had been told by Nolan himself how she had handled the truth about her father and was deeply impressed and moved. *This girl, with no training at all, has true greatness and puts us all to shame.*

When Kolyn and Addie entered the circular room, the Guardians stood up respectfully. Two chairs had been added to the circle in preparation for their arrival. Once they were all seated, Kolyn nodded to Addie. Standing up poised but determined, she looked at all the members in turn, her eyes commanding their attention.

"Thank-you for meeting with us," she began simply. "It is not our intention to tell you how to carry out your duties but we need your help. For centuries now, you have held this Kingdom secure against harm but there is another danger coming our way which directly affects the Royal family."

As if suddenly linked by an invisible thread the Guardians leaned forward imperceptibly, curiosity mirrored in their eyes.

"There have been amongst us two individuals who upon learning of our impending arrival, fled the island. This you are already aware of. But their kind does not give up easily and they will return. It is my belief that they will try to prevent my union with Kolyn and this through our daughter, Trinity."

This time, her words created the desired effect breaking their careful stance, the most notable in Dimitri. His face went ashen and then flushed with anger.

She let them digest this information briefly before continuing.

"At some point before the wedding, they will attempt to approach the little princess and lure her away with lies and promises. They will not hurt her but they could hold her captive. We *cannot* let this happen for all of our sake… Please! Help us!"

Addie sat down abruptly, her composure shattered. Kolyn silently took her frozen hands rubbing them gently.

The force of her plea pierced the souls of all present. The leader looked at each member in turn getting affirmative nods from all of them.

Rising with great dignity, he addressed Addie, "My lady, it is in our power to help you and we will protect the little princess with all of our combined resources."

She mutely thanked him with her beautiful green eyes bright with unshed tears.

The logistics were worked out rapidly. They left the chamber satisfied they were doing all they could. Kolyn was extremely relieved, not only for his daughter's sake but for Addie's too. *She loves my daughter as much as I do... Our daughter*, he amended happily.

Needing some relief from the morning's tension, Addie changed into her favourite jeans, tied her long hair in a pony tail and went to find Trinity. She found her in the study hall, her lessons just finishing.

"Would you like to play Frisbee with me in the garden?" she asked twirling the object on her finger.

Her shriek of delight was all the answer Addie needed. Skipping excitedly, Trinity was going on a mile a minute. Watching her indulgently, Addie didn't see Kolyn, also changed, standing there in the middle of the hallway until she rammed into his hard body. Dropping the Frisbee, she lost her balance but he caught her in his arms kissing her fiercely.

"Where are you two running off to?" he teased noting with satisfaction that once again, their thoughts and actions were on the same wavelength.

"To the garden to play Frisbee," announced Trinity, dancing from foot to foot in her excitement.

"Can I join you?" he pleaded putting on a sad puppy face.

Laughing, Addie replied, "Sure – if you promise to play fair."

"I promise!" he said raising his hand in a boy's scout fashion. Laughing freely, he hoisted Trinity onto his shoulders and grasped Addie's hand. "I get to play with my favourite girls!" he declared squeezing her hand.

Their laughter and giggles could be heard ringing throughout the garden and into the castle. Love was in the air!

Chapter Nineteen

Long Lost Love

Addie's audience with the King was for 1:00 pm and she didn't want to be late. Walking quickly, she arrived slightly out of breath mostly due to her nervousness. She took a deep breath and walked in with some trepidation not sure how to act or what to say to him as a king or even as Kolyn's father. She was apparently wasting a good worry as he immediately put her at ease.

"Welcome my dear Addie. Please make yourself comfortable."

"Thank-you, Sir," she replied formally sitting down in a chair facing the King.

He looked at her thoughtfully wondering where to start. There seemed to be so many things he wished to tell her all of a sudden. Her big green eyes were steady as she gazed at him kindly.

"Addie, on behalf of the Kingdom of Cebrae, I wish to express my heartfelt gratitude for your aid in ridding this castle of the evil within it. It is in large part due to your courage and perspicacity that I am alive and well today."

"Thank-you, Sir, for your kind words. I am happy for your sake and Kolyn's as well. He loves you very much," she said smiling gently.

She is so selfless! "Yes – and my son is very much in love with you," he countered in a guarded tone making her cheeks blush delicately at his straightforwardness.

Thinking of Kolyn made her feel warm and safe. Her eyes took on a glow of their own as she said softly, "I love Kolyn with all my heart and soul."

The King now had the answer he had been seeking except for one little puzzling detail. Smiling at how she had not answered this question before, he put it to her again. "How *did* you meet my son?"

With a frank but thoughtful look, she began, "I'm not sure but… I don't think it was coincidence."

Pausing to coordinate her thoughts, she continued, "I was clearing the snow off our front sidewalk when this large white dog appeared out of nowhere. He had deep blue eyes. But then my father yelled from the house and he disappeared into thin air it seemed… The next day, I was walking through the mall with my friend Jo Dubois when I missed a step and fell. A tall guy with deep blue eyes extended his hand to help me up. On the following Saturday, I'm skating and run into a little girl with deep blue eyes. You can imagine that by this time, I'm questioning my own sanity, seeing deep blue eyes everywhere. I finally met Kolyn for real that afternoon at the skating rink after Trinity left with the Sanchez. Little did I know that I would see him again at the Dubois' place that very night."

Lost in her own thoughts, she pictured again the subsequent blooming of their love and his promise to come for her. Various emotions passed swiftly across her beautiful features – love, sadness, pain and back to the radiant love she now had.

Watching her, the King was stirred by her simple account in which she had managed to convey a love so strong it could not be destroyed despite the few times she had actually been with his son.

"If it's not a coincidence, what do you think it is?" he asked gently.

She stared at the King, calculating his possible reaction to her answer and decided against it. "With your permission, Sir, this is one question I'd rather not answer. Sooner or later someone is going to have me incarcerated for having too much imagination," she finally replied with a big grin.

Laughing at her honest answer, he reached for her hand and holding it gently, said, "You already have Kolyn and Trinity's trust but it seems that I must earn yours. And rightly so! When Kolyn told me that you suspected the Sanchez' of treason, I did not believe him. It took hard core evidence to open up my eyes to the truth of the matter and this only after you had been hurt and I was near my deathbed. I was in a position to do something about it and did nothing. I was blind and set in my ways. Addie, just like you have touched everyone else in your life, so have you touched me. Now, I feel hope for the future something I have not felt in a very long time. This you have restored to me by your great love for my son and his daughter. Thank-you...my daughter," he finished off eloquently.

Addie was so moved that tears sprang in her eyes and in a spontaneous gesture, hugged him affectionately.

Smiling happily, she declared, "You may be King, Sir, but you are also Kolyn's father and for that I will be eternally grateful to you."

"And speaking of which, it would please me greatly if you called me 'father' when we're with family."

A secret smile formed on her lips. *Kolyn was right!* She nodded and said softly, "Father."

"Now, will you tell me what you think it is?" he reiterated patiently.

Chuckling, Addie said candidly, "I can see where Kolyn gets his tenacity for getting his questions answered!"

Regaining some seriousness, she said, "I believe the Guardians have had a hand in it. They guided me and protected me something Kolyn said had never been done before for an individual outside the realm of the kingdom."

Shaking her head at the wonder of it all, she added in a whisper, "I don't know how or why they chose me… but I am so incredibly happy, it doesn't matter." Her whole face was beaming with love and joy.

"I do believe you're right. One day we may find out but until then I am very happy you have found your way to us," he said sincerely.

She took her leave of the King shortly after that and picking up a warm sweater from her room, headed out to the gardens. She had a couple of hours to kill before meeting Kolyn and needed some time to absorb all the changes that had occurred in her life in the last few days.

Following the various paths, she ended up in a section of the gardens that had been left to grow in its natural state – huge trees with tall grasses growing at their feet, vines interlacing their branches; several types of flowers she wasn't familiar with hung over the trail, vying for a spot in the sun. Coming around a bend, she spotted an arbour holding up a wrought iron garden swing complete with cushions nestled amidst a riot of yellow blooms growing on the vines.

Enchanted, she stretched out in it leaving one toe on the ground to keep the swing gently rocking and with her sweater bundled up under her head, laid there listening to the songbirds thinking of nothing. In no time, she was fast asleep.

Kolyn's meeting had ended earlier than expected of which he was secretly glad as he wanted to spend some extra time with Addie. Wanting to surprise her, he decided to arrive unannounced but he couldn't find her anywhere. Checking with his father, he was informed that she had left him over an hour and a half ago. *"Where is she?"* he wondered starting to feel a bit anxious. Heading out to the gardens, he intercepted the head gardener.

"Have you seen Addie?"

"Yes but that was about an hour ago, Sir. Maybe you could check with my young apprentice. He's by the greenhouse," he replied trying to be helpful.

Sean, watching Kolyn approach noticed the tension in him right away and guessing the source of his concern, met him halfway.

"Have you—?"

"Sir," he said right away cutting him off, "she is in the back garden arbour asleep in the big swing."

The relief he felt was like the rush of an outgoing tide leaving him slightly dizzy.

"Thank-you! I was getting worried!" he admitted.

"There's no need for that, Sir – we are continuing to watch over her."

The gratitude in the prince's eyes was reward enough making his duty as a Guardian a pleasure. Kolyn walked swiftly to his destination not wanting to waste any more time away from his love. He approached the arbour silent as a cat and rounding the same bend Addie had earlier, he was struck by the peace and serenity of the scene before his eyes.

Two colourful songbirds perched on the swing by her head looked at him curiously. *Even the birds are watching over her!* He stood there gazing at her sleeping there so relaxed. Her long eyelashes rested peacefully against her cheeks; her brow smooth as alabaster. His jaw tightened when he took in the bandaged arm again lying across her stomach while her other arm was folded behind her head. A small breeze picked up a strand of her golden hair moving it across her throat. Kolyn reached out and gently placed it back along her shoulder.

Ugly purple, green and yellow bruises stared at him. The vivid reminder of the tragedy and near loss was like a physical blow. Overcome with emotion, he fell to his knees hiding the tears that sprang to his eyes. Pain, grief and hate twisted themselves in his tortured mind. His heart got tight and black, murder flickering through his mind at those responsible but also knowing that he was just as responsible for not being there to protect her. *I came so close to losing you, my love. How can anyone even think of hurting you – I hate them! I'm so sorry I left you behind...* It felt like he was falling in a twisting abyss where no redemption was possible... deeper and deeper... his heart burning...

In the depths of his despair, something bumped his head. Slowly raising his head, he was faced with

Addie's outstretched hand which had fallen outward in her sleep. Latching on to it like a drowning man, he pressed his lips against her palm not wanting to let go of this precious lifeline. When he finally looked up, she was watching him with a steady, peaceful gaze. A slow smile formed on her lips reaching up to her beautiful green eyes, illuminating her whole face. Sliding gracefully to her knees in front of him, she cupped his face tenderly, timeless love and understanding in her eyes.

"My dearest Kolyn, do not grieve for what has past or what might have been. We are here together now and we have a beautiful future ahead of us."

Cradling his dark head against her chest, her hair forming a golden curtain around them as she laid her cheek on his dark head, she added, "I sense that we have loved each other for a very, very long time and there is *nothing* that can tear us apart. You told me once, my love, that we were meant to be together and we will be from here on out," she whispered fiercely.

Something she said pulled him out of the downward spiral he had been headed into and with a strange glow in his deep blue eyes, stared at her as if truly seeing her for the first time. Getting up to his feet, he drew Addie into his arms holding her in his warm embrace.

"Ariadne, my long lost love," he whispered reverently, "I have been searching and waiting for you forever it seems. I think I got a little help because I wasn't expecting to go to Canada last Christmas."

"Strange… that's what I told Father earlier today that it wasn't a coincidence!"

"Father?!" he queried picking up on her relationship with the King.

"Uh huh," she answered smugly, a wide smile on her face and a twinkle in her eyes.

"You are so amazing and beautiful and MINE. I don't care who else falls in love with you, no one will ever love you as I do!" he declared passionately, kissing her over and over.

Locked in each others' arms, time became meaningless as two old souls were once again reunited.

On their way back to the castle they were met by Trinity who was overjoyed to see them. When Addie reached down to give her a hug, Kolyn was startled to hear her murmur, "And where do you fit in my little one?"

"Interesting question! Is there a connection?" he thought rocked by such a possibility.

Dinner that night was an interesting affair. The king was startled several times when they said the same thing at the same time. It was uncanny. *Something has changed in their relationship. It's more profound and ...peaceful – like something got sorted out.*

Later, as the two were taking a shortcut through the main hall which served as a ballroom on special occasions, Kolyn stopped and turned toward her. "Addie how would you like to go on a short trip with me?"

Her eyes lit up with pleasure at the thought. "I would love that!" she replied beaming.

"Good – then it's decided! Next weekend, I have some business to attend to in Madrid on Saturday morning and early afternoon and I thought you might like the opportunity to get some personal shopping done."

Addie was of mixed reactions to that plan as she wanted him all to herself *the whole time* but she also wanted to pick up a few gifts and things. Her face must have been quite transparent because Kolyn started chuckling as he hugged her close.

Pulling back slightly, his deep blue eyes teasing, he added, "And after that, I want to take *my girl* out on a date!"

For a second, Addie just stared at him. Spontaneously throwing her arms around his neck, she exclaimed, "You sure know how to make a girl happy! Do you realize," she disclosed openly, "that this will be my first date? — No, my second – there was the brunch with you too."

It was his turn to stare at her. *I'm the only guy she's ever gone out with?!* Secretly, he was thrilled to the bone.

"Well, my princess, I am doubly honoured," he said grinning widely. "Is there anything you would like to do on this special occasion?"

That stumped her. The little she knew about things you did on dates came from books and movies.

"Actually, I'm somewhat culturally deprived but I do enjoy classical music and dance although I don't really know how to do that very well. The sum total of my dancing experience is what we were taught in gym class," she admitted regretfully, not sure how he would take all that.

"Well!" he muttered, "I'm glad we're having this conversation now!"

Looking up at him, she saw that he was teasing her and in her relief broke out in giggles.

"What an amazing woman! She can face down the lions and woo kings but she can't dance!"

He kissed her tenderly and smoothly led her into a grand waltz. There were a couple of miss-steps but Addie's natural sense of rhythm stood her in good stead. Keeping to the basic steps, he could feel her relax becoming soft and pliant in his arms. Kolyn was on cloud nine. Never before had he held such a beautiful woman who responded so readily to his slightest pressure as he guided her across the floor to the sound of a silent orchestra playing just for them.

CHAPTER TWENTY

The Date

Madrid -

Kolyn knocked softly at the door to her suite. Carmelita promptly answered, a big smile on her face.

"G-Good evening, Sir," she stuttered making way for him to enter, her usual composure shaken by this tall, dark and handsome prince.

"Good evening, Carmelita," he answered pleasantly smiling indulgently as she stared at him in wonder. "Could you please let Addie know that I am here?"

Cheeks flushed, she backed up a couple of steps before fleeing to announce him to the princess. She burst into the sitting room where Addie was waiting and stood there wide-eyed and speechless.

"What's the matter?" Addie asked rising to her feet with celerity.

"Oh, my lady," she exclaimed putting her hands over her heart dramatically, "your prince is so gorgeous!"

Laughing, Addie gave her a quick hug and whispered, "Yes!" With a twinkle in her eyes, she went to meet her "date". When she saw him, she totally understood Carmelita's reaction. He looked every bit a prince as described in Fairy Tales, tall and proud with the most gorgeous deep blue eyes. Her heart started beating in her chest like a hummingbird and a flush of pleasure coloured her cheeks.

"Hello, Kolyn!" she said happily.

"Addie, you are so beautiful! You take my breath away!" he said admiringly. Her sleeveless black gown hugged her body up to her hips and then gradually flared out falling in soft folds down to her sandaled feet. She seemed to float as she gracefully walked toward him her golden hair flowing loosely down her back. Two braids held in place at the back of her head by a satin ribbon topped with some orchids created the impression of a crown.

He kissed her, softly running his hands down her arms.

"No bandage?" he asked just realizing she had taken it off.

Shaking her head, she answered, "It didn't match the dress!" Seeing that he was somewhat concerned she added quickly, "My arm doesn't hurt anymore. I just need to make sure I don't bang it."

Looking at her again, he noticed with satisfaction that the only jewellery she was wearing were two small zircon diamond studs and their engagement ring.

"My lovely Addie, there is something I meant to give you later but tonight will be just perfect. I'll be right back," he said mysteriously giving her a quick kiss before leaving the room rapidly.

He came back almost right away carrying two small black velvet jewellery cases. The first one contained a pair of very unique earrings. The stud part boasted three small diamonds set in a triangular formation from which were suspended two interlaced triangles at the end of a short delicate chain.

She was silent for a long time staring at the beautiful earrings nestled in the palm of her hands, her throat tight with emotion.

"Addie?" Kolyn questioned softly unsure what was happening.

Looking up at him, her eyes moist with suppressed tears, she said, "I received my first pair of earrings on my 12th birthday. My mother had taken me to get a haircut and get my ears pierced. Little did I know it would be the last gift from my beautiful mother. I wear them all the time."

Misunderstanding, he said, "You don't have to wear these if you don't want to. I understand."

Shaking her head, she gave him a wide smile. "Oh no – I will be proud to wear this beautiful gift from you. I know in my heart that my mother is very happy that I have found you. Thank-you so much," she said giving him a hug and a kiss. "Will you help me put them on?"

The earrings securely affixed to her ears, Kolyn opened the second box and took out a solid white-gold bracelet and clasped it to her slender wrist. The motif was the same as the earrings and the engagement ring! An unending row of triangles placed end to end circled the whole band and a runway of closely set diamonds lined both edges.

"I had these made and designed especially for you, my love," he said smiling tenderly.

"Thank-you! It is so beautiful!" she exclaimed wrapping her arms around his neck, her body pressed close against his. Holding her tight, he could feel his blood pulsing through his veins, wanting her more than ever. The heat between them was escalating. *If we don't go soon, we'll never get out of here!*

Breaking up the embrace, he asked with a smile in his voice, "Are you ready to go out on your date?"

Excited, Addie replied, "You bet! I'll just get my jacket."

He helped her with her gold embroidered bolero-style jacket and offering his arm, said gallantly, "My love, you are a vision to behold!"

As they exited the elevators into the main lobby, a reverent hush fell over the place. Seeing such grace and beauty, the hotel guests could not help but feel they were in the presence of greatness. Awed gazes followed their progress out the door, their problems and concerns momentarily forgotten.

Their entrance in the fancy restaurant caused much the same effect. It was like an unspoken current had passed through the patrons and as they were escorted to their table, several men half rose out of their chair astounded by the vision floating by, earning themselves a few glares from their wives or dates.   As Kolyn assisted Addie with her chair, his lips were twitching with amusement. He was not without knowing the kind of effect their passage had just created.

"Do you ever get used to this?" she asked rhetorically, her cheeks more flushed than usual.

Laughing gently, he said, "Addie, you are so beautiful. Everyone here tonight has already been marked by your presence. Don't be surprised if several people come to our table simply to satisfy their curiosity about the goddess they have just seen. I'm glad I decided not to go dancing with you tonight. I wouldn't have had a single dance with you!" he declared with a chagrined expression.

Grinning at him, Addie whispered, "Looks like the parade has started."

Sure enough, a portly gentleman and his heavily-jewelled wife were approaching their table. Kolyn rose, quietly signalling to Addie to remain seated.

"Prince Kolyn, what a pleasure to see you again," he said sincerely, shaking the prince's hand.

"Likewise, Monsieur Bastien," he replied genuinely pleased to see him.

"I'm sure you remember my lovely wife, Marguerite."

"Enchanté," he said taking her hand and kissing it lightly. "And may I present my fiancée, Addie Cargill. Monsieur Bastien and his wife own a winery in southern France and provide the castle with some of the best wine in the world."

"I'm very pleased to meet you," she said as M Bastien kissed her hand and then shaking Marguerite's she noted the strong grasp of working hands. "You must love your vineyard very much to get such excellent wine," she said astutely dazzling them with a big smile.

Her kind words pleased them enormously and taking their leave, Marguerite said, "Congratulations on your engagement. We are planning to come to your wedding."

Not sure what had just happened to them, they peacefully returned to their own table with a sense of pride and happiness.

Kolyn was looking at Addie thoughtfully when their meal arrived.

Waiting impatiently for the Maitre D' to wrap up, he continued to gaze at her, wonder in his eyes.

Finally they were alone and he blurted out, "How do you do that? How do you always seem to say the exact right thing?"

"Kolyn," she said reaching to take his hand, "it's easy. I just pay attention to small details. With Monsieur Bastien and his wife, I could tell that you were very happy to see them for one, and when I shook their hands, I noticed that they both have strong working hands. I just assumed that theirs is a family business with everyone pitching in."

"Wow! I'm impressed! And you're quite right about it being a family business. It's a gorgeous vineyard – I will have to take you there someday," he promised.

The meal was excellent and no one interrupted until they were done but while they were waiting for their desert and coffee, another couple approached. They were from the Netherlands and had known Kolyn and his father for a long time. In fact, his best man, Vincent Crane was their first cousin and working for them in their luxury cruise ship enterprise. At this moment, he was on one of the cruises and would be back just in time for the wedding which they were also planning to attend.

After they left, Addie inquired, "What's with Vincent? Did something happen to him?"

Shocked, Kolyn stared at her. *She is too good to be true. How does she pick up on these things?!* "I will answer your question but first tell me, what makes you ask?"

It was her turn to look at him thoughtfully, her beautiful green eyes serious as she said, "When you spoke of him, there seemed to be an uncomfortable moment between the three of you."

"Yes – Vincent fell deeply in love with a beautiful girl he met on one of the cruises. It lasted three months and Vince was planning to ask her to marry him when she ditched him. He took it very hard and his family was quite concerned about his state of mind and so we invited him to recover on our peaceful little island. He is fine now. He's a good guy, hard working and actually has a great sense of humour."

Just then, a short balding man came up to their table. Addie didn't like him on sight. Kolyn introduced him as Sir Ronald Degg, a cultural attaché to the British embassy in Spain. He grasped her hand in his sweaty palms kissing it wetly, ogling her as he oozed compliments in her direction. Pulling her hand out of his, she surreptitiously wiped it on the napkin resting on her lap.

"May I join you?" he asked but didn't wait for permission before sitting down.

They looked at each other in dismay. Addie moved her head to the left and Kolyn moved his in the opposite direction completing a negative shake of the head. Smiling at each other in total understanding, they simultaneously turned to Sir Degg, dazzling him with their beautiful eyes and said in unison, "Perhaps another time."

Overwhelmed, and feeling like he had just received an order, he murmured, "Of course." Slightly shaken, he got up and left without as much as a by-your-leave.

Exhilarated, Addie felt like giving Kolyn a high five.

"We make a great team!" he said taking the words out of her mouth. Joining hands across the table, they gazed into each others' eyes.

"Let's get out of here so I can kiss you like I've wanted to do all night," he whispered, his deep blue eyes shining with love.

Once in the car, he did just that. The fifteen minute drive to the *Teatro Real*, the Royal Theatre where the ballet presentation of *Sleeping Beauty* was currently playing, was just too short in Kolyn's estimation.

"I'm the luckiest man in the world and I love you so much, my beautiful Addie."

She was feeling warm and fuzzy from Kolyn's passionate kisses and blissfully unaware of how radiant she looked. As he escorted her through the crowd, it parted like the Red Sea, the patrons unconsciously making way for the royal couple.

"Who are they?" Addie heard someone whisper.

"Prince Kolyn of Cebrae and …and…his escort," the other whispered back lamely.

Kolyn looked at Addie his eyes shining with love and pride. However, the person's vague answer alerted him to the fact that he had better fill in the void. *If they don't know who she is, they'll make up something and that is never good!* Being tall had its advantages. Surveying the crowd he spotted the ABC logo sticking up from a reporter's camera. *I suppose that will have to do*, he thought not looking forward to this at all. After presenting their tickets, he handed the attendant his business card.

"Please have the ABC reporter come to our box at the second intermission," he ordered.

The man glanced at the card with a blasé attitude when it suddenly registered that this couple was *royalty*! Fawning admiration, he assured him that he would handle it personally and was there anything else he could do—?

Kolyn cut him off with an abrupt "Thank-you" and left him standing there still holding the business card. Addie could feel his tenseness in her arm and a swift peek at his expression told her he was brooding over something. He gave her a quick smile but it didn't reach his eyes.

Once safely seated in their private box, she took his hands in hers and said gently, "Kolyn, when we're together we can overcome anything. Now will you please tell me what's worrying you? I don't like seeing you unhappy."

His deep blue eyes troubled, he admitted, "I wanted this to be a perfect evening for you but something has come up that needs to be addressed right away. It's better to face this kind of thing head-on."

Quick of mind, Addie immediately made the link between the reporter and the whispers.

"You're talking about the fact that people don't know who I am, right?"

Surprised at how fast she had grasped the situation, he chuckled, "Addie, you never cease to amaze me. I keep thinking I have to protect you or shield you from all the bad things in this world but you seem to hold your own quite nicely."

His good humour restored, he went on to explain, "Now that you are part of our family, you are also in the limelight and I'd much rather they get their story straight about you."

"What kind of questions is he going to ask?"

"The usual – where are you from, how long have we known each other, what's our relationship, and probably a few others."

"Well, the relationship one is easily handled and… I've been a friend of the family for a long time —

"You have?"

"Sure – through the Dubois," she replied grinning.

Grinning back, he said teasingly, "Okay, how long have we known each other?"

"Forever it seems but we met again last Christmas—

"We did!?"

"Uh-huh! We met on Monday and *again* on Saturday," she responded barely able to contain her laughter.

This time, Kolyn laughed outright. "And are we having a traditional wedding?"

"Of course – virgins and all!" By this time, both of them were practically in glee.

"You know, next time I'm worried about something, I'll come and see you for comic relief!" Then he added on a more serious note, "You make me so happy. I don't recall ever having such a good time on a date!" he declared giving her a hug and a quick kiss.

"Me neither." Kolyn raised his eyebrows. "I mean, I can just be myself when I'm with you."

Just then the lights dimmed and taking full advantage, he gave her a long, warm kiss. "I love you," he said softly.

The audience rose to welcome the Maestro and the orchestra struck their first chords. Settling back in their seats, Kolyn kept his arm around Addie's shoulders. Leaning contentedly against him, she was prepared to thoroughly enjoy this ballet presentation of *Sleeping Beauty.*

Although she was familiar with the basic story line, the "death" of Princess Aurora still left her close to tears but the breaking point came when the wicked sorceress captured the prince barring any hope of rescue for the sleeping princess. As if to ascertain that *her* prince was truly there, she turned to Kolyn her eyes bright with tears. Softly, he kissed her wet eyelashes.

"I'm here, my love," he whispered in her ear.

Comforted, she gave him a radiant smile and went back to watching the ballet. By the time the second intermission came, she was back on an even keel.

The reporter came and it went just as expected. He left feeling cheated. *It's just like they rehearsed the damn thing! Well, at least I have a photo and a bit of a story,* he grumbled in disappointment. Little did he know!

It was quite late when the presentation ended and Addie was starting to feel the effects of so much adrenaline. In the car, he held her close, her head resting on his shoulder. He leaned his head against hers wishing they were already married.

At the door to her suite, he took her in his arms and said, "Addie, thank-you for this wonderful evening."

And he kissed her softly but her uninhibited response put an end to any control he had left. Holding her tight against his body, his hungry kisses left her trembling with desire. Shaken, they gazed at each other silently knowing they were dangerously close to crossing the line. The sound of an opening elevator tipped the balance.

"I will see you tomorrow, my love."

Opening the door for her, he gave her one last kiss and left. Dazed, Addie slowly entered the room and softly closed the door.

CHAPTER TWENTY-ONE

Happy Birthday

Jo and her parents finally arrived on April 27th, a week later than planned. When Kolyn had told Addie about the delay, she had been extremely disappointed.

"They have a few more things to take care of but I promise you they will be here before the end of the month."

Addie nodded miserably, trying to put on a brave face.

"You love Jo and her parents very much, don't you?"

"Yes – they're my family and Jo is like a sister to me. I didn't realize how much I would miss them!"

"I know," he said squeezing her hand sympathetically. "By the way, I have good news for you – Mr Dubois has found a companion for your father."

"He did?! That's great!" she said snapping out of her misery. "Who is he?"

"*She* is a widow in her mid-forties who was having a hard time making ends meet and this position was like a godsend. She is of Ukrainian descent – Mrs Mary Drakiw and per her credentials has done a fair amount of volunteer social work in her community. All of her references checked out beautifully. Mr Dubois interviewed her personally and was quite impressed. He said 'She's a kind and gentle soul who likes to tell people what to do'," he reported with a grin.

"She sounds just perfect! And I trust Mr Dubois – he's a good judge of character." She jumped up and gave him a big kiss. "Thank-you, Kolyn. I am so relieved to know that my father is being cared for."

"For you, my love, I would do anything," he said smiling widely. "You are so easy to please!"

And now they were here! Addie was beside herself with joy. She was reading in his study when he came to tell her. She got up in a flash and prepared to dash to the front door but he grabbed her hand and WALKED down the halls with her. Frowning, she looked at him puzzled.

"A little decorum, my dear," he admonished his eyes sparkling with mischief. That earned him another stare. *"Since when is he concerned with decorum?"* she thought belligerently. Resigned, she gave a big sigh and matched her pace to his.

Chuckling to himself, Kolyn had the impression of hanging on to a wild mustang. If he let go, she would make a run for it. That's exactly what she did when she saw Jo standing there with her parents. Nothing could have stopped her! With a cry of delight, she ran to her friend, both of them crying and laughing as they hugged each other. It was one superlative after the next!

"I missed you *so* much! I'm *so* glad you are here!"

"You look *great*!"

With tears of happiness, she hugged Mr and Mrs Dubois warmly. Kolyn was grinning as he watched

Addie going from one to the other like an excited puppy. He cocked an eyebrow at Mr Dubois who smiled and nodded.

Imprisoning her in his arms as she passed near him, he announced, "We're throwing a party Saturday night to welcome your family and our cousins. *And* you can show them how well you can dance now!" he added mischievously.

"You can dance?!" Jo exclaimed.

Blushing prettily, Addie just nodded as she leaned more securely into Kolyn's arms.

"Will you teach me, please?" she pleaded with a woebegone expression her hands joined in prayer.

Chuckling at her, Addie looked up at Kolyn, a question in her eyes.

Dropping a kiss on her brow, he challenged Jo, "Of course! We'll see if you learn as fast as Addie – you've only got three days!"

"Yes!" Jo said jubilantly raising a victory fist.

They dispersed shortly after, Mr and Mrs Dubois going to their quarters and Jo following Addie to her room.

"I've never seen Addie look so radiant," said Mrs Dubois.

"Yes," replied Mr Dubois, "it will be another match made in heaven." Taking her in his arms, he gave her a tender, loving kiss.

Smiling like a school girl, she said, "I think their great love is rubbing off on us. Jo will be happy here and find love too."

"It will have to be a strong man who can tame our wilful daughter," he concluded chuckling.

Meanwhile, the girls in question were sitting Indian-style on Addie's bed catching up on the latest as they had stayed in touch via e-mail.

"Addie, I wasn't kidding when I said you look great! You look so happy and peaceful!"

"I am – very, very happy! When I'm in Kolyn's arms, I feel whole but then when I'm away from him, it's like I've left part of me behind. We understand each other so well. Sometimes we even say the same thing at the same time just like you and I do."

This reminded her of her date and laughing she proceeded to relate the incident when they got rid of the British ambassador and then later how they handled the reporter.

They were laughing so hard, they had tears in their eyes. Wiping them, Addie said, "It's so good to see you. I wish you could stay forever."

"Yeah – it's such a gorgeous island but I don't know if I could stand watching you two love-birds all the time," Jo kidded a big smile on her face.

"Well, you'll just have to find a love of your own then," she teased back.

"Maybe I will!" declared Jo.

Addie glanced at her watch. "We need to get ready for dinner. You have to at least comb your hair, wash your hands and wear a dress. Otherwise, it's pretty informal. Where is your room?"

"It's in the same wing as Trinity's room."

"Good!"

Jo detected some emotion or innuendo in her tone and gave her a puzzled look.

"I'll explain later – it's kind of long," Addie promised.

She got ready quickly and went to pick up Trinity from her room. This was a routine they had established ever since she had arrived. Sometimes, it was Trinity who came to get her. But they always arrived together for dinner holding hands. This time though, they stopped by Jo's room and all three girls made their way to the dining room. Today was just family. Mr and Mrs Dubois were already there chatting with the King and Kolyn when they arrived. Addie was quiet at first feeling somewhat emotional at having all the people she loved sitting there with her at the same table. All in all it was a very pleasant evening. The dancing "lessons" were to begin the next day!

Kolyn had shanghaied Nolan and Sean to help out as Trinity wanted to learn too. That made four couples counting Mr and Mrs Dubois who professed they needed lessons also. There were a lot of giggles and faux pas as Kolyn taught Jo the basic steps of the grand waltz. Although, she too had excellent rhythm and learned quickly, Kolyn couldn't help but feel the difference between Jo and Addie. *I have to work so much harder!* he complained mentally. Addie danced with Nolan, Mr Dubois and Sean, teaching them as she had somehow been declared an expert.

After about half an hour of lessons, it was each to their own – Kolyn was anxious to dance with Addie and hold her lithe body in his arms. With *The Emperor's Waltz* playing softly, he took her hand and gazing into her beautiful green eyes, masterfully led her in the first steps of the dance. The love and passion in his deep blue eyes was her sole focus as she surrendered body and soul to him. Lost in their own world, neither was aware that they now had the floor to themselves, the other couples watching in awe the magic unfolding before their eyes. There was a visible aura surrounding them as they twirled gracefully. A feeling of serenity spread into the room and one by one the other couples joined in again equally affected. As the last chords were sounding, Kolyn slowed down and holding Addie close to his heart, whispered against her lips, "I love you now and forever."

By the end of Friday night's lesson, the dancers felt ready for a party and a ball. Everyone was quite looking forward to it.

Addie woke up early the next morning refreshed and feeling on top of the world. She took a long shower and by the time she stepped out Carmelita had arrived to dress her hair. She was just wrapping up when Jo and Trinity burst into the room singing Happy Birthday enthusiastically.

"It's the 1st of May! Wow! I totally lost track of time."

"I'm not surprised! Happy Birthday, my dearest friend," said Jo giving her a warm hug.

Trinity climbed on a chair and extended her arms to Addie, "Happy Birthday, Mommy – I love you." Addie kissed her sweet face and gave her a big hug.

'My beautiful daughter, I love you too, very much!"

"I have a present for you but it was too big to carry so I left it in my room," she said with a serious expression.

"And I have something for you too!" Jo said handing her a small box.

When Addie opened it, she was stunned. She stared at the beautiful locket nestled on its velvet cushion.

"That's amazing!" she murmured to herself. Picking it up gently, she read the inscription on the back – Eternally Yours.

"It's perfect, absolutely perfect!"

"Open it!"

Inside were two miniature photos – one of her and Kolyn dancing and the other of Trinity in her father's arms their deep blue eyes sending their love. Deeply moved, she silently hugged her friend.

"Thank-you so much! But I need to show you something – you won't believe this," Addie said rummaging in her drawer.

She pulled out a jewellery box and handed it to her friend. Curious, Jo flipped it open and laying there on black velvet was the exact same locket!

Stunned, she asked, "Where did you get this one?"

"In Madrid."

"I got yours in Bilbao – did you get something engraved on the back?" she asked as she turned it over. The message was essentially the same – I love you Now and Forever.

"I bought it for Kolyn. I wanted to give him something on our wedding day."

"That is truly amazing," Jo declared as they stared at the identical lockets now resting in the palms of Trinity's small hands.

Addie put Kolyn's away mentioning, "I still need to get something for inside – something special."

"I'll keep my eyes open," Jo answered pushing her out of the door. "Let's go see what Trinity got you."

On her bed, was a large flat box nicely wrapped with a red bow.

"That's a big box alright," she agreed as she unwrapped the present. Inside was a large framed watercolour! The pastel blues, pinks, yellows and greens merged into one another like dancing Northern Lights but this wasn't a picture of the sky.

Trinity had drawn her family – Kolyn in dark blues standing next to Addie in a pink gown, her long hair forming a golden aura around them both with herself standing in front of them. Her light blue gown blended in with the pink and darker blue on either side of her. The faint trees in the background gave the impression of a protective shell. There was an ethereal quality to the whole painting, a softness and love totally captured. The only sharp features were their deep blue eyes and Addie's beautiful green eyes.

"Wow!" She propped the painting against the headboard and went to stand at the foot of the bed. Jo who was equally impressed joined her. They stood there gazing at this work of art reverently.

Tears in her eyes, Addie held her daughter close to her heart. "Thank-you, Trinity – it is so beautiful. You have given me a priceless gift – my own family. I am so happy to have you and Kolyn in my life. I love you both dearly," she declared passionately. "We will have to find the perfect place to hang it where I can see it everyday."

They made their way to breakfast, throwing various suggestions as to the best place, some rather preposterous.

Kolyn heard their excited chatter and his heart started beating faster. Every morning, for the last month, he awaited her arrival with impatience and throughout the day, he would listen for her footsteps and hope to hear her voice or her laughter; he'd go out of his way to meet up with her, to smile at her and see his love reflected in her beautiful green eyes.

When the three girls entered, he only had eyes for his lovely Addie. A blush of pleasure rose in her cheeks and her eyes lit up when she saw him waiting there for her.

"Good morning, Addie," as he wrapped her tightly in his arms, "and Happy Birthday, my love."

If ever there was an excuse to kiss her, this was it. He gave her a long, deep kiss that left her blushing at the intimacy of it. Still holding her in the circle of his arms, he said, "I have two presents for you. The first one you will get after breakfast and the second one tonight."

Trinity was so excited she was prancing around and ended up on her backside as she tripped over her own feet letting out a "woof" as she fell. Kolyn picked her up and gently put his finger on her lips cautioning her with his eyes.

Laughing, she wrapped her arms around his neck and said, "I won't tell."

Watching them, Addie was struck by the love between them and her heart twisted as she remembered the ever present threat hanging over their heads. Kolyn noticed her expression and included her in his arms.

"Today, you are not allowed to worry about anything, my love," he whispered in her ear.

As he looked into her beautiful eyes, he could see the fear and worry being replaced by her blazing love for him.

She flashed him a big smile and said with a twinkle in her eyes, "As you wish, my prince."

Breakfast was a lively affair but no one got a chance to linger over coffee. As soon as Trinity saw that Addie was finished eating, she grabbed her hand and pulled her out of her chair.

"Papa will show you your present now," she commanded.

Laughing, he took her hand saying, "Yes, my impatient daughter."

They walked out into the garden toward the greenhouse. When Trinity saw Sean, she ran to him crying out, "Sean, they're coming!" Grinning, he held the hand of this exuberant little girl as they waited for their cue. As soon as they were close enough, Kolyn nodded and they both disappeared into the greenhouse. Sean emerged carrying a bundle and put it in Addie's arms. There was a soft whine from the warm blanket.

"A puppy! You're giving me a puppy!"

Tears of joy in her eyes, she dropped to her knees and took off the blanket. Curious dark brown eyes stared at her, the tip of his little pink tongue sticking out. Amazed, she stared at this gorgeous Rottweiler puppy.

"Woof"

"Well hello to you too!" she said kissing his soft head.

He squirmed around and licked her face. Beaming, she looked at Kolyn who was kneeling in front of her.

"Thank-you! I... I'm... How did you know?" she finally formulated.

He placed his hands on her shoulders and kissed her above the puppy's head.

"My sweet Addie, you love life – all of it," he told her simply.

Overwhelmed by such understanding, she buried her face in the puppy's furry coat, unbidden tears forming in her eyes.

"What's his name?" she asked getting her emotions under control.

"He doesn't have one yet. We thought you would like to name him."

Thoughtfully, she gazed at her puppy for a moment. Everyone was silently waiting for the verdict.

Finally a big smile on her face, she announced, "Zeus."

The name was greeted with cheers of approval. Even the puppy seemed to be in favour and now that the formalities were over, he squirmed off her lap and waddled over to a delighted Trinity. Jo and Sean were equally captivated by the cute bundle of fur leaving Addie alone with Kolyn. She reached for his hands and together they rose to stand face to face.

"Kolyn, I love you for who you are; I love you for the incredible understanding you have of me. You could easily have given me jewellery and baubles which would have been nice. But you chose to give me something much closer to my heart, something live…"

Her beautiful green eyes shone with love as she took his handsome face between her hands and kissed him tenderly. In a rush of emotion, he squeezed her against his chest, kissing her with restrained passion.

"My beautiful Addie, you are part of my soul, you complete me. When your heart beats in unison to mine, I am so incredibly happy, I go out of my head."

A warm glow formed around them as they gazed into each others' eyes silently. A soft whine brought them back to earth. Zeus was sitting at their feet begging for their attention. Jo, Sean and Trinity were standing there quietly, also drawn by the magnetism emanating from them. Addie picked up the puppy who proceeded to nuzzle her neck and burrow in her hair. Giggling, she put him down again. He sat there waiting expectantly.

She walked several feet away and called him, "Zeus, come."

As if he'd been released from some form of restraint, he ran to her exuberantly, tripping over his own feet. Shaking his head, he crossed the remaining distance and stood there looking extremely pleased with himself.

"What a smart puppy," she exclaimed patting his head.

In his excitement, he grabbed a mouthful of her long hair and tugged on it. Everyone burst out laughing at his antics. Disentangling her hair from his mouth, she told him, "We have to go now but I'll come and see you later."

As she walked to the greenhouse, the puppy followed close on her heels. Kolyn was watching with amazement at the ease with which she controlled this small animal. *No one and nothing can resist her! Her wish is her command. She is my queen!*

The rest of the day passed pleasantly. The three girls finally agreed on the perfect place to hang the painting and then converged in Addie's room to get ready for the party. With Carmelita's assistance, they helped each other with their hair, put on nail polish and make-up, eyeing each other critically till everyone was perfect. Addie wore the beautiful earrings and bracelet Kolyn had given her on their date. Dressed in flattering gowns, the three headed down.

Kolyn and Sean were busy regaling Nolan with the antics of the puppy when the girls walked in. Each was a vision in their own right and the men gazed at them in wonder. Nolan walked toward Jo, admiration in his blue eyes making her blush with pleasure.

"You are beautiful, Lady Jo," he said sincerely. "You will have to save me a dance or two or I'll turn green with jealousy," he added with a twinkle in his eye.

Laughing softly, she said, "Nolan, you can have as many dances as you like. I wouldn't want you turning green, after all."

At ease with him, Jo placed her hand on his arm, feeling pleasantly warm inside. With a smile, he led her to where her parents were standing.

Trinity went chatting away with Sean happy to have him there as her friend amidst all these adults.

Kolyn raised Addie's hand to his lips, his deep blue eyes never leaving hers.

"My beautiful princess, how I love you," he murmured for her ears only.

Giving her a dazzling smile, he placed her hand in the crook of his arm and led her toward his father. The room was teeming with guests, the tuxedos offset by a rainbow of colourful gowns.

"This is my first ball," she said her eyes flashing with excitement.

"It makes my heart sing when you say it's your first of something and I'm the one with you. There will be more firsts," he added with a knowing look making her blush at the thought.

Chuckling at her reaction, he patted the hand resting on his arm.

Dinner was served with full pomp and pageantry. Again as desert was being served, the King rose getting everyone's attention. A hush fell over the guests.

"My friends, it is with great pleasure that I welcome our cousins Mr Paul and Mrs Hélène Dubois and their lovely daughter, Jo-Anne. I hope you will enjoy your stay with us on our beautiful island of Cebrae."

The guests applauded heartily and raised a toast in welcome. Addie heard the King but something didn't sound right.

At that point, Kolyn stood up beside his father and announced, "My dear Addie, it has been arranged for your adopted family to remain with us forever."

She stared at him, her mind slowly absorbing this information.

Clarifying, he added, "They have moved here and this will be their permanent residence."

Her face went various shades of white and red as she struggled with her emotions. She looked at Jo as if to confirm what Kolyn had just said. She nodded, smiling broadly. Still unable to accept the evidence, she turned her big green eyes toward Mr and Mrs Dubois. Love in their eyes, they smiled at her and nodded.

She stood unsteadily and clutching Kolyn's hands, asked, "Is it true?" fear, hope and joy fighting for supremacy in her eyes.

"Yes – it was decided the day we got engaged. That's why there was a bit of delay in their arrival," he said smiling at her tenderly.

"They're staying?" she questioned again sort of dazed.

Jo and her parents had made their way to where she stood and turning to them, she was slowly starting to accept what her mind understood but her heart dare not believe.

"It was Kolyn's idea and we were all in favour!" said Mr Dubois.

For some reason, his words ended the conflict between head and heart.

"YOU'RE STAYING!!!!" Laughing and crying, they hugged joyously.

Breaking apart, the Dubois returned to their seat and Addie approached Kolyn, her eyes moist with emotion.

"Thank-you so much. I am so happy," giving him a heartfelt kiss. In a whisper, she added, "I will thank you much better later."

Smiling at each other, they sat down to eat their desert, although they were both privately thinking that any desert paled in comparison to just being alone together.

The King and Mrs Dubois officially opened the ball followed by Kolyn and Addie along with Mr Dubois and Jo. The protocol having been observed, everyone joined in, the orchestra playing all-time favourites. Addie and Jo were much in demand leaving Kolyn and Nolan no other choice but to dance with other girls and women to their great delight.

However, when Kolyn heard the first bars of *The Emperor's Waltz*, he skilfully manoeuvred his partner next to Addie. With a debonair attitude, he cut in and switched partners smooth as can be. Her dazzling smile was reward enough for his efforts.

"This is *our* dance, my love," he said to her.

Apparently, Nolan had done the same thing, claiming Jo for this special dance. But once in Kolyn's arms she lost focus of the rest of the world. It was just the two of them floating in a space of their own. The masterful execution of the dance by this tall, graceful couple earned them most of the floor as others melted to the side lines to watch.

Their eyes never leaving the other, a thousand small currents ran between them as mind and soul merged. There was something mystic happening that left the guests mesmerized. A love so pure invariably caused anyone in its vicinity to be imbued with the grace and beauty it radiated and when the ball ended, it was the general consensus that this one had been the best, the most fun, the most uplifting.

As Addie got ready for bed, she felt strangely lonely. Kolyn's passionate kisses before leaving her only intensified the feeling. It was like he had taken her soul with him. *I should be happy – I have my family, Kolyn, Trinity and my new puppy.*

On the spur of the moment, Addie put on her jeans, a warm sweater and headed to the greenhouse.

The night security smiled when she told him, "I'm going to see my puppy."

The moon was shining brightly and she walked quietly along the path. The door to the greenhouse was obviously well oiled as it made no sound when she opened it. Turning on her small flashlight, she found Zeus sitting up watchfully. Recognizing her, his whole body started shaking with joy.

"Hello, Zeus," she said cuddling his soft body.

Finding an old blanket, she sat down on it her back to the door. He curled up into the circle of her crossed legs, his head resting on her thigh. For a while, Addie just petted him gently and then started talking to him, pouring out her soul.

Kolyn, meanwhile, made his way downstairs and told security he was going for a walk.

"Sir, Princess Addie is out," the guard informed him.

"She is?!" surprise on his face.

"She said she was going to see her puppy."

Smiling, Kolyn thanked him and went toward the greenhouse. Knowing the layout well, he did not need any light and as he neared the puppy's space, he heard Addie talking softly.

"I don't know what's wrong with me. I have all the love and riches in the world and yet I feel ...incomplete. I love him so much, sometimes it scares me. He's the best thing that's ever happened to me. When he holds me in his arms, I feel like I'm floating. But when he goes, it's like my heart stops beating... You have no idea how precious you are my little puppy. You will keep me from going insane when he's away. How he knew I would need that, I'll never know," she whispered tears silently rolling down her cheeks.

Thoroughly moved, Kolyn swallowed painfully against his tight throat.

"Addie," he called out softly as he moved toward her.

Slightly startled, she turned her head quickly at the sound of his voice.

"Kolyn!" she whispered.

Seeing her tear-streaked face and wet eyelashes, he nearly lost it. Putting the puppy back on its bedding, he pulled her into his arms and kissed her – a long, seductive kiss that made them both dizzy.

Pulling back, Addie smiled and told him candidly, "Kolyn, you drive me crazy with wanting you but you have an unfair advantage."

"I do?"

"Yes – You seem to have enough control to stop but I don't think I could if things got beyond a certain point."

"*Seem* is the correct term. You have no idea how hard it is sometimes to stop. But you're right, my love," he said sitting down on the blanket she had been using earlier.

She sat next to him and leaned her head on his shoulder. Hands intertwined, they talked quietly, peacefully. There were so many things to find out about each other.

"Kolyn, what happened to your mother?" she asked gently looking into his eyes.

His whole body tensed and he gripped her tightly against him. Watching the emotions flashing across his handsome face, she was sorry she had asked but then he relaxed and said, "You have a right to know."

Taking a deep breath, he began, "When I was Trinity's age, my mother went to visit some friends in France and never came back. She... she abandoned me and my father for someone else. Father was devastated and I was sent to a fancy boarding school. I would come home for the summers but during my fourth year there, I got very sick. My father came for me. It was a turning point in our lives. When Trinity was born, I swore I would not let the same thing happen to her and decided to raise her myself."

Addie looked at him silently, commiseration in her eyes. "Your opinion of women has been sorely tested," she finally said. "Aren't you afraid that I —?"

He put his finger gently over her lips cutting her off. "Addie that is one thing I'm dead sure will never happen."

"How...?"

"Because, my sweet love, your eyes don't lie. Because you loved my daughter and cared for her even before you knew me and ...when we were skating and I told you who Trinity was, your first reaction was to think of her mother and not the pain it was causing you!"

Staring at each other, they both knew it was the truth. Their love had a redeeming and healing quality for both of them.

"I love you," she murmured against his lips.

"You are my life and together we can conquer universes," he said kissing her tenderly.

They got up and walked back to the castle at peace and secure in their love.

CHAPTER TWENTY-TWO

Teamwork

Four days before the wedding -

Addie woke up with a start and sat there staring in the dark, listening intently, her heart pounding so loudly she had to hold her breath to hear anything. It was dead quiet. Nothing was moving. Slowly turning her head, she glanced at the clock – 2:40 am!

"Ugh," she groaned and flopped back down on her pillow. Closing her eyes again, she willed herself back to sleep. Not being comfortable, she twisted onto her side and pulled the covers over her head. *Can't breathe!* Frustrated, she lay there staring into the black of the room. Strangely anxious, her heart started beating faster, her body tensing. *Something's wrong!*

Suddenly, she was in the grips of a full blown panic! Flinging back the covers, she struggled into her housecoat and searching on all fours found her slippers. She slipped out of her room, half running down the hall, the thick carpet muting her flight. *I've got to find Kolyn...* Turning down another hallway, she met one of the guests coming her way carrying a small platter of food but didn't pay much attention to him. He looked at her curiously but she didn't care. Her chest was tight and she had trouble breathing.

Reaching Kolyn's room, she quickly entered. Closing the door quietly behind her, she stood there letting her eyes adjust and her breathing slow down. After what seemed like an eternity, she took a tentative step in the darkness. A hand suddenly closed over her mouth stifling the scream of terror rising in her throat as strong arms grabbed her. Fighting like a wildcat, she kicked out and struck his shins. The pain brought tears to her eyes and she suddenly went limp.

"Addie!" he whispered urgently.

"Kolyn?" Grabbing on to him, she started sobbing out of sheer relief.

"Sshhh, my darling," he whispered holding her tight against his body, rocking her gently.

The rhythmic motion calmed her down but standing there in the dark, his awareness of her scantily clad body was driving him crazy. Totally aroused, he loosened his grip but Addie wouldn't have that. Out of some desperate need, she coiled her arms around his neck and kissed him feverishly. Groaning with desire, he scooped her up and carried her to the bed. Sitting her down, he regretfully disentangled her arms from around his neck and holding her hands imprisoned in his, gently brushed his lips against hers.

Turning on the bedside light, he asked, "Addie, why are you here? What's happening?"

"I don't know... I had to find you!" she replied uncertainly. "I woke up all of a sudden but I couldn't get back to sleep and then... then I just panicked. I don't know why."

Confused, she stared at him, her big green eyes still troubled.

"It's all right – you're safe here," he said putting an arm around her shoulders and hugging her close.

Warm and safe, Addie snuggled even closer moving her hand over his chest. He was just thinking, *"God, I want her!"* when she pulled back puzzled.

"How come you're all dressed?"

"I guess I'm not the only one who couldn't sleep," he answered grinning. "How are your toes?" he asked out of the blue.

"Remind me next time to wear shoes!" she chuckled. "I should have followed the example of that guest I crossed on my way here. He had good sturdy ___."

She broke off suddenly, dread and horror flooding her whole body. "Oh my god! TRINITY!!" she choked out.

Jumping up, she grabbed Kolyn's hand, "Let's go!"

Needing no further urging, her panic communicating itself straight to his heart, they ran full tilt down the halls to Trinity's room. Flinging the door open, Kolyn flicked on the light switch and they stopped dead. EMPTY! The room was empty! Speechless, they stared at each other for a split second.

Addie broke into a dead run toward her room, yelling over her shoulder, "I'm getting dressed – give me one minute."

Kolyn rang security. "Sound the alarm – Trinity has been abducted!"

Within minutes, they were all assembled in front of the castle – the Royal Guard, Kolyn and Addie, staff and even some guests. The Captain quickly organized his men and sent several in various directions. Addie, holding on tightly to Kolyn's hand, closed her eyes to shut out the confusion and concentrate.

"Garden… side gate…," she murmured opening her eyes to stare at him.

Kolyn stared back. *How does she know about that secret gate?* Then he heard an urgent voice inside his head, *TRUST HER!*

Driven into action, he ordered, "Captain! Follow us!" and raced with Addie towards the gate. It was already open…

Sean had been restless all day. *The girls going to the market today was a bad idea – too many people, too many chances of them getting separated and …* He didn't even want to imagine the rest.

For most of the afternoon, he'd been pacing in the garden, unable to concentrate on anything useful. By the time they came back laughing and loaded with packages, he was fit to be tied. He stood there rigidly, glad they were back safe and sound but he couldn't seem to let go of his earlier worry. Trinity had perceived his upset and putting down her small bag had crossed the short distance separating them. Kneeling, he hugged her tight, her little arms circling his neck.

"Sean, I'm okay!" she whispered in his ear and then kissed his cheek.

Her simple words made his eyes prickle with unshed tears of relief. Giving her a shaky smile, he stared into her trusting eyes and knew, then and there, that he would never love another. Shaken to the core of his being, he had stood up slowly and looked at Addie with wonder in his soft dove-grey eyes. She had smiled at him, ancient wisdom in the depths of her green eyes.

Now in the middle of the night, he was still gripped by an unreasoning fear. Getting dressed quietly, he slipped out of the house and headed toward the side gate of the castle's garden. He had almost reached his destination when a sixth sense alerted him to the presence of another. Ducking behind a large tree, he waited. The man came to a stop just a few feet from his hiding place and Sean noted with relief that it was another Guardian – Nolan.

Stepping out silently, he whispered soundlessly, "Glad to see you. Where are the others?"

"Close by and on full alert. Something is going down tonight!"

"I was headed to the side gate."

Nolan nodded and fell into step beside him. Quiet as ghosts, their passage absorbed by the night, they approached the gate. Just then, the little door started to open cautiously and the two Guardians melted into the nearby shrubbery. A tall man with sturdy shoes walked out carrying a large bundle. An iron grip on his arm prevented Sean from jumping out, freezing him in place. Unable to move, he could only stand there helplessly while the man carried away his little Trinity!

The man walked rapidly despite the added weight of the child.

As he rounded the first bend, Nolan released Sean and whispered, "He's not working alone! We have to catch all those involved."

Silently they followed. Something had changed while he was "frozen". The earlier feeling of helplessness had been replaced by one of hope and… power. *That's it! The Guardians are working together!* Utterly confident, he found he could relax and concentrate for the first time on what needed to be done.

At that moment, the castle erupted in lights, the warning siren waking everybody up. The man stumbled slightly in surprise and broke into a run his bundle tucked under his arm like a football. The waiting car was just ahead in the small clearing and he sprinted to his goal. The door was flung open and he unceremoniously dumped the child in the back seat. He jumped in slamming the door.

"GO!" he yelled at the driver but the latter was staring fixedly out the windshield his face an unhealthy hue.

Facing the car in a semi-circle were five big white dogs shimmering in the darkness. Panic stricken, the man and a woman attempted to bolt from the car and make a run for it but Nolan having just arrived froze the whole scene.

Nodding to Sean, he said, "Go get the princess."

Sprinting to the car, he jerked the door open and pulled Trinity out swiftly. Running back a short ways, he gently laid her on the ground and quickly removed the bag covering her. She lay there limp, eyes closed, her dark eyelashes contrasting sharply with the pallor of her face.

"Trinity! Wake up, Trinity!" he pleaded.

"They drugged her. She'll be all right soon but keep her warm," advised Nolan who was still holding the culprits in his force field.

Sean raised her limp body gently and wrapped her in his coat. Cradling her tenderly, he became conscious that the Guardians had resumed their human form and what sounded like an army was fast approaching the clearing.

Kolyn and Addie were first on the scene and zeroed in on Sean and Trinity. Neither one said anything. Very carefully, Kolyn took his daughter from the young Guardian's arms, coat and all, giving him a heartfelt but silent *"Thank-you!"* Addie hugged him fiercely and whispered, "Please come to the castle – all of you."

Seeing that the King's Royal Guard was now handling the logistics of the capture, he nodded his assent. Looking over the prisoners, he was not surprised to be confronted with Mr and Mrs Sanchez. The other man he did not know.

He felt intoxicated by the power of the Guardians, by the swiftness of the events and his love for Trinity.

Slightly light-headed, he shook Nolan's hand saying, "Well done my friend."

Nolan's reply was totally unexpected. "If Addie hadn't forgiven me for what I did to her father, I don't know if I would have had the courage or the ability to use my power again. She gave me back my trust in myself."

Smiling inwardly, he left Sean staring at his retreating back. Coming back to earth, he caught up to the Guardians who were leaving for the castle. They followed the same path as before and once in the garden, Sean split from the group heading in a different direction.

"Where are you going? Aren't you coming with us?" asked Nolan.

"I'll be joining you shortly, but first - a special tea for Trinity."

The leader, hearing Sean's answer, smiled proudly. *He will be a strong Guardian — thoughtful, selfless and I'm afraid very much in love with the little princess... which reminds me...*

Turning to the Guardian next to him, he asked in an amazed voice, "How did Kolyn and Addie get there so fast?"

"AND that's not all ... the man was barely out of the garden gate when the alarm was sounded!" piped in Nolan equally amazed.

Shaking their heads in wonder, they set off for the castle with renewed purpose. When they entered, it was like someone had thrown an impromptu party with sandwiches and hot drinks being dispensed liberally. Several guests in various states of dress were taking advantage of this elite gathering at 4:00 in the morning feeling part of the "in-crowd". Nolan spotted the King sitting with Mr and Mrs Dubois near the fireplace, Kolyn and Addie ensconced in a large armchair next to them.

At the other end of the room, the big double doors swung open and Jo stepped into the room holding a large platter of freshly made sandwiches over her shoulder like a seasoned Maitre D'. Eyes sparkling with amusement, she noticed Nolan with five other men who had just arrived and bee-lined in their direction.

Smiling cheerfully, she put down the platter and said, "Gentlemen – Enjoy!"

She seemed to dance across the room to where her parents were sitting and, crouched down with her arms resting on each of their chairs, looked fondly at Kolyn and Addie. Nolan saw her turn to the King as he addressed her. Swinging her long, straight brown hair over her shoulder, she turned to gaze at their group. Wonder in her eyes, she stared at Nolan as she made her way back to them. *He's a Guardian!*

Smiling, she announced, "The King would like you to join him by the fireside."

All right, thought several of them, *now we get the whole story!* Following their host, they formed a semi circle in front of the King. Noticing that Jo was standing, Nolan pulled up a chair for her and positioned it in such a way that he could see her. *She is so ...so free-spirited...*

At that moment, the King stood up effectively relegating this train of thought to later.

"Dear Guardians, Kolyn and Addie... tonight we have shown true team work, working together to overcome —" Breaking off abruptly, he queried, "Where's Sean?"

"Sir, he's preparing a special tea for Trinity," the leader said with a smile.

Knowing exactly what those special teas could do to counteract poisons and drugs in a body, he sat down announcing, "As you were gentlemen. We will continue when young Sean arrives. Let us talk amongst friends."

The six Guardians got themselves some chairs, bringing a spare one for Sean, and relaxed in the pleasant company. Jo was sitting comfortably, her legs curled under her, sipping a hot cider. Being in such elite company did not intimidate her in the least. Looking around interestedly, she was starting to figure out who was who when Dimitri, the leader, asked of Kolyn and Addie, "How did you know so quickly that Trinity was missing?"

His question caused some unexpected reactions – Kolyn chuckled as he turned to look at Addie who blushed prettily as if caught in some misdeed.

Taking pity on her, he answered, "Addie woke up suddenly in the middle of the night and knowing that something was wrong came to warn me. We ran to Trinity's room only to find her already gone."

The Guardians were gazing at her with wonder when Kolyn added in a soft voice, "We were all standing outside the castle not really knowing in which direction to search when Addie said to take ... *the garden gate!*"

The Guardians' composure shattered completely. Various emotions could be read on their faces – shock, incredulity, awe but most of all respect. *She is gifted! What power! She truly belongs here! She must love Trinity very much*, this last thought coming from Sean who had arrived just in time to hear the last part.

"Sean, welcome to our circle. How's little Trinity?" asked the King.

"She woke up long enough to drink the tea, Sir, and then went out like a light. She is sleeping peacefully now."

When he had entered her room she had been asleep. He very quietly set the cup on her night table and was standing there not willing to go just yet when she opened her big blue eyes.

Seeing him there, she reached out calling his name, "Sean!"

Taking her hand, he sat on the edge of the bed and asked, "How are you doing?"

"My head hurts," she complained.

"I made you a special tea that will make the headache go away."

He propped her up against the pillows and handed her the tea. She peered at him over the rim of the cup, her deep blue eyes troubled. Not sure what to do or say, Sean waited. Her eyes filled with tears, the cup threatening to spill in her trembling hands. Rescuing the tea, he held out his arms to her as she started to sob.

"I was so scared when I saw him in my room and he put something over my mouth and I couldn't breathe."

Sean held her against his chest, rubbing her back gently till she calmed down. He was sorry she had been put through this but was eternally grateful that she was safe.

"I knew you would come," she said smiling tearfully at him.

"I don't ever want to lose you, my sweet little girl," he said kissing her brow. "Now, are you ready to finish your tea?"

With the tea done, he tucked her in and in no time she was fast asleep.

He suddenly realized that he had missed most of what the King was saying.

"...the protection of the Guardians is deeply appreciated. Thank-you for being there," he ended off simply.

Addie, warm and snug against Kolyn, was having a hard time keeping her eyes open.

Glancing down at her, he said softly, "Time to get this princess to her bed."

She looked up at him, her beautiful eyes saying it all. Gazing back at her, he felt his love burst forth and there was just the two of them. The rest of the world melted into insignificance, a soft shimmering glow forming around them.

Once again, the Guardians and the King witnessed the power of this great love while The Dubois stared in amazement. Feeling like intruders, they quietly left.

Kolyn kissed her temple tenderly. Hand in hand, walking in a bubble of happiness, they arrived at her bedroom door. It was almost physically painful to let go. Desire overruling, he crushed her in his arms and kissed her passionately. Abandoning all caution, she pressed her body hard against his, needing him, wanting him.

"I love you so much!" she said against his lips.

Both taking a ragged breath, they stepped apart regretfully knowing this was not the time and place. She turned to enter her room but then Kolyn stopped her.

"Oh! One more thing, Addie," he said putting his arms on either side of her shoulders and pinning her to the wall with his body. "If you ever decide to visit me in my room again in the middle of the night, I will not be held responsible for what happens."

His eyes smouldering with desire, he gave her a swift kiss and left her standing there tingling with awakened passions.

"Me neither," she murmured loud enough for him to hear.

Chuckling, Kolyn literally floated to his room.

CHAPTER TWENTY-THREE

A Few Hurdles

Later, much later that morning, Kolyn was sharing a light breakfast with Jo going over the events of the night. She was fascinated with the Guardians' role in the rescue, especially Nolan's.

"Do all the Guardians have a special power?"

"It's not that they have special powers per se, but they have innate abilities that they have recovered over time and with the right training are now able to control it and use it at will."

"Like what?"

"Well, take Sean for example. Although he is fairly young and new to the Council, he does have a special gift for healing. Nolan, on his part, can project a force field that will 'freeze' whoever is inside which is actually how he saved Addie from getting hurt even more..."

Mentioning her name made him wish that she was with him right now.

"Have you seen Addie or Trinity this morning?"

"Your girls are sleeping... Actually," she said grabbing his arm, pulling him out of his chair, "this is something you gotta see. Follow me!"

At a brisk pace, she led him to Addie's room and signalling him to silence, quietly opened the door and let him peek in.

It was all he could do to stay put. Both of them were still sound asleep, Addie's arm resting protectively over Trinity's body, the latter's small back snuggled comfortably against her. Feeling sort of left out, yearning to be with them, he took the tiniest step into the room but Jo grabbed his arm and pulled him back shaking her head.

"Let them sleep," she whispered.

Reluctantly, he stepped back, closing the door softly. "I wish I had a camera handy."

"Been there – done that!" Jo told him smugly grinning at him.

"Ever so practical," he chuckled. "When you get the pictures developed, I want a copy so I can put it in a locket for those times I will have to be away from home." *My sleeping beauties will always be close to my heart!*

Silently, they retraced their steps and sat down to finish their hastily abandoned breakfast. Both were lost in their own dreams of love and happiness, when Kolyn suddenly announced out of the blue, "By the way, Vincent will be arriving around 1:00 today. He'll be just in time for the afternoon rehearsal."

"And who is Vincent?" she asked feeling slightly irritated at having her pleasant fantasy cut short.

"My best man and your escort, of course," he said surprised that she didn't know.

"Oh!" Hiding her expressive eyes in the bottom of her coffee cup, she took a long sip. *Why am I so resentful about this? I don't like him already! ... Well, it's not like somebody is asking me to marry him! It's just for the wedding.* She became aware that Kolyn was watching her closely, his lips twitching in amusement as if he knew exactly what she was thinking. It was impossible to stay upset with this Greek god who was apparently able to read all her thoughts. Her lips formed into a reluctant smile and she broke out in a hearty laugh.

"Okay, tell me about him," she conceded.

As he started to extol the virtues of his friend, Jo was mentally adding her own comments.

"He's tall,

Good – short men give me a kink in the back.

"Blond,

Hope he doesn't hold true to form!

"Brown eyes,

Not deep blue eyes... Jo was now seeing a totally different picture.

"And you're prepared to hate him on sight!" he threw in unexpectedly.

"Busted!" she said bursting out laughing. But another man's image floated before her eyes filling her mind.

"It's not like we're asking you to marry him!"

"Who?" she asked totally off track.

"Why, Vincent of course," he explained starting to get confused. Looking at her with a perplexed expression, he started, "Jo—" but she cut him off.

"Don't worry, I'll be nice."

Getting up, she announced, "I'm going to see if Addie's up" and literally fled the room.

Kolyn stared after her not quite sure what that was all about. *Whatever it is, it will get sorted out at some point. Right now, I'm going for a walk!*

Jo was mentally chastising herself for the way she'd handled the whole conversation. *Remind me in the future not to get stuck alone with Kolyn...or even Addie for that matter when it comes to my love life. They're way too perspicacious!* I *don't even know how I really feel! It's funny... but when you're around them, you get caught up in their happiness and you just want some of the same for yourself...*

As she neared Addie's room, she could hear them giggling and laughing. *Good, they're awake.* Opening the door, she was met with a scene of total disarray. The bed was a tangle of sheets and blankets, legs and arms sticking out every which way with little Trinity trying to pin Addie long enough to tickle her sides.

"Good morning, princesses," she called out cheerfully.

They stopped in mid motion, took one scheming look at each other and scrambling off the bed, ganged up on Jo. A new victim! Pulling her down on the bed, they proceeded to tickle her till she cried mercy. Their laughter and mock protests could be heard resonating down the hall causing the cleaning maids to smile indulgently at their joy and exuberance. Nonetheless, they went about their work with a lighter step and a song on their lips.

Some time later, Addie and Trinity being presentable again were sharing a late breakfast with Jo basking in their joy.

"What are the plans for today?" asked Addie

"The rehearsal. The best man is arriving early this afternoon," replied Jo in a disgruntled tone.

Surprised, Addie gave her a perplexed look. *What's up here?* "Vincent is a very close friend of Kolyn's. Do you know anything about him?"

"Sure – he's tall, blond, brown eyes…" she recited thinking back to her earlier conversation with Kolyn. Her tone had Addie laughing uproariously.

"Well at least your *back* is safe!" she said knowing her friend well.

Bursting out in giggles at such complete understanding, all feelings of resentment fled out the window.

"I promised Kolyn I'd be nice," she said with a twinkle in her eyes.

"Wonder what he did to make you promise something like that!" teased Addie.

"*I* didn't do anything!" the latter protested jokingly having just come in from his walk. Giving Addie a sound kiss, he picked up his daughter.

"How's my little girl, today?"

"Great! I slept with Addie. I got cold and she let me sleep in her bed. Then she tickled me!"

"Like this…?" he asked tickling her briefly, distracted with images of *his* arms wrapped securely around the body of a warm golden-haired princess floating before his eyes. Giggling, Trinity squirmed out of his arms and returned to her chair. He became aware that Jo was looking at him with suppressed mirth, apparently her turn to read his mind.

Grinning, Kolyn cocked an eyebrow at her as if to say "*Well what do you expect… a man can dream.*" It

171

had been years since he had felt so carefree and light-hearted. Exhilarated, he grabbed Addie in a big hug swinging her off her feet.

From the very first moment when she fell on her knees in front of him in the mall up until now, she had irrevocably changed his life and those close to her. The Kingdom was freed of suppression, his father was alive and well in no small degree due to her warnings; Trinity would now have a loving mother and he had found the love of his life – his soul mate but even that sounded trite. Their love was so much more than that. There was just no language to describe it.

They decided to all head to the gardens for a game of Frisbee. Vincent, who had arrived a bit earlier than expected, followed the sound of their laughter. Kolyn spotted him first and sent him a swift throw which he caught easily. Rapidly eyeing the small group, he sent Jo a mean low throw which she caught like a true professional at a full run to the cheers of the others.

Laughing, she spun around and sent it flying to Addie. The Frisbee was gaining altitude and with impeccable timing, the latter lifted off and caught it on the tip of her finger rapidly reaching up with her other hand to stabilize it. She came down gracefully her arms opening out like wings, the Frisbee secure in her hand.

Spontaneous applause and cries of wonder broke out from the onlookers as they ran to congratulate her on the superb catch. Kolyn got there first and hugging her tight to his chest whirled her around and around in total ecstasy. Coming to a stop they stood there gazing at each other, flushed, their eyes bright with excitement and love.

"You are so amazing! God, I love you," and he crushed his lips on hers in a swift kiss.

Holding her close to him, he turned to present her to his friend who stood there gaping at them. The joy and happiness emanating from them was like a physical assault on his senses.

"Earth to Vincent!" Kolyn said grinning from ear to ear.

"Wow!" was all he could come up with.

Laughing, Kolyn made the introductions leaving Jo to the last.

"And this is Jo Dubois, Addie's close friend and my cousin," he announced watching her with a humorous glint in his eyes.

Knowing that he was watching her, Jo winked at him before turning to "the best man" and said pleasantly, "Hello Vincent and welcome to the wonderful Kingdom of Cebrae where love knows no bounds."

Grinning at Addie and Kolyn, she took Trinity's hand and proposed, "Anyone for a cool refreshing drink?"

Her suggestion was greeted with cheers of approval and the small party made their way to the cool shade where ice teas and refreshments were promptly served.

Watching the dynamics of their small group as the conversation ebbed and flowed, it suddenly dawned on Vincent that it was Addie and not Kolyn who bound them all together. It was like she had drawn this network of invisible threads of love bonding them to her and to each other. Trinity sat on her lap contentedly tracing the outlines of the delicate triangles of the ring on Addie's finger while Kolyn gently caressed her golden hair, letting the luxuriant strands flow through his fingers like silk. The sensual motion was waking up emotions and desires he had long steeled himself against not wanting to get caught up in another disastrous love affair.

Kolyn's friendship had saved him from total despair some three years past and he had spent six months on this beautiful island rediscovering once again who he really was and what his goals in life were. It had been a hard fought battle but now, faced with the force of their love, a deep yearning crept into his heart. Uncomfortable and miserable, he just wanted to run away.

Addie sensed his withdrawal and gave Kolyn's hand an infinitesimal squeeze letting him know of his friend's distress. Searching in the depths of her green eyes, he understood immediately what was happening.

Giving her a quick hug, he smiled at his friend. "Vince, let's take our leave of these charming ladies for now. I need to catch you up on a few things and I'm sure you would like to freshen up from your travels."

Addie put Trinity down and rising gracefully, shared a brief kiss with Kolyn.

Turning to look at Vincent, she smiled as she shook his hand. "We'll see you later."

Her luminous green eyes shining with contained love was almost his undoing. He felt as if his heart had just cracked open. Swallowing convulsively, he inclined his head and turned away abruptly.

Having gone a few paces down the path, Kolyn looked at his friend's shattered expression and wondered if asking him to be his best man had been a mistake.

"Vincent, I'm sorry – I didn't realize…" he started awkwardly.

"Kolyn, my friend, I'll be fine. Your beautiful Addie is a goddess and a sorceress!" he admitted. "You should have warned me!" he growled giving him a mock punch on the shoulder.

"You wouldn't have believed me."

"You're right! There's something about her – about the way she looks at you that crumbles all your defences… leaves you feeling rather vulnerable."

A couple of steps later he added seriously, "I wouldn't want to be her enemy!"

Chuckling, Kolyn filled him in on her brief encounters with the Sanchez and how she had been the one to pinpoint the source of trouble in the Kingdom.

"They sure messed with the wrong girl this time to their own detriment," he concluded proudly.

Vincent whistled appreciatively. "Little Trinity seems to like her all right," he said conversationally.

Kolyn came to an abrupt stop and staring at his friend, gave him the truth of the matter.

"No – It's much more than that! I have known many people who shared a strong bond but never before have I seen the kind of bond that exists between Addie and Trinity. It transcends time and distance. They sense when something is wrong and look out for each other."

Seeing that his friend was looking at him blankly, he decided to fill him in on the time his daughter had sensed that Addie was "missing" and, in reverse, when Addie knew that Trinity had been abducted omitting the role of the Guardians.

"I understand now," he said slowly a bit overwhelmed by this amazing information and the emotions he'd just experienced. "These last few months haven't been easy for you," he remarked with renewed respect for his long time friend.

"No - but it has been worth every bit of the fight. I love Addie so much! When I'm with her nothing else seems to exist - it's like we're on our own little island."

"I noticed!" exclaimed Vincent grinning at him.

Having reached their quarters, the men rapidly freshened up and headed back down to meet with the girls for the wedding rehearsal.

Jo and Addie were standing close together looking out over the garden, deep in discussion. Trinity's greeting warned them of their approach. They looked at each other in consternation abruptly cutting short their conversation. Kolyn saw Jo raise an eyebrow at Addie and the latter shrug back as if saying *I don't know.* When they turned around both were blushing furiously looking embarrassed.

They were in the middle of the rehearsal, when Kolyn, eyeing Addie in a peculiar way, gave her a loaded, "Oh!" having just figured out their puzzling behaviour. Mortified, she turned brick red and wouldn't look at him for the longest time. *What a cad I've been! Of course she's nervous about the wedding night.* Thankfully the rehearsal was almost done and he managed to slip a whispered *"I have to see Addie alone"* to Jo thereby clearing the way to speak privately with his fiancée.

Taking her hand, he asked, "Addie, will you walk with me?"

She nodded but there was a constraint about her making her walk stiffly at his side. In silence, Kolyn led her to a secluded area of the garden where they were not likely to be interrupted by guests. Addie felt miserable but she didn't know what to do about it. For the first time, she felt let down – not understood by Kolyn and this hurt. On the other hand, she justifiably couldn't blame him as it wasn't his problem. *I'm so confused – I just want to hide somewhere! Why does it have to be so complicated? He probably thinks I'm an idiot.* She was close to tears by now.

Kolyn steered her to a comfortable garden bench and sat down next to her. She was staring at the greenery, trying to get her emotions under control, when he gently turned her face towards him. He was struck by the misery and despair in her eyes making him feel even worse.

"Addie... I'm truly sorry I embarrassed you. I acted like an insensitive cad and I apologize. Will you forgive me?" he said contritely his blue eyes pleading with her.

The remorse in his beautiful eyes was unmistakable and it wrenched her heart to be causing him such needless pain. Throwing her arms around his neck, she started to cry.

"I don't know what to do. I'm scared," she managed to get out between sobs.

Having finally put a name to her fears and uncertainties, she calmed right down and raising her beautiful green eyes to Kolyn, she whispered, "I'm the one who is sorry for upsetting you."

"Addie – listen to me," he said gently. "The very first time I saw you in the mall, your smile took my heart away and when you gave me your hand again at the skating rink after I explained to you about Trinity's mother, I was beside myself with joy and happiness. When you were hurt, you have no idea how sorry I was that I wasn't there to protect you. When I see you, I feel such pride and love sometimes I think the world is too small to hold all my happiness. But when I hold you in my arms and kiss you, I forget who I am – I only think of you my beautiful and sensitive Addie. I love you so much!"

Throwing caution to the wind, her lithe body held securely against his, he took possession of her lips and her heart and soul. Trembling with desire, their passion rose to a feverish pitch. Addie couldn't tell where her body ended and his started. She just wanted to merge with him. Still wild with desire they broke apart hunger in their eyes as they gazed at each other.

"We will work this out… *together*," he murmured.

"I don't think it's going to be a problem," she whispered wonder in her beautiful green eyes.

"We should get back," he said regretfully still holding her in his arms.

"We've had so little time together – just the two of us."

"How true," he agreed looking back at those precious few stolen moments. "When I was raising Trinity, I made a point of spending some time with her every day unless I was away on business but even then I would call her. Which reminds me," he said just remembering the locket he was going to have made. "This morning I got a rare opportunity of seeing you sleeping with our daughter."

Surprised, Addie narrowed her eyes at him and with a hint of a smile, demanded, "And how did that come about, Sir? Were you sleepwalking or did you get lost in your own castle?"

"It was Jo's fault," he protested in his own defence. "You see, I mentioned your name and that made me long to have you at my side so I asked her if she'd seen either one of you. Instead of answering, she dragged me to your room so I could see *'my sleeping girls'*."

His deep blue eyes burned with desire and yearning, the image fresh again in his mind. The compelling force of his love pulled her inexorably closer to him. Slipping his hand under her thick hair, he softly stroked the back of her neck causing shivers of pleasure to cascade down her back and arms.

"I wanted to be with you so much," he admitted in a low voice. "It took everything I had not to join you right there and then!"

Heat coursing through her body, she pressed herself hard against his body, her heart hammering in her chest.

"Knowing what I know now, I wouldn't have sent you away," she confided, love and desire shining in her eyes.

A groan escaped his lips. "Addie, you have no idea what you're doing to me – you're driving me crazy," he confessed giving her a hard kiss before resolutely moving her body away from his.

Holding hands, they slowly followed the path back to the castle.

"The point I was trying to make before I got so thoroughly distracted," he said winking at her, "is that we need to make time for just the two of us every day!"

"I like that plan! But Kolyn," she began in a mildly curious tone, the corners of her mouth twitching all the while keeping her expressive eyes down "is this special time over and above the *bed* time?"

She heard his sharp intake of breath and peering at his slightly stunned expression, she broke out in giggles. A cunning look came into his eyes and he made to grab her but Addie, expecting that, jumped away and ran. In a few long strides, he caught her by the waist and held her slender body in the circle of his arms.

"You wanton woman, behave," he cautioned lovingly his eyes twinkling with laughter and joy. "We have an audience."

Sure enough, they had reached a more populated area of the garden, with numerous guests strolling about, cocktails in their hands. The sound of her laughter had attracted some curious stares.

"Oh – I'll behave all right!" she responded with a loaded look, her beautiful green eyes brimming with love and promises.

"And to answer your question – the answer is yes, definitely yes!"

Addie's deep sigh of contentment had the strangest effect on him. He felt himself explode out of his head the only thing holding him down in this insignificant universe being the extraordinary individual in his arms.

"I love you," he whispered tenderly brushing her brow with the softest kiss. Clasping her hand in his warm grasp they walked across the front lawns of the castle. Between them a thousand little currents flowed forming a soft glow around them. No one present remained immune to the strength and power of Kolyn and Addie's love.

CHAPTER TWENTY-FOUR

The Wedding

May 15th - 6:00 am. Addie was wide awake. *Today I'm getting married!* Knowing that staying in bed would be useless, she got dressed rapidly and put her hair up in a pony tail. Lightly, she made her way out of the castle and headed to the greenhouses. The dew-covered grass and flowers sparkled in the early morning sun, the air was crisp and clean. She felt like doing cartwheels but not knowing how, she settled for a small dance in the middle of the path. Laughing softly out of sheer joy, she entered the greenhouse.

"Zeus, I'm here!" she called out happily.

Expecting the usual excited welcoming bark and rush of pattering feet, she was surprised when nothing happened. Checking his bedding space, she saw that effectively he was not there. Slightly annoyed, she figured that Sean had probably taken him out for a walk. *Well, I'm just going to have to get him back!* she thought grinning. Standing outside the door of the greenhouse she put two fingers in her mouth and let out a piercing whistle.

The puppy stopped dead in its tracks and started pulling on his leash in the direction of the sound. Then another whistle came. Whining, he looked at Kolyn plainly wanting to be let loose.

Chuckling, he said, "She calls and we come!" as he unhooked the leash from the puppy's collar. Freed, Zeus raced to find Addie as Kolyn followed at a leisure pace.

Addie crouched down expectantly when she heard her puppy coming. He never slowed down and ran right into her. Losing her balance she lay there on her back, laughing as Zeus tried to lick her face.

"You sweet little monster," she said affectionately.

Kolyn was just in time to see her try to get up but the puppy was stepping on her hair and she only got up part ways before flopping back down.

"Hey!" she protested as she grabbed the puppy. Holding him against her chest, she swung onto her knees coming to a rest on her heels.

"Where did Sean take you? You could have waited for me, you know," she gently remonstrated.

Clearing his throat, Kolyn said, "It wasn't Sean."

Addie's heart missed a beat or two when she heard his voice.

"Kolyn!" she cried joyously as she immediately put Zeus down and ran to him.

He met her halfway and lifted her off her feet in a bear hug.

"I'm so glad to see you. I thought I wouldn't see you today!" she said.

Laughing, he kissed her tenderly. "We're getting married today in case you forgot," he teased.

Her eyes twinkling with merriment, she said, "Let's see if my memory is intact. The Cathedral at 4:00

o'clock –I'm supposed to meet Kolyn Roy of Cebrae, tall, dark and handsome prince."

Kissing her hard, he declared, "Your memory is perfect and if *I* remember right her name is Ariadne Renée soon to be *of Cebrae.* She is my golden-haired, green-eyed princess!"

The tenderness and love pouring from his deep blue eyes made her feel weak and dizzy. Wrapping her arms around his neck, she laid her head next to his and softly kissed his cheek.

"I really thought I wouldn't see you till the wedding and I just couldn't bear that," she whispered.

"Me too," he whispered back. "But someone forgot to inform the bride and groom about that little tradition not that it would have made any difference as we keep showing up at the same place at the oddest hours!" he added smiling into her eyes.

"Like magnets – We could probably find each other even if we were lost in the forest in the middle of the night," she chuckled.

"You're no doubt right, not that I would want to test that theory, particularly," he replied shuddering at the thought. "I almost lost you once, my love and that was one time too many."

Very gently, he traced the outline of her beautiful eyes and down her jaw and neck sending shivers over her body. Cupping her face in his palms, he lowered his head slowly and moved his lips over hers in a tantalizing kiss. He could feel her body heat up with desire, her eyes yearning for more.

"Tonight, I will make love to you, Addie and there will be no stopping," he whispered against her lips.

He pressed his lips hard against hers and then walked away.

"I love you, Kolyn Roy of Cebrae," she whispered softly to his retreating back.

The leash lay at her feet and she automatically picked it up and called Zeus. He wasn't far and came running right away.

"Do you want to go for a walk?"

He let out a short bark obviously pleased with the idea. Snapping on his leash, she told him, "I'm going away with Kolyn so I won't see you for a while. You will be staying with Trinity and Sean - they'll take care of you."

After about fifteen minutes, Addie suddenly felt anxious to get the day going plus her stomach was growling. She dropped off Zeus and headed to the castle.

Jo and Vincent were already having breakfast when she arrived, laughing over something. *Looks like Jo is over her annoyance regarding the best man. That's good!*

"Good morning, everyone," Addie called out.

Vincent stood up and pulled out her chair.

"Hi," answered Jo, "Where have you been? I looked for you in your room but you weren't there!"

"I woke up early and took Zeus for a walk."

Vincent and Jo exchanged a knowing glance.

"And did you happen to see the groom?" Vincent inquired smiling.

Addie's cheeks turned pink thinking of Kolyn's last words.

"Yes, but it wasn't planned, I swear."

Jo laughed and said, "I totally believe you. You two are like magnets only you don't just pull in each other - others are affected too!"

"You sure understand me," she said giving her friend a hug. "I told Kolyn as much earlier this morning."

Vincent stared at the two, trying to fathom the feelings stirring up in him. A few days ago, he hadn't met either and now it felt like his view on life had shifted irrevocably. The depth and purity of their friendship healed his broken heart and he found himself able to breathe normally for once in the presence of women. A tremendous weight seemed to have lifted.

Grinning, he said, "Ladies, shall we eat? My eggs are getting cold."

Following a very light-hearted breakfast, he sought out Kolyn, whistling a happy tune. The latter perceived the change immediately. There was peace in his friend's eyes and tranquility to his features that had not been there since the disastrous break-up.

Kolyn looked at him frankly and said softly, "Welcome back, my friend."

The other knew exactly what he was talking about. "Yes, I'm back!" he declared with a wide smile.

Kolyn wasn't going to pry but he was dying of curiosity.

"Curiosity killed the cat," Vincent warned with a wink.

"But satisfaction brought him back," completed Kolyn laughing.

"I'm not even sure myself what happened but I was watching Jo and Addie during breakfast and I was struck by the simplicity of their friendship. There was nothing

catty or phony - just plain honest love for each other
and I felt totally included. I didn't have to watch how
or what I said; I didn't have to pretend I was enjoying
myself although I really was. I could just be *me* and
that, my friend, is priceless."

"I am very happy for you. What do you think of
Jo?"

"Well now that I can think straight on the subject,
I can say I like Jo as a friend. She's funny and
straightforward but she's not my type. We're too much
alike – we both like to have our own way and that would
never work."

Chuckling inwardly, Kolyn thought of how
he and Addie were so much alike, operating on the
same wavelength most of the time. A warm feeling
coursed through his body thinking of her. His whole
physiognomy took on a glow of its own.

The morning crept by slowly but the afternoon sped
by. There was so much to do but shortly before 4:00
o'clock, Kolyn and Vincent were standing at the front of
the cathedral. Both tall and good looking, it was Kolyn
who took every one's breath away. Dressed in a navy
blue double-breasted blazer with epaulettes, his Royal
sash across his chest, he had every girl and women's
heart beating double time.

The organist struck the first chords of the Wedding
March and all heads craned to the rear expectantly. Trinity
solemnly led the procession until she saw her father standing
there smiling at her. Her face broke into a beautiful smile.
Clad in a royal blue gown which matched her eyes to
perfection, her long raven hair decorated with a crown of
small white flowers, she stole the heart of many.

Tall and slim, Jo caused a stir of her own. Several admiring whispers erupted as she gracefully traversed the distance.

But when Addie appeared a reverent hush fell over the congregation. They had the impression of seeing an angel. Her white satin dress shimmered in the light, a golden cloud over her shoulders. She seemed to float as she walked on the arm of Mr Dubois, her luminous green eyes focussed exclusively on her beloved prince.

When he gave her away to Kolyn, it was all he could do not to kiss her right there and then.

"My princess," he whispered, "you are so beautiful!"

Her answering smile left him somewhat light-headed. Her warm hand was the only thing keeping him grounded. As the ceremony progressed, the energy flowing between them increased exponentially. A faint glow was starting to form around them causing several in the audience to rub their eyes in disbelief.

"Do you, Prince Kolyn, take Ariadne Renée Cargill to be your beloved wife, to love and to cherish from here on out?"

"I do," he declared firmly as he placed the wedding band on her finger.

"And do you, Addie take Prince Kolyn Roy of Cebrae to be your lawfully wedded husband, to love and to cherish from here on out?"

"I do," she declared equally firmly, love shining in her eyes. Smiling at Trinity, she took the ring from the cushion she was holding and placed it on Kolyn finger.

"I now declare you man and wife. You may kiss the bride," the minister instructed the groom.

Kolyn needed no such instruction. Pride and love shining in his eyes, he took Addie in his arms possessively and kissed her tenderly.

"I love you, my beautiful wife," he said softly, deeply moved.

Eyes moist with emotion, she whispered, "We are together forever now."

Dimly aware that the minister was asking them to sign the registers, he took Addie's hand and guided her to the table where the forms were.

Pen in hand, Addie stared at the form, her name and Kolyn's joined on paper. She smiled at him and with a twinkle in her eyes said for his ears only, "That's a very royal name, your majesty."

A huge smile lit up his face as he replied, "And I share it with you now."

As she signed *Ariadne Renée of Cebrae*, a feeling of peace and belonging descended upon her.

Once outside the cathedral, a thunderous cheer rose from the huge crowd assembled to congratulate the royal couple. It seemed like the whole Kingdom of Cebrae was there, it being the main focus of attention for this mid-May Fête.

Walking down the steps, Addie's attention was drawn into the crowd. Her smile froze on her lips and she stiffened as she met the hateful glare coming from the dark eyes of a beautiful black-haired women. Her hand tightened on Kolyn's arm.

Seeing her troubled expression, he asked slightly concerned, "What is it?"

She looked back into the crowd but the woman was gone.

"Later…" she answered.

Taking her hand off his arm, he clasped it in his warm hand and smiled into her eyes. The love and joy radiating from him more than compensated for her slight upset and she flashed him a wide smile.

"You make me so happy, I feel like my heart is going to jump out," she told him.

"If it does, I will catch it," he promised. "I don't ever want your heart to be broken!"

They reached the carriages that would take the royal party back to the castle. Kolyn and Addie rode in the first one, the King and Trinity along with Vincent and Jo in the second, Mr and Mrs Dubois in the last one. As soon as the six horses started pulling away, Kolyn kissed his bride again to the cheers and applause from the crowd.

"I can't wait to be alone with you, my love, so I can show you how I really feel," he said passionately.

"Are we going somewhere after?"

"Yes…after I dance with you and everyone has a chance to see how lovely you are. Our final destination is a surprise!"

"Speaking of surprises, I have a small gift for you," she announced. "I will have to get it from my room."

"Good! Then you can meet me in my quarters – *our* quarters now," he corrected his eyes sparkling with anticipation.

When Addie entered, her heart was thumping furiously. Staring into Kolyn's deep blue eyes, she knew that their love would never end. A tremendous feeling of serenity filled her whole being as she moved towards him. She handed him the small box but he had other things in mind. Putting the present on a table, he caught her in his strong arms and kissed her over and over. Shivers of pleasure ran through her as his hands caressed her back and neck. Running her fingers through his thick black hair, she pressed her body against his. A soft moan escaped her lips as his hands moved freely over her body. Trembling with desire, Kolyn stopped and stared into her beautiful green eyes. Taking her hand he placed it over his heart. She could feel it pounding in his chest, strong and true.

"As long as this heart shall beat, I will love you and when it quits, I will find another one and continue loving you," he promised, his deep blue eyes burning with love.

"And no matter where you go or where I am, I will find you," she whispered softly.

Gathering her in his arms, he kissed her tenderly sealing their eternal love.

"Now, let's see what's in the little box," he said letting her go reluctantly. When he opened it, he stared at the beautiful locket, stunned.

"It's identical to yours!"

He gently pried apart the two halves of the heart. His throat tightened with emotion when he saw the photo of his sleeping beauties on the one half and Addie's beautiful green eyes sending her love on the other.

"It's perfect! Thank-you, my love – I will wear this close to my heart all the time." He kissed her deeply then asked, "How did you know?"

"I had a little help," she replied grinning.

Smiling, he put on the locket and tucked it under his shirt. "There!" he said patting it gently.

Taking her hand, he said, "We should be going down."

Addie took a long look at him and a slow smile formed on her lips. "I think you will need to comb your hair first. It's in passionate disarray," she determined.

Chuckling, he quickly brushed his hair and then walking back to her, brush in hand, proceeded to smooth out her long hair. Addie blushed at the intimacy of this simple gesture while a strange heat built up in her loins.

"Your hair is like silk," he marvelled. Turning her to face him, he said, "You look totally presentable now and the colour in your cheeks is adorable."

When they made their entrance, Jo and Vincent were waiting for them impatiently. Vincent eyed Kolyn noting that everything was still in order and said quietly, "Needed a bit of time together?"

"Yah – I wouldn't have made it through the night without making a spectacle of myself."

The two smiled at each other knowingly and turned to look at Jo and Addie.

"There doesn't seem to be too much damage done and your hair looks fine," Jo said as she examined the bride with a discerning look.

Her comment about her hair caused a new wave of colour to flood Addie's complexion. Guessing shrewdly, she hugged her friend and whispered in her ear, "Kolyn brushed it, right?"

Addie nodded but the glow in her eyes was answer enough.

At that moment, Trinity and Sean joined their group. She headed straight for Addie, a big smile on her face.

"Mommy! You're really my mommy now!" she said happily.

Addie kissed and hugged her tightly, "And you are truly my daughter – we are family, my precious Trinity!"

Kolyn put his arms around both, his heart in his throat.

"Yes – we are a complete family now and I love you both dearly," he said in a choked voice.

After almost six years, Trinity finally had a mother, one who loved her like her own. He could only imagine what it meant for his daughter, but he knew what it meant for him. He felt himself go out of his head and a warm feeling enveloped him as Addie joined him. A shimmering glow formed over the trio as they held each other.

An awed hush fell over the astounded guests. The force of their love expanded into the room touching all with its peace and beauty. Even though the King and several others had witnessed this particular phenomenon before, they were still astonished by how much more powerful it was.

Dimitri, leader of the Guardians turned to Nolan and said cryptically, "It was a wise choice."

For this occasion, the Guardians were wearing a tuxedo sporting a cummerbund the color of their respective tunics. They made an impressive group when they stood together, exuding a quiet power of their own.

Nodding in acknowledgement, Nolan stated, "The Kingdom will flourish and prosper under this family."

They took their place, three to a side forming a Royal Guard with the King waiting at the end as the bridal party made their way for the formal reception line. He embraced Kolyn and Addie.

"My son and daughter, to see you two so happy makes my heart sing. You make me proud."

They took their place on the King's right, Trinity next to Addie, followed by Vincent and Jo then Mr and Mrs Dubois.

It took most of an hour to get through all the guests. Addie knew very few of them but she was very happy to see M and Mme Bastien again.

"We hope you will come and visit us in the near future," said Mme Bastien which Kolyn assured them would be soon.

She was also pleased to see the couple from the Netherlands, Mr and Mrs Crane. But by the time it was all over, Addie felt somewhat light-headed from lack of food and standing for so long. Thankfully, dinner was being served right away. Once seated, she surreptitiously slipped off her shoes wriggling her toes in delight. Looking over at Jo, she realized that she had done the same thing. They grinned at each other in complete understanding.

"What was that about?" asked Kolyn curiously.

"Just a girl thing," she replied still grinning.

He raised an eyebrow, his eyes smiling at her. She was unprepared for the tinkling glasses. As he helped her rise for the traditional kiss, she bit her lip in consternation. He noticed immediately that she was a couple of inches shorter and it took all he had not to break out in laughter.

"I see," he murmured and when he kissed her, she could feel his suppressed mirth against her lips. Their eyes twinkling, they looked at each other barely able to maintain the necessary etiquette.

"That's the advantage of long dresses," she told him with a big smile once they were seated again.

"I love your simplicity, your sense of humour – I love you," he said giving her a quick kiss.

Addie felt totally exhilarated and out of some unknown compulsion, rubbed a bare foot against his leg. He almost choked on his wine. When he turned to look at her he was met by the most candid look you had ever seen on anyone. The desire in her beautiful green eyes made his head swim.

"Addie, if you keep this up, we will not be doing any dancing," he warned with a smile.

She gave him a thoughtful look before deciding, "I want to dance in your arms."

For a moment there, he wished they had eloped.

"Alright, you will dance in *my* arms," he promised with a warm smile.

The rest of the meal was uneventful as Addie kept her feet to herself. Twice more they kissed but it was carefully monitored by both.

When the girls retired to freshen up, Jo asked, "What's happening between you and Kolyn? There seems to be some kind of ... of barrier or something."

Throwing her arms around her friend, Addie's emotions let loose. Crying and laughing, she managed to tell Jo what was happening.

"I love him so much. I want him as much as he wants me and it's taking all the control we can muster to not make a spectacle of ourselves. *We* are creating this quote barrier so we don't offend others' sensibilities."

Relieved, Jo chuckled, "Your love is so strong. You should have seen the glow surrounding the three of you when you were together before the reception line. The whole room lit up and I think everyone there experienced an epiphany."

Startled, Addie stated, "Actually, it felt like I wasn't even in my body and neither was Kolyn."

Jo gazed at her in wonder. "Wow!" she said in amazement. Staring at Addie, she noticed that her make-up needed repair. "We need to fix your face – it looks like you've been crying," she said in a light tone.

The repairs were completed amidst laughter and giggles. "How are your feet doing?" Addie asked.

"Great! They just needed about an hour and a half to cool down!" she said laughing.

"Mine too! Kolyn noticed right away and he almost burst out laughing." Thinking of him made her long to be with him – alone. "How long do we have to stay at the reception?"

"Till the last guest has left," replied Jo with great seriousness.

Shocked, Addie frowned causing the other to break out in a fit of giggles.

"I'm kidding. You can leave after the first hour if you want."

"That's a relief – you had me going there. I would have perished," she declared dramatically.

Laughing, the girls returned arm in arm to the great hall. When Kolyn saw her, he said, "Excuse me" and promptly left the men he was talking with.

"You're back!" he said happily as he kissed her briefly. "The first dance is ours then you will dance with father and I will be with Trinity. After that it's Vincent and Mr Dubois for you, Jo and Mrs Dubois for me. Then the rest of the evening it's me, then Kolyn, then me and so on," he said his eyes sparkling with mischief.

Laughing, Addie asked, "I love your programming. When do we start?"

"As soon as father arrives."

The King made his appearance a few minutes later and was greeted with a warm welcome by all. The number of guests had dramatically increased, word of mouth rapidly informing the newcomers on the magical powers of the royal couple. They were not going to be disappointed as the opening bars to *The Emperor's Waltz* were heard. Kolyn held out his hand to Addie and with a graceful curtsy, she placed hers in his. Holding her lightly, they moved gracefully to the beautiful waltz, lost in each other's eyes. At one point, he lowered his noble head and kissed her softly.

That's when the magic happened – two earthly bodies dancing as though under a volition of its own, an aura forming around them spreading into the room. When the dance ended, Kolyn looked at Addie, exhilarated. "When I'm with you, I feel so powerful, so big I could fill this whole room."

"I know and… I think we do!" she revealed her beautiful eyes luminous with love. Kolyn stared at her in amazement.

There was a moment of stunned silence when the waltz finished, then the usual polite applause was replaced with thunderous cheers and laughter. Everyone started talking to each other wanting to share this wonder with someone. It felt like the wedding reception had just taken a life of its own.

Smiling broadly, the King held out his hand to Addie. She looked at him with such love, he was practically moved to tears. As they danced, he told her, "Addie, your love for my son is beyond description. Your tremendous ability to love others is a precious gift. You have brought peace to this whole kingdom."

"I feel so much at home here, so loved by everyone. I belong here!" The truth of what she was saying suddenly dawning on her. Staring at her father-in-law, she repeated wonder in her voice, "I belong here!" Her eyes shone with joy as a slow smile spread across her face.

"There is no doubt about that, my dear. You truly belong here!" he declared as a deep happiness welled inside of him.

When the dance ended, he gallantly kissed her hand and said, "Enjoy your honeymoon."

The evening passed in a blur. Everyone wanted to dance with her. Thankfully, Kolyn cut in and rescued her.

"I think my body is going to drop soon," she confided to him.

"I'm not surprised – 6 am makes a pretty long day. Are you ready to leave?"

Her response was immediate and unmistakable.

Smiling at her gently, he said, "Then let's go."

Vincent was nearby and catching his eye, signalled to him that they were planning to leave. Jo appeared out of nowhere and the two made their way to her room.

Carmelita was there to help and they made short order of getting Addie ready for their departure. Getting her hair brushed out nearly put her to sleep – it was so relaxing!

They met Kolyn on the first landing. Knowing that she would not have another chance, she said, "I'd like to say goodbye to Trinity before we go down."

Silently, he took her hand and turned about leading her to their daughter's room. Trinity was sleeping but when Addie gently brushed her hair away from her cheek, she woke up.

"Mommy, Papa," she exclaimed throwing her arms around Addie's neck.

"We didn't want to leave without saying goodbye, sweetheart," Kolyn said caressing her back.

"We love you, sweet daughter and we'll be back soon," said Addie giving her a hug and a kiss.

"I love you too. I'm very happy we're together now," she said kissing her back.

She then wound her arms around her father's neck and said, "Thank-you for giving me a mommy – I love you."

Choked, he kissed her forehead tenderly and put her down on her bed.

Holding Kolyn's hand, Addie said, "Trinity, I would like you and Sean to take care of Zeus for me while we're gone. Could you do that?"

"Yes, I'll take good care of him," she promised and happily went back to bed.

Once outside the room, Kolyn took Addie in his arms and kissed her ardently.

"You are wonderful, my love. Giving her that little responsibility made it so much easier for her to accept our leaving."

"That puppy will definitely earn his keep," she said wisely. Not wanting to think of the times when he would be gone, she kissed him just as passionately as he had just done. "I love you."

"We should go. We have a short flight to the mainland then a longer one. You can sleep on the plane," he announced smiling.

CHAPTER TWENTY-FIVE

The Honeymoon

They said goodbye to the guests and left in the small plane shortly after. It was really a skip and jump to the mainland leaving them with about an hour wait for their main flight. Sitting together, her head resting on his shoulder, Kolyn was the happiest man on the planet. Going over the day, he suddenly remembered her troubled eyes as they had walked out of the cathedral.

"Addie, what upset you outside the church as we were walking down the steps?"

"There was a woman who looked at me with such hate in her eyes, it shocked me."

"What did she look like?"

"Very beautiful, tall, black hair, dark eyes, full lips—"

Kolyn eyes went black as he whipped out his cell phone and rapidly punched in a number.

"Dimitri, we may have an undesirable on the island. Addie has just described to me what appears to be Marietta Lopez. She saw her when we were walking out of the cathedral. I had given this woman express orders never to set foot on the island again." He listened for a while, said "Thank-you very much" and hung up.

Addie was watching him with big eyes, totally awake by now.

"Who is she?"

"Mrs Sanchez' troublemaker niece," he stated point-blank.

It was so out of character for him to insert pejorative comments when speaking of another that Addie was starting to get alarmed. She picked up his clenched fist and worked her hand into his. He was completely introverted, his eyes black with anger and pain.

"Kolyn, what did she do?"

He shook his head, not sure how she would take what needed to be said. Looking into her trusting eyes, he knew he couldn't withhold any part of it, not if he wanted to live in peace with himself.

"Kolyn?"

Closing his eyes momentarily, he thought, *"What a way to start our honeymoon!"* When he looked at her again, he was struck by the unfathomable depth in her beautiful green eyes, demanding – no commanding an answer.

Haltingly, he said, "She came at the invitation of the Sanchez to supposedly recover from a broken engagement. From the start, I knew that she was up to no good. She was jealous of you and wanted me for herself."

Staring at Addie, he told her the whole story – her use of every feminine wile in an attempt to seduce him, her use of Trinity to get near him, her treacherous kiss and his daughter's heartbreak.

"It was the same night your father beat you," he whispered hanging his head in remorse.

Addie had listened to his account getting angrier and angrier.

"That witch!" she blurted out heatedly. "How could she possibly think she could get you away from me?!"

Shocked at this uncharacteristic display of anger from his sweet-tempered love, he looked into her furious eyes. A smile spread across his face, his eyes once again deep blue.

"You are utterly gorgeous when you're angry," he said caressing her face.

His touch softened her expression considerably.

"I love you, my little tigress," he said softly as he kissed her.

Her big green eyes were shining with love as she kissed him back.

"We will be boarding soon. I need to make a quick trip to the washrooms but I'll be right back."

He gave her a quick kiss and walked to the washrooms which were only some 20 feet away.

Addie leaned her head back and closed her eyes. She was exhausted.

"Senora!" someone said.

Opening her eyes, she was faced with a man in an airport security uniform. Sitting up, she looked at him inquiringly.

"Senora, you need to come with me. There's some confusion regarding your seats and boarding pass."

Groaning inwardly, Addie said, "Alright, as soon as my husband comes back, we'll go."

"I'm sorry but the plane is scheduled to leave soon and this needs to be handled immediately," he said somewhat forcefully.

Digging in her heels, Addie shook her head negatively. His lips tightened in anger and he grabbed her arm, jerking her to her feet.

Stunned, she tried to shake his hand off but he was holding on tightly. *Something's wrong!*

Flashing him a big smile, she said, "Okay, let me just get my purse." As soon as he let go of her arm, she put two fingers to her mouth and let out a piercing whistle. Angrily, he grabbed her arm in a vice-like grip and started to drag her away.

"Let me go!" she shouted as she struggled against him.

The other passengers were simply watching curiously not wanting to get involved.

"ADDIE!"

Her relief was so great she suddenly went limp. Thrown off balance, the man tripped into her legs and they crashed to the floor. As he was trying to get up, he was hit by a powerful blow to the jaw and he crumpled in a heap. Kolyn picked up a stunned Addie and held her tightly in his arms. By that time, security had been alerted and several arrived at the same time.

"What's going on here?" one of them demanded.

"This man tried to abduct my wife!" Kolyn declared.

They stared at him and the uniformed man who was just regaining consciousness. A trapped look came into the latter's eyes. Rubbing his jaw, he got to his feet and pointed at Kolyn accusingly. "This man hit me!"

"Enough! All of you, come with me," the security ordered.

Exasperated, Kolyn gritted his teeth and looked at Addie apologetically. Her big green eyes stood out in her face pale from shock. However, she still had enough presence of mind to remind him they needed to get their on-board luggage which had been left by their seats unattended.

The whole group went with them so they could get their bags and then they were escorted to the main security office. The Chief of Security was waiting for them, a big burly man with a large moustache.

Addressing Kolyn he asked, "Name please?"

Silently, he handed him their passports. He was angry and frustrated and was going to use his status to the hilt to get out of this situation. As the Chief read the information in the passports, his face registered his astonishment. He looked up at Kolyn who stared back at him unflinching.

"Where are you flying to?"

Again, Kolyn dug out the boarding passes and handed them to him silently. The man looked at them briefly then checked his watch. A chagrined expression crossed his face. *"That's right – this bastard made us miss our flight!"* he raged silently.

"Tell me what happened," the Chief asked of Addie.

"I was waiting for my husband when that man," she said nodding in his direction, "approached me saying I had to go with him to handle something that was wrong with our boarding passes. I wanted to wait till my husband got back but he insisted and grabbed my arm. So, I warned Kolyn and then he got mad and started dragging me."

"Where were you when this was going on?" he said eyeing Kolyn.

"Washrooms."

Knowing the layout of the airport well, he turned back to look at Addie. "How did you warn him?"

"I whistled," she replied mortified, bright red spots appearing on her cheeks.

"You whistled?" he repeated in a puzzled tone. "And you heard her from inside the washrooms?"

This is not going the way it should - he's getting suspicious. Kolyn looked at Addie regretfully and said, "Show him."

Resigned, she let out a sharp, piercing whistle shattering the quiet of the room. Startled, the Chief stared at this beautiful, tall girl in amazement. Her deep green eyes stared back defiantly, daring him to even comment on this. His moustache was twitching but he simply nodded at her.

"I see," he said finally.

Looking at the report on his desk, he turned to the prince, "This man claims you struck him."

Kolyn didn't bother to answer but he lifted his eyebrows eloquently intimating he could have done a lot worse.

Gazing at this beautiful couple, there was no doubt in the Chief's mind as to who was the guilty party. Secretly, he concurred wholeheartedly with the prince's action.

"Sir," he said standing up, "please step aside so I may question the other party."

Holding Addie close to him, he led her to a chair so she could sit down. He remained standing next to her, his hand on her shoulder.

The other "security" man was brought forward.

"Name?" the Chief said gruffly.

"Miguel Lopez."

Kolyn's eyes narrowed to slits and his hand tightened on Addie's shoulder. She nodded silently.

"Do you have any ID?" he barked.

Like a cornered animal, he looked around in fear searching for an exit.

"I-DEN-TI-FI-CA-TION?" he repeated as if talking to someone mentally challenged.

"I …I seem to have misplaced it," he announced after a futile search in his pockets.

"What unit are you with?" he asked as he punched something in the computer in front of him.

Again, the man could not come up with a suitable answer.

Out of patience, the Chief ordered, "Take this man into custody for further questioning."

At that, Miguel went several shades paler. This may not have been the times of the Inquisition, but he knew that there was little hope for him. He glared at Kolyn and Addie as he was removed from the room.

The Chief came over to them apologizing profusely.

"I am terribly sorry for this mix-up. Unfortunately, you have missed your flight. We will need to rebook for the next available flight."

"Sir, my wife is exhausted. Are there any accommodations nearby?"

"Yes – There's the Palazzo Hotel which is just 10 minutes from here! I can call them to let them know you are coming, if you wish. There will be no charge, Sir."

"Thank-you and yes, please call the hotel. I will take care of rebooking our flight. Goodnight," he said shaking the Chief's hand. "Also, could we be informed as to the outcome of the inquiry?" he requested as he handed the Chief his business card with his royal crest on it.

"Certainly, Sir," replied the other with authority.

They left and Kolyn rebooked their flight for 2:00 pm the next day. He waved down a cab and gave the driver their destination. Addie was strangely quiet, her head resting on his shoulder. He stroked her hair softly, his mind disturbed by the recent events.

The hotel had prepared their best suite for them which suited Kolyn just fine.

When they got to the room, Addie looked at him, tears forming in her eyes.

"I'm so sorry, Kolyn, I just want to sleep but I want you to hold me in your arms," she said sobbing, the recent events and exhaustion catching up to her.

"Addie, my love, we will sleep together. You are exhausted. I want you fully conscious when I make love to you," he said smiling at her.

She gave him a shaky smile and kissed him softly.

"Go to bed, my darling. I will join you shortly after I talk to Dimitri."

She got ready and slipped into bed, the satin sheets felt cool and soft on her exhausted but heated body. She was almost asleep when Kolyn joined her. Very gently, he turned her toward him and kissed her.

"Goodnight, my love," he whispered. Holding her close, he heard her sigh contentedly and in no time she was fast asleep.

He woke up at some point in the night to find her beautiful green eyes watching him. Slowly, she caressed his face, love and desire radiating from her whole body. Her hand moved down to his neck and shoulders sending shivers of pleasure through his entire body.

"I love you so much, Kolyn," she whispered, moving her body the length of his.

He pulled her in even closer, running his hand softly over her back and down her thigh making her catch her breath. Smiling at her tenderly, he continued to explore her body.

Dizzy with sensation, she suddenly wanted to touch him. Drowning in his deep blue eyes, she stroked his chest with her fingertips. He stopped breathing. Emboldened, she moved her hand down to his flat stomach and around his hip. Groaning with desire, he rolled her onto her back, kissing her passionately.

Addie's uninhibited responses drove him to the brink time and time again. There was hardly any resistance when he moved into her. Her beautiful green eyes widened imperceptibly and then with fiery passion, she thrust her hips up to let him in all the way. Shuddering, he made love to her, slowly, gently.

"Kolyn!" she breathed, her body vibrating with her need for him.

"Addie, you are mine!" he whispered, his love filling her body and soul as they became one.

Eyes moist with happiness, they gazed at each other in wonder.

"I had no idea it would be so beautiful," she said in a dazed voice.

"Addie, you fulfill my wildest dreams. I have never felt so complete in my whole life. Thank-you, my love... my wife."

They slept some more and made love again. Addie was blissfully happy as she lay in Kolyn's arms. *I never want this to end* she thought but then her stomach growled loudly.

"Hungry?"

"Yah - but we'll see which one wins - my stomach or my heart," she said as she moved her lips tantalizingly over his.

He instantly held her head securely kissing her long and hard. Her stomach rumbled in protest. Laughing, they decided breakfast was in order. After a long warm shower, Kolyn brushed Addie's long hair. This was almost their undoing as passions threatened to override them. The arrival of their breakfast cooled things down a bit.

"We had an interesting start to our honeymoon," Kolyn observed with a big smile. "I have a feeling life will never be dull with you around."

"I'm going to have to learn some form of self-defence," Addie retorted with a chuckle.

"Where did you learn to whistle like that?"

"When I was about 10, there was a girl in our neighbourhood who had a lot of cousins. They must have taught her and she taught me. Every now and then when I went for a walk, I'd try it out to make sure I didn't forget how to do it. It would scare all the birds away," she recalled with a grin.

"You're amazing! Is there anything you don't know how to do?"

"Yes…but I learn fast," giving him a knowing look.

"That you do, my darling," he chuckled. "What would you like to learn?"

Looking at him seriously, she said, "I'd like learn how to drive a car and I don't know how to swim—"

"You can't swim?!" surprise in his eyes.

Shaking her head, she clarified, "Remember, I come from a landlocked city and I never took swimming lessons."

He gave her a strange smile as if she had just played a good joke on him.

"It looks like I will have to teach you," he said cryptically.

She gave him a speculative look and asked, "Are we going swimming?"

He laughed as he avoided the question. "You will be living on an island and so you need to learn how to swim," he said categorically.

"You didn't answer my question," she laughed, "but that's okay. I'll find out soon enough where we're going!"

Smiling broadly, he pulled her into his arms and kissed her. "You are so refreshing. I love the times I spend with you!"

Looking at his watch, he announced, "We have a good hour before we need to be at the airport. What would you like to do?"

She looked at the bed then she looked at Kolyn back and forth and said playfully, "Go for a walk?"

"And how far were you planning to walk?" he teased his eyes sparkling with laughter.

"Actually, as much as I would like to make love to you right now, I feel the need to walk outside."

"My sentiments exactly," he declared kissing her passionately.

It was quite a few minutes before they made it out the door. They stopped by the front desk to inform the staff they would be back in about 45 minutes and would check out at that time.

"Was the suite to your satisfaction, Sir?" the lady asked.

"Yes - Everything was perfect," he answered smiling at her.

Addie ducked her head biting her lower lip to avoid bursting out in giggles. Kolyn's tone of voice meant something entirely different. Her hand twitched in his and she was aware that he glanced at her but there was no way she could meet his eyes right now without breaking up.

As they walked away, he was chuckling quietly. She looked up at him, mischief in her sparkling eyes.

"Addie, it's almost impossible for me to keep a straight face when I know you're just about ready to explode."

"I'm sorry but I'm so happy I want to sing and dance and run and kiss you over and over again," she informed him cheerfully.

"Well, it's a good thing we're going for a walk so we can *both* burn off some of this extra energy - otherwise, we'd never make it through the day!" he declared, holding her hand tighter.

The walk did help a lot but their awareness of each other was simply intensified. The perfect coordination of their steps made it seem like a graceful dance. It was impossible to tell which one had decided to turn or stop so closely were they attuned.

Returning to the hotel, they collected their belongings and left for the airport. Being first class passengers, check in was rapidly taken care of. As they made their way to the proper gate, an interesting phenomenon took place – the hectic pace and anxious expression of those around them seem to mellow. Men and women unconsciously made way for the royal couple, admiring their class and grace. Their passage left in its wake a feeling of hope and calm, the general turbulence of that section of the airport considerably abated.

They were almost at their gate when the Chief of Security hailed them.

"Good afternoon, Sir," he said and then turning to Addie, he was struck speechless. Last night, he thought she was very pretty but today she was stunning - her big green eyes radiated with love, her cheeks a perfect pink graced with a soft smile.

"G-Good afternoon, Princess," he stammered.

She flashed him a wide happy smile which threw him off balance even more.

Blinking, he informed Kolyn that they had a report ready.

"Excellent. Please have it sent to my Chief of Security in Cebrae," giving him Dimitri's number.

He assured them it would be sent right away and took his leave. Boarding for the first class passengers had just been announced. Once in their seats, Kolyn gently clasped Addie's hands and eyed her seriously.

"You have no idea how utterly beautiful you are and the effect you have on men."

Unsure as to how to take this double-edged compliment, she frowned. "I'm not trying to create an effect on men," she assured him stiffly. *How could he even think that?!*

Seeing her troubled eyes and stiff demeanour, he quickly realized a misunderstanding had just occurred between them.

"Addie, I'm sorry. This was not meant as a criticism of you at all but rather of my kind," he said deprecatingly.

She continued to look at him with a baffled expression.

"Men in general," he continued, "are infatuated with themselves and when a beautiful woman smiles at them, they tend to jump to conclusions, misconstruing her intentions."

She relaxed slightly but he could see she was still unhappy about something.

"Kolyn, what am I supposed to do? I am what I am."

He stared at his beautiful wife helplessly. "I don't know," he replied frustrated.

The plane was taxiing down the runway for take-off and they both sat back in their seat, silent. Kolyn sat there ruminating on the problem. "*I don't want her to change. Her spontaneity and natural charm are the most endearing things about her. But that's exactly what's going to get her in trouble. Men are drawn to her like moths to a flame. I don't want her hurt but I also don't want to tell her how to act - she is her own person. I guess the only thing I can do is to be there for her when it happens,"* he finally concluded at peace with his decision.

Head back, Addie was also mulling this over. *I don't get it - why is Kolyn worried about whether I smile at men or not? He must know I'll never love but him. It doesn't make sense... I went through most of High School without a single boy asking me out on a date - not that I could have, but still... No one seemed to be jumping to conclusions then. So what has changed?* Closing her eyes, she thought of her love for Kolyn and how incredibly happy she was; how she felt on top of the world most of the time. Sighing, as she was no closer to understanding the issue, she turned to look at him.

He was watching her with a tender expression, his deep blue eyes peaceful. Addie's heart somersaulted in her chest and her eyes blazed in response.

"Kolyn, I don't have a clue what to do about this situation but I want you to know that you are the first and only man I ever fell in love with and there will never be another," she declared passionately.

"My sweet and sensitive Addie, even if you grew a third eye, you would still remain my only love. I cannot bear a future without you in it," he said with a catch in his voice.

Sliding his hand under her thick hair, he held her nape as he gave her a long deep kiss.

"I love you," he whispered fervently against her lips.

"Have you figured out where we're going yet?" he asked after a while.

"I think I can make an educated guess," she replied not saying anymore.

"Yes?"

"We're going on a floating island – one of the Crane's cruise ships possibly as a wedding gift," she elaborated with a self-satisfied smile.

"Wow! I don't know how you figured all that out but I'm impressed!"

"You said I live on an island, I would need to learn how to swim, we're headed to Amsterdam, need I say more?" she said laughing.

"What a mind! We should make you Chief Detective of Cebrae!" he said jokingly.

The rest of the flight was spent reminiscing on the trouble they got into as kids. There was a lot of laughter interspersed with kisses. The plane arrived on schedule and they were whisked straight to the ship which had actually delayed its departure by a few hours on their account.

The Captain was waiting for them as they boarded.

"Prince Kolyn and Princess Addie, welcome aboard. I heard about your little adventure. I trust you will enjoy your cruise and honeymoon," he said all in one breath.

"We're happy to be here safe and sound," Kolyn said. "I hope we haven't caused you too much inconvenience."

"Not at all but I must go now. You're invited to dine at the Captain's table tomorrow night," he said a twinkle in his eye.

"It will be our pleasure," they both said at the same time.

Chuckling, the Captain left. *This is going to be an interesting cruise with those two aboard!*

The steward escorted them to their cabin which was really a luxury suite. You would never know you were on a ship. As Addie looked around marvelling at its beauty and comfort, Kolyn followed her with his eyes. Sometimes he forgot that this was all new to her.

The image of her home in Canada flashed in his mind. The one time he had seen its interior, he hadn't been in a very good frame of mind and the discovery he made there did not endear him to the place at all. Looking back at it now, he recalled the cold, utilitarian aspect of the kitchen and living room space with its mismatched furniture and TV in the middle of the room. Her room had been different, though. He sensed this had been her sanctuary, the one area where she could be herself. Clean and well-organized, she had managed to imbue the room with a quiet beauty just waiting for that ray of sunshine to reveal its inner peace and glory.

And here she was today, unimaginable riches at her disposition, desiring only the love of the individuals in her life. He knew to the very core of his being that she loved him for who he was and not because of his title or status or wealth. *She loves ME!* His heart expanded in his chest and he called out softly to her, "Addie," reaching out a hand in her direction.

Her beautiful green eyes searched his questioningly and then exploded in a blaze of love. He felt himself go out of his head as he took her in his arms. He kissed her softly running his hand over her long silken hair. Staring into her eyes, he unbuttoned her jacket and slipped it off her shoulders. Her heated body burned his as he took her in his arms again. He saw the wild desire in her eyes, her lips trembling with emotion. With one hand, he undid the buttons on her blouse as he continued to kiss her. Her sudden intake of breath when he touched her breast caused a burning sensation in his loins. The bed was not far.

Dizzy with passion, their love escalated to a feverish pitch, a glow forming above them as they were consumed by the fire burning in them.

"I think I've died and gone to heaven," he told her, love still blazing in his deep blue eyes.

A radiant smile spread across her features as she murmured, "Then I must be there with you."

"We will always be together no matter where we are. There is no time or distance that separates us. In fact, when I think of you, it's like you're right there with me close to my head and I can feel the warmth of your love embracing me."

"I get a warm feeling too when I think of you. And if I concentrate a bit more, I can sense your arms around me and see your love and soul pouring out of your beautiful blue eyes. It's almost as if you were physically present," she said wonder in her voice.

They gazed at each other not fully grasping the meaning of it all yet comforted by the thought that each could sense the love and presence of the other.

"What time is it in Cebrae right now?" Addie asked suddenly.

"It would be an hour earlier so ... 6:15," he said having picked up his watch from the nearby night stand.

"Can we call Trinity? I miss her all of a sudden and I'm not sure why," she said with a puzzled expression.

"Of course," he answered an unfathomable look in his eyes. *"I wonder what she is sensing now from this progeny of mine. How will she be with our children...?"* Slipping on his housecoat, he got his cell phone and dialled the number. As it was ringing, he handed it to Addie who was now also wrapped in her housecoat sitting cross-legged against the head board. A smile of pleasure lit up his face seeing her so relaxed and at ease like they'd been married for years - not days.

"Hello," answered Jo.

"Hi, it's Addie. Just thought we'd call home and say hello."

"Addie, you really are psychic!" she exclaimed. "Trinity was just saying 'Mommy and Papa are very happy. I miss them and I wish they would call.' And here you are calling not five minutes later. It's uncanny."

"Wow!" she said giving Kolyn a stunned look. "Can you put her on?"

As she waited for the transfer, she whispered, "Trinity was wishing we would call." He watched her as she listened and replied to his daughter's questions in monosyllables.

"Mommy, I'm so glad you called. Papa loves you very much," she stated.

"Yes!" Addie replied fervently, worship in her eyes as she gazed at him.

"And you love him just as much," she also declared.

"Yes!"

"I can feel it," she announced. Then she asked, "Mommy, will I have a baby brother or sister?"

Addie's complexion coloured delicately as she answered, "Yes."

Kolyn was dying of curiosity and impatiently waiting for his turn.

"I love you very much and thank-you for taking care of Zeus for me."

She handed him the phone a mystified expression on her face. He looked at her curiously as he said hello to his daughter.

"Hello, sweetheart! How are you doing?"

"I'm doing great! Jo taught me how to do or-orgamy! I made a little bird."

"That's good – now you can teach me."

She laughed and then asked, "When are you and mommy coming home?"

"In about 12 days. Right now we're on a very big ship out on the ocean."

"Papa," she said seriously, "please take good care of my mommy." Her tone of voice seemed to contain a caution of some kind making him glance at Addie quickly.

"I will certainly do that," he assured her.

They chatted a bit more and then said goodbye. After he hung up, they looked at each other silently both wondering what the other half of the conversation had been and also unsure what should be revealed and what should be kept secret. Addie solved the problem for both.

"I think our daughter is watching over us," she suddenly realized. "We have our own little guardian angel."

Kolyn, thinking of the 'warning' she had given him concurred wholeheartedly although he couldn't quite shake the feeling of foreboding she had stirred up in him.

"What did she ask you to do?"

"She said to take good care of you," he answered lightly as he gave her a warm kiss.

"You certainly do that!" Addie said happily.

She gave him a tender kiss and announced that she wanted to explore the ship. Kolyn agreed readily for which she was secretly glad as she didn't want him questioning her about *her* conversation with Trinity.

They explored the ship and met up with the Cruise Director who informed them of the various activities available on board and of the ports they would be stopping at. They looked at all the choices day by day and then the decision making began. The Cruise Director watched them dumbfounded. Never, in his long career had he ever seen two people decide a whole week of activity without some kind of debate over one or another of the choices. With Kolyn and Addie, the whole process took about ten minutes without a single word being spoken. Every now and then, they would look at each other, smile and would either skip the activity or check it off. When they were done, she handed their card to the Cruise Director who accepted it without a single change or suggestion. It was perfect the way it was. He handed a copy back to her which she promptly gave to Kolyn. Seeing them interact, he was struck by the level of understanding that existed between them.

"Tomorrow morning, swimming lessons for you, my love," he said giving her a hug.

She raised her beautiful green eyes to him asking, "Will *you* be my instructor for this *first* time?"

This obviously meant something more to them as he smiled into her eyes before murmuring, "Definitely!" They were glowing as he kissed her temple tenderly.

After they left, the Cruise Director automatically started entering the data in his master lists but his attention was elsewhere. The Captain found him staring into space, his pencil poised in mid air.

"Good evening, Thor."

Startled, he dropped his pencil and stood up, a strange expression on his face.

"Captain," he returned politely.

"Is everything all right?"

"Y-yes, Sir," he stammered. The Captain raised a bushy eyebrow. "Prince Kolyn and his wife were just here deciding on the activities they wished to participate in during the cruise."

Ah! Wonder what they did to rattle my Cruise Director who never gets fazed by anything?

"Was there a problem?" inquired the Captain.

"Not at all - in fact it was too easy. I didn't have to do or say anything. The whole thing took only a few minutes without a single word between the two! It - it was like they were communicating telepathically or something. I have never seen anything like it!" he concluded shaking his head.

Keeping his own counsel, the Captain chuckled and said, "I see!" and left the poor man to figure it out on his own. *"Who's next to fall under their spell?"* he thought rubbing his hands in anticipation.

The next day the lessons started. Kolyn was an excellent swimming instructor, patient and understanding. Today, he simply taught her to relax in the water. She had braided her long hair into one thick plait and then looped it back on itself which she secured with a big barrette. Her one piece bathing suit simply accentuated her slimness and long legs. *She looks so young and innocent*, he thought looking at her float on her back. He caressed her cheek tenderly and earned himself a huge smile.

He was barely supporting her back when she asked quietly, "Kolyn, can you make love in the water?"

The blaze of passion that lit up his eyes was her answer. Her eyes twinkling with mischief, she splashed water at him and rolled away like an eel from his grasp. He caught her leg and she went under. She came up spluttering. It was his turn to laugh as he whispered in her ear, "If you tease me, you will have to pay the price."

"Does that mean a near-drowning and being rescued by a handsome prince?"

"That is just the tip of the iceberg," he informed her as he calculatingly moved his leg against hers. Her body broke out in goose-bumps, his deep blue eyes laughing at her response.

In mid-afternoon, they played badminton as a couple against other pairs. They got soundly beat the first game but by the end of it they had figured out how to play as a team. Kolyn appreciated her competitive nature and her sportsmanship - she was a good loser. Sitting on the benches before their next set, they planned their strategy.

When they were called up again, he said, "Let's dance!"

That's exactly what it looked like to the spectators. As in a ballet, they moved around each other gracefully returning the birdie time and time again. It didn't seem to matter what strategy their opponents used, one of them was always there seemingly waiting for that exact move. It was match point and Kolyn rescued a spike from the back court. Addie was standing facing the net, right in the birdie's return trajectory. With an uncanny sense of timing, she suddenly crouched down, the birdie barely clearing her head and then the net!

There was a standing ovation from the crowd which had somehow doubled in size. That ended the game! Kolyn caught Addie in his arms and gave her a big kiss to the delight and cheers of the spectators.

They decided to cool off with a stroll on the deck but they were being constantly stopped by people who had seen the game and wanted to congratulate them. Unconsciously, they cut short their promenade and escaped to the sanctity of their quarters.

Safe in their room, they shared an ice tea going over the last play of that game. There was something Kolyn couldn't quite figure out.

"What made you get down right at that instant?" he asked curiously.

"You told me to duck!" she replied puzzled by his question.

"I didn't *say* anything – I just thought it!" he denied with a smile.

"You didn't use words?! That's amazing – it came loud and clear!" she marvelled.

They looked at each other like accomplices and broke out into uproarious laughter.

"I guess the joke is on them," she said wiping tears of laughter from her eyes.

Kolyn wrapped his arms around her tightly and kissed her enthusiastically. "Addie, you are so special! I love you! I love you! I love you!" he declared punctuating each declaration with a kiss.

She twisted her arms around his neck and asked meaningfully, "Are you up for a bit more exercise?"

No answer was needed as he kissed her passionately. There was nothing serious about this love making. Adrenaline was still running high as they playfully teased and tickled each other. The end result was nonetheless just as climactic. It was sometime later when they realized they had better get ready for dinner with the Captain or they would be late. After a quick shower, Kolyn helped Addie dry her long hair and within half an hour they were both ready looking very much the part of prince and princess.

"I have never known anyone spend as little time as you do getting ready and yet achieve such astounding results," he complimented her.

"I had help," she replied with a grin.

"Ready?" he asked. She nodded and took his hand as they walked out the room.

Their arrival caused the usual stir. "*I'm getting used to this,*" thought Addie. Kolyn looked at her with a knowing smile and said softly, "You are!" She gently squeezed his hand, her eyes bright with her love for him.

Captain Lärsson stood up as well as the three other men present at the table. Introductions were made. The

225

first couple, Mr Jack and Eva Thull, were middle-aged British entrepreneurs specializing in finding unique locations around the world for Bed & Breakfast resorts. The other couple was even more interesting. They were an American archaeologist team, Mr Lucas Drake and Danielle Montpetit. Addie finally figured out that they were married only she had kept her maiden name. He was tall and lanky with sharp grey eyes, his face darkly tanned and a ready smile. In contrast, Danielle was five foot some with short spiky hair. She looked like a doll but when Addie shook her hand, she noticed the wiry muscles in her arms and her strong grip. The two girls felt a sense of kinship as they smiled at each other. And then there was the 1st mate, Bjørg. He was a true Norwegian! Tall and broad shouldered, he moved with the ease of a big man comfortable in his own skin.

The guests were no sooner seated, when the Captain turned to Addie who was on his immediate left. "I got word you two play a mean game of badminton!"

"We certainly had a lot of fun but I think that by the time the story gets to the Captain, the fish has grown wings," she chuckled.

Everyone erupted in laughter and the tone was set for a very pleasant evening. The Thulls and the other couple had travelled extensively and regaled all with some of their adventures. Not to be outdone, the 1st mate and the Captain shared some of the funnier moments that happened on the ship.

Addie was enthralled, her big green eyes bright with interest. However, Kolyn distracted her at one point. He moved his foot under hers, his eyebrows slightly raised. *"Just checking!"* he thought at her with a smile. She looked back at him and with an impish smile thought, "*Yes, my shoes are on!*" He winked, his deep blue eyes twinkling at their private joke.

Just then the Captain asked him, "How's your daughter?"

Addie, still a bit distracted by how well they understood each other, replied at the same time as Kolyn, "Great! – she's an angel." There was a momentary pause as six pairs of eyes focussed on them in amazement.

"*They did it again!*" thought the Captain. He saw her look at Kolyn briefly and when she turned to him, he was struck by the love radiating from her.

"I love little Trinity as my own," she explained, her heart in her eyes.

The force of her emotion affected him in a way that left him a bit short on breath. Smiling, he simply nodded making a mental note to speak to Kolyn privately.

The opportunity arose sooner than expected. When the meal ended, Danielle and Addie headed to the ladies washroom while the Thull's took their leave. His 1st mate was talking with Lucas.

"Kolyn, may I have a word with you?"

He nodded and fell into step with Captain Lärsson.

"I trust you will not take offence from an old sea-captain by what I wish to tell you," he started.

Kolyn assured him that he'd been a friend of the family far too long for that to happen.

"Good – Your wife is very beautiful and … innocent. I'm afraid she might get hurt by—."

"You need say no more," said Kolyn cutting him off. "I'm quite aware of the effect she has on men and when I mentioned it to her, we had our first and only misunderstanding. She told me, 'What am I supposed to do? I am what I am!' It's frustrating!" After a pause, he confided, "I, too, am afraid she will be hurt but I can only be there for her when it happens."

"You're right, my friend, you cannot grow up for her. However, you two have a very special connection – it will turn out right," he assured him.

They parted company on that note. A sombre Kolyn found Addie talking with Lucas and Danielle. When he put his arm around her shoulder, an irrational fear gripped him.

That night, he made love to her with an intensity and desperateness he had never experienced before, trying to hold at bay this feeling of loss.

Chapter Twenty-Six

Innocence Lost

Kolyn and Addie's "following" grew day by day. No matter what activity they were involved in or where they went, there were more and more people drawn to them. Their uncanny propensity to voice things at the same time was the talk of the ship. But there was also an intangible quality to their love that spread to those around them making them feel part of something special.

Unfortunately, it had necessitated that Kolyn and Addie work out some form of signal as to which one should reply to the numerous questions and compliments they were bombarded with, especially when it was addressed to them as a couple.

After escaping to their own quarters once again, they relaxed in each other's company. Kolyn was gazing at Addie softly tracing the contours of her face as her head rested on his lap. Her beautiful green eyes were soft as she stared at him.

"I love you, my beautiful Addie. You are part of me and I am part of you," he murmured.

"We are one," she agreed. "Sometimes, it feels like my life is charmed. When you hold me, when you touch me, I feel so safe, so incredibly happy I think I'm in paradise."

"When I see my love reflected just as strongly in the depths of your eyes, I forget I'm a mortal man. I could slay dragons with one hand and conquer this whole cockeyed universe," he declared brandishing a mock sword.

"But that would leave me with nothing to do," she objected as she sat up.

"Not quite," he said narrowing his eyes at her. "You could take care of your hero!"

"Like this?" she teased, twisting her arms about his neck but not quite kissing him.

"Mmmm – a little closer, princess," he directed in a seductive voice.

She approached to within a hair's breath from his lips, "Now?"

In a flash, he imprisoned her face between his hands and crushed his lips on hers. "Now!" as he kissed her passionately moving on to more serious business.

The settee was obviously not made for that kind of activity and they ended up in a tangled heap on the floor. Green eyes met blue eyes in surprise. As they realized that no harm had been done to either party, they started laughing helplessly.

"My hero, you bring laughter and adventure to my life," giggled Addie.

Kolyn suddenly rolled on top of her and holding her hands pinned above her head in one of his, started to stroke her body erotically.

"You are the first and only dragon I want to tangle with," he said lovingly. He lowered his body gently over hers and kissed her tenderly.

Much later, they went for dinner. Addie had arranged with Danielle to save them a couple of seats at their table. She felt comfortable with her new friend and found they shared a lot of common interests.

"Are you two attending the Grand Ball tomorrow night?" Danielle asked.

"We wouldn't miss it," they answered.

Lucas and Danielle both broke out laughing. "I can't wait to see you dance!" she said her eyes twinkling in anticipation.

"I wanted to do something with my hair but the line-ups at the salons will probably be more than I care to withstand," she said regretfully.

Kolyn saw Lucas nod at his wife, a big smile on his face.

"Addie, I can do your hair if you want. Before meeting Lucas I was a professional hairdresser!"

"You can?! Thank-you! You have just saved me hours of torture."

The girls decided to meet after lunch the next day at Addie's place since it was bigger.

"In that case, I will evacuate," Kolyn said with a grin. "How many hours do you need?"

"Two," replied Danielle decisively.

With the men having also organized their afternoon, the four parted company in high spirits.

The next day, Danielle arrived promptly at 1:00 a handful of white ribbon in her hand and a small case in the other. Addie showed her the gown she would be wearing and also mentioned that she could do whatever she wanted with her hair other than pile it on her head.

"It gets too heavy and my neck hurts from holding my head up!" she said laughing.

"I understand. I know just what to do," she announced rapidly explaining to Addie what she had in mind. The next two hours went by fast, the two finding more and more things to like about each other.

"I don't know how this works yet, but I would like to invite both you and Lucas to visit us in Cebrae."

"I would love that! Do you need to check with Kolyn?"

"Not exactly – I'm sure he'd be fine with having you over. It's just that I'm new to this and I don't know if there's any protocol to observe or not."

Smiling, Danielle gave her a hug and said, "You look so much like a fairy tale princess, we tend to forget you weren't born into it."

"Sometimes it feels like a fairy tale – I love Kolyn so much!" she said softly.

"A blind man could see the love you two have for each other." Pausing, she stared at Addie before saying the rest, "Your love is bigger than the two of you."

"Wow, Danielle, that's very perceptive of you. Sometimes when we're together especially when we dance, it's like we fill the whole room."

"Well, I'm really looking forward to watching you dance, now!" she said winking at Addie. "Your hair is done and it's gorgeous even if I say so myself!"

Using very slim braids intertwined with strands of hair and the white ribbon cleverly laced into the whole, the effect was quite stunning.

Hardly any length had been sacrificed which pleased Addie enormously.

"Thank-you so much!" she said giving her a hug, "It is perfect!"

They said goodbye with promises to find each other at the ball. Addie was busy polishing her nails when Kolyn came back. He was smiling broadly as if he was very pleased about something. She looked at him inquiringly but he didn't volunteer any data. He just gently pulled her off her chair and said, "Tonight, my dear, we are going to dance!"

She looked at him askance, wondering what he was up to. But he continued to smile mysteriously.

"By the way, I've invited Lucas and his wife to visit us in Cebrae."

Shocked, she stared at him for a split second and began to laugh, "Oh boy! I wish I was a fly on the wall!"

"Addie, you're a step ahead of me," he chuckled.

"I *also* invited Danielle and her husband!"

Quickly catching on, he burst out laughing as he hugged her. "You'd be the prettiest fly ever!"

Once all dressed up for the ball, there was no doubt they were royalty. Addie in her white ballroom gown truly epitomized the princess of everyone's dreams while Kolyn in his long-tail black tuxedo, cut a dashing figure – one that stole all the women's hearts.

Their arrival caused more than a stir this time. As he led her toward the table where Lucas and Danielle were already seated, there were cheers and applause greeting them. Addie looked up at Kolyn, her beautiful green eyes shining with love.

He bent his dark head closer to hers and said softly, "You are so beautiful, my love!" Their progress was slowed by the many who wanted to greet them personally and also try to get their name on her dance card. When Kolyn saw what was happening, he deftly plucked the card out of her hand and started filling his own name every fourth dance. She watched him biting her lower lip. *I wanted to dance with him only!* He caught her wistful expression and whispered to her, "If I don't let others dance with you it will start a war!"

He put an asterisk by the 3rd instance of his name and said," There will be a break before this one. I'll meet you at our table."

Between the first and fourth number with Kolyn, Addie danced with the Captain and Lucas, who was a surprisingly good partner. There were others that she knew from seeing as part of their "entourage" but her main focus was to get through those and back in Kolyn's arms.

Finally there was a brief intermission and she hurried to join him at the table. When he saw her coming, he met her half way and gave her a tender kiss, hugging her tight against his chest. "I love you," he whispered.

"I only wanted to dance with you," she confessed wistfully.

"Me too!" he agreed wholeheartedly. "After this break we will waltz to *our* dance!"

At that, Addie's whole face lit up and she beamed at him. "Just you and I," she said already losing herself in his deep blue eyes.

Danielle noticed how Addie had brightened up and looked at Lucas, a question in her eyes.

"The next number is their favourite dance. Kolyn arranged it with the orchestra yesterday. This is the one you've been waiting to see," he said smiling at her tenderly.

The two couples relaxed with cool drinks as they exchanged pleasantries. Danielle turned to Addie and smiled at her saying, "I guess you know enough about protocol. Thank-you for the invitation. Lucas and I have tentatively decided to visit next spring about this time. And if you ever find yourself in the area of Massachusetts, you are most welcome to drop by."

Then Lucas added, "We had a good laugh when we realized we both had been invited at about the same time apparently without you having discussed it first!"

Kolyn and Addie chuckled, "We did too!" All four of them exploded in uproarious laughter causing nearby tables to look over curiously. The announcement that the orchestra would resume shortly was thoroughly welcomed by all as couples made their way back onto the dance floor. Kolyn's arm was warm against her bare back and she felt loved and secure. The floor was packed and as the music started, he held her closer than usual his deep blue eyes never leaving her face as he smoothly led her into the first steps of the *Emperor's Waltz*.

Gazing into her beautiful green eyes, he was powerfully reminded of how precious she was to him and how much a vital part of his life she had become. His eyes blazed with sudden intensity and he felt her tremble in response. "When I hold you in my arms, I don't feel the ground," he told her softly.

"I feel so light, so close to you, my dearest Kolyn," she whispered back.

"I love you!" both voicing it at the same time. Kolyn felt himself explode out of his head and Addie was filled with the warm sensation of Kolyn wrapping himself around her. In a world of their own, they twirled to the music gracefully, harmoniously totally unaware that a golden aura was forming around them. More and more couples left the dance floor to gaze in wonder at this phenomenon. Their warmth spread into the room, a feeling of serenity enveloping those touched by their love. As the dance came to a close, Kolyn held Addie close to his heart and kissed her tenderly. Two ladies fainted when their heart went into overdrive effectively ending the magic for the mesmerized guests.

Smiling into Addie's eyes, Kolyn silently handed her over to her next partner, a young man he didn't know by name and went to find Danielle who was his next partner.

Addie was on cloud nine, her feet barely touching the ground. She was still feeling warm from being in Kolyn's arm, her beautiful green eyes glowing softly. As they danced, she smiled lost in her own world. She was totally unprepared for his next move.

He hugged her tight and crushed his lips on hers, kissing her passionately. Stunned, she came to a dead stop and stared at him her eyes wide with shock. Freeing herself from his grasp, she gasped, "How dare you?!"

"You are so beautiful!" he replied.

Out of an age-old reflex, she slapped him hard across the cheek and walked away stiffly. Numb, not really seeing or knowing where she was going, she escaped from the ballroom through the first door and found herself on the outside deck. Like an automaton, she reached the railing and held on to it her arms stretched out stiffly. She shivered in the cold air but she didn't care. It just meant she was unfortunately still alive. Her mind refused to function as she looked out vacantly at the ocean. She felt humiliated, violated. Her world had come to a stop.

Kolyn missed a step nearly tripping his partner as he felt a sharp pain in his head. Nimble on her feet, Danielle averted a complete fall down.

"I'm sorry," he apologized holding his head between his hands, his eyes filled with pain.

"Kolyn, what's wrong?" she cried out in alarm.

"I don't know," he said in agony. "Where's Addie?"

Being too short to see past anyone's chest and guessing that Kolyn couldn't see for the pain he was in, she called Lucas. Not unlike Addie, she let out a peculiar high pitch whistle. He stared at her in shock, his feeling of loss intensifying. Lucas arrived promptly and taking one look at Kolyn, turned to his wife equally alarmed.

"We need to find Addie!"

Nodding in understanding, he stood on his tip toes and scanned the room. Coming down on his heels, he said regretfully, "I don't see her in here." Holding Kolyn between them, they headed to an exit.

They were near the door, when someone said, "She's outside on the deck."

They found her, a frozen figure still holding on to the railing, her white dress billowing in the wind.

"ADDIE!" cried Kolyn as he rushed to her.

Prying her hands off the rail, he wrapped his arms around her frozen body.

"Addie," he said desperately, "Addie, what happened?"

Her face was deathly white as she looked at him, her eyes lifeless. "Kolyn, you were right," she replied dully.

"Right? – What happened?" he repeated, a feeling of dread washing over him.

"He kissed me," she said in a monotone voice.

He felt her shiver in his arms and his head exploded with rage. *That bastard!!*

"My poor Addie, I am so sorry," he murmured, his heart wrenching with her pain.

He bent his head to kiss her but she turned her head, his lips ending up on her cheek. At a loss, he held her tight for a moment.

"Come, let's go to our room."

She nodded, letting him lead her. As they went by Danielle and Lucas, he thanked them for their help, his eyes dark with worry.

"Let us know if you need anything," she said gently.

He nodded and they were gone. Kolyn and Addie returned to their room silently. It felt like he was holding onto a deserted shell.

Once in the room, she undressed robotically and put on her robe. Sitting in front of the mirror, she stared vacantly at herself as she tried to take the braids and ribbons out of her hair. Kolyn gently took over for her and then brushed it lovingly. She relaxed ever so slightly.

"Thank-you," she said in a quiet voice getting up to go brush her teeth and wash her face.

Kolyn watched her get into bed and lay on her back looking fixedly at the ceiling. He got ready for bed quickly and joined her. Turning her face gently so he could look into her eyes, he said softly, "Addie, I love you and I always will."

She looked at him, her eyes softening slightly, "I know," she whispered, "but I don't love myself any more."

He held her as she fell asleep. *I can only be there for her when it happens,* he reminded himself. He must have fallen asleep too. He woke up in the middle of the night, hot and sweaty.

"Kolyn…" she mumbled tossing her head on her pillow.

She's burning up! Her whole body was on fire as she continued to moan in her sleep, "Don't go…" Then her body went rigid and she cried out, "No-o-o!"

Alarmed, he tried to wake her up but she was unresponsive. *She needs a doctor!* Whipping on his housecoat, he ran to the bathroom for a cold wash cloth. His hands were shaking as he twisted out the extra water. *I have to find a doctor* he thought desperately, walking back to Addie. As he wiped down her forehead and face, she quieted down and seemed to go back to sleep.

Unconsciously, he grabbed his cell phone on the way to find the ship's doctor. Quietly shutting the door behind him, he leaned his back against it, experiencing a sense of loss so deep it nearly brought him to his knees. Like a dazed man, he started down the corridor hoping he'd meet someone who could help him. He was so startled when his cell phone buzzed in his hand, he nearly dropped it.

Automatically, he answered, "Hello?"

"Papa!"

"Trinity!" he exclaimed grabbing the railing weakly.

"Papa, Addie is hurting!" she cried.

The need to talk to someone was so great, he blurted out what happened, "Another man kissed her and now she has a fever." Taking a ragged breath he told his daughter in an agonized voice, "She won't let me kiss her."

There was a moment of silence then Trinity's clear voice came through the line. "Papa, I want you to put your arms around her like I do and give her a kiss for me. Tell her 'I love you mommy'."

Speechless, Kolyn gaped at the phone in his hand. "Hello!? – Papa, are you there?" he heard from far away.

Something shifted in his universe and a calming sensation penetrated his panicked heart.

"Trinity, my sweet daughter, I love you! Thank-you! I will do as you say."

They said goodbye and he moved away from the wall feeling hopeful once again. He had taken two steps when he heard his name being called.

"Kolyn!" Lucas was fast approaching.

"Wh—?"

"I was worried man but… you look better," he said taking a look at his friend. "How's Addie?"

"She has a fever and I need to find a doctor."

Taking the phone from Kolyn's hand, he dialled the emergency number and told them a doctor was needed for Prince Kolyn's wife. Smiling, he gave it back to him.

"Why didn't I think of that? Thank-you, Lucas. You are a friend."

"You're welcome! Now I should be able to sleep!" he admitted still smiling but with a puzzled look in his eyes.

Kolyn was now able to think clearly and he perceived that Lucas was too polite to voice his curiosity.

"You want to know what change?" he asked startling him by the accuracy of the question. "I just talked to my daughter, Trinity. She told me what to do to help Addie."

Lucas stared at him completely baffled by that answer. Seeing the look on his face, Kolyn chuckled.

"I will tell you about Addie and Trinity before the trip is over, I promise. Then you will understand."

They shook hands and went their separate ways. The Doctor arrived shortly after he got back to the room. After examining her, he said she had the start of pneumonia and gave her an injection of antibiotics.

CHAPTER TWENTY-SEVEN

Recovery

Addie slept after that. Her fever broke by morning. Kolyn found her watching him when he woke up. Her eyes were clear but there was a guarded expression about them that told him everything was not all right.

"Good morning, Addie," he said softly, "How are you doing?"

She paused as if mentally taking stock of her condition before answering, "I feel like I've been to Hell and back."

Hesitantly, Kolyn reached toward her and gently brushed the side of her face with the back of his fingers. She swallowed, running her tongue over her dry lips. Without a word, he got up and got her a glass of water. Leaning against the headboard, pillow at her back, she closed her eyes and slowly sipped some of the water.

"Thank-you," she said handing him the glass.

He set the water aside and took her hands in his. She saw the concern and worry in his eyes.

"Kolyn, please don't worry," she said touching his face lightly. "I'll get over it," she added in an apathetic tone.

He nodded silently, his heart breaking at the change in her.

"Addie, last night I spoke to Trinity," he said watching her expression carefully.

A rush of colour came into her cheeks and her eyes got bright with unshed tears.

"You called her in the middle of the night?" she said disapproval in her voice.

Shaking his head, he said, "No, she called me!"

As he let that sink in, there were various emotions flickering in her eyes – pain, sorrow and …hope.

"She asked me to give you something on her part."

Addie looked at him silently waiting.

"This is from your daughter."

Just as Trinity had instructed, he wound his arms about her neck as he said, "I love you, Mommy," and he kissed her.

Addie started trembling and with a strangled sob cried out, "My daughter – my beautiful, sweet little daughter."

Her eyes filled with tears and she fell apart. Hanging on to Kolyn, she sobbed her heart out unleashing her pain and loss. She cried for a long time finally choking out her feelings.

"I was so happy, feeling so high but when he grabbed me and kissed me it was like my world came apart." Cringing at the memory, she continued, "I felt physically assaulted, outraged and then I slapped him."

Visualizing the scene again, she burst into fresh tears. "He said I was so beautiful but I felt ugly after that – I didn't want to be me. I just wanted to get out of there!"

Looking up at him, her eyelashes and cheeks shiny with tears, she said remorsefully, "Kolyn, I am so sorry. I never wanted to cause you any pain."

"Addie, my love, the only pain you caused me was the one I felt coming from you."

Very slowly, she leaned forward and kissed him. "Make love to me, Kolyn! I feel so empty!"

A fierce light came into his eyes as he took her in his arms and kissed her softly.

"No!" she said as she grabbed his hair and kissed him hard, digging her nails in his shoulder, "Make me forget!"

Abandoning all restraint, they made wild, demanding love, at times punishing in its intensity. Their need for each other drove them to the edge of reason as they battled the demons within themselves. No quarter was asked and none given. Culminating in an explosion of senses, they collapse next to each other wasted yet at peace. They slept in each others arms waking to make love again, only this time tender and caring.

After a warm cleansing shower, they ordered breakfast. Addie ate with a good appetite making Kolyn smile at her amazing ability to recuperate from the worst possible situation. Her beautiful green eyes were blazing with her love for him.

"Kolyn, I need to know *why* he kissed me."

Shocked, he stared at her dumbfounded. *Why does she want to go there?!*

As if reading his thoughts, she said, "If I don't, I'll never know if it's something I did or if it's his problem."

Understanding her need to know the truth, he agreed. "When do you want to meet him and where?"

"The sooner the better. I'd like to meet him here with you present."

"Alright! What's his name?"

"David ... I'm sorry I don't remember or know his last name."

"Not to worry – *I* remember what he looks like. I'm sure the ship has a record of everyone aboard with their picture. I'll go find him and bring him back say in about an hour?"

"That would be fine," she said a bit nervously.

"Would you like Danielle to come over?" he asked perceiving that she didn't want to be alone for all that time.

"Kolyn, I love you! You understand me so well!" she said kissing him adoringly.

"And you are the bravest, most courageous person I've ever known. I love you, my beautiful Addie." As he was leaving, he said, "I'll find and send Danielle first."

He found her in the restaurant talking quietly with Lucas. They shared a brief glance in amazement. *He seems happy!*

"Hello, you two," said Kolyn cheerfully.

"Hi!" they responded at the same time causing all three to smile broadly.

"Danielle, I'm on an errand for Addie but she was wondering if you could spend some time with her while I do that?"

"Of course! I'd love to. How is she doing today?"

"You'll see," he said with a mysterious smile as she was leaving.

"Lucas, I could probably use your help."

"Sure," he agreed simply, a questioning look in his eyes.

"I need to find the guy who kissed her last night. Addie wants to know why he did it."

Equally dumbfounded, he thought, *"Why does she need to turn the knife in the wound?"*

His expression must have been quite transparent because Kolyn gave him a pat on the shoulder.

"That was my exact reaction. She said, 'I need to know if it's something I did wrong or if it's his problem'."

"Amazing – not many would face that kind of challenge or issue head on!"

"For all her innocence with our kind, she understands people and their motives like no other. Twice she saved the Kingdom of Cebrae from a crippling loss and nearly paid for it with her own life," he said, a strong emotion overcoming him.

Lucas gaped at him, his opinion of the royal couple rising in leaps and bounds with their trials and tribulations only hinted at. Hoping to pull Kolyn out of his dark mood, he smiled and said, "You have me in a total mystery!"

That did the trick and he snapped out of it.

Chuckling, he asked, "Do you and Danielle have plans for tonight?"

Lucas shook his head negatively.

"Good! After dinner if you would join us in our room, we'll fill in the blanks."

"Sure but only if Addie has equally asked Danielle," he said laughing at their in-joke.

They ended up stopping at the Cruise Director's desk figuring that he would know just about everybody. They weren't disappointed. As Thor watched them approach, he was astonished at how happy they both seemed. *Well, that's more than I can say for the other guy!* After the usual greetings, Kolyn asked if he knew David's last name and where he could be found.

Guessing that the Cruise Director was probably imagining the worst, he quickly allayed his fears. "We mean him no harm but my wife wants to talk to him."

"That's quite magnanimous of her," Thor said. "I don't know what you said to him but he's hiding in his room officially ostracized by just about everyone aboard."

"I assure you I haven't spoken to him or to anyone about this. Last night, my only concern was for Addie and you're the first person I speak to this morning except for Lucas here," he said in amazement.

Convinced of the sincerity and truthfulness of Kolyn's statement, he gave them the name and room number – David Yardow, C Deck - Rm 321. He watched them leave and then placed a call to the Captain.

When David opened his door to find Kolyn and Lucas standing there, he was shocked and only a quick foot in the door prevented it from closing altogether. Both tall and strong it was no problem gaining entry. David was no slouch either but he seemed to shrink into himself faced by what he thought were his executioners.

Eyeing him coldly, Kolyn said, "We will not harm you. I know you kissed my wife last night and I don't condone that kind of behaviour. However, Princess Addie wants to see you."

As the man started to shake his head in refusal, he added in a commanding tone, "You owe her that much!"

Resigned, he acquiesced silently, his shoulders dropping in despair. "We will escort you to our room, now."

Lucas was watching Kolyn as this was going on. Standing straight and tall, his imperial bearing commanded respect as he decisively took control. Here was man used to taking charge and getting compliance to his orders. *Prince Kolyn is not a man you want to cross especially when it comes to his wife! I am really looking forward to tonight!*

When they arrived at the Prince's quarters, Lucas picked up his wife. She was smiling at him like a cat that had gotten into the cream.

"All right – spill!" he said laughing.

Raising her eyebrows, she said, "Addie invited us over after dinner."

Shaking his head in disbelief, he told her about Kolyn's invitation and what he had said. "Those two are unbelievable! Looks like things are back to normal between them!"

"I don't think the word *normal* is quite right," Danielle said laughing softly. Hugging his wife, he concurred wholeheartedly.

Meanwhile, Addie greeted David pleasantly enough and bade him sit in a chair facing hers. Kolyn sat to the side out of his line of vision.

"I have asked you here so you can tell me why you kissed me," she began without any preamble.

Looking at her, he was struck again by how beautiful she was. Taking a deep breath, he said hesitantly, "I don't know …because you are so beautiful."

She narrowed her eyes at this and declared, "There were many very beautiful women there last night. You could have kissed anyone of them – why me knowing I am married?"

Seeing the passion in her eyes, he realized what it was. Haltingly, he told her, "I wanted some of your love. I wanted to see how it would make me feel."

She looked at him commiseratively and said gently, "David, love does not work that way. Love is never about oneself. Until you can love another for who they are without any thought for what's coming back to you, you will not be happy. When your love is wholly for the other, you will find it is *then* returned a hundred fold.

"You are not a bad person, David and I hope you will forgive yourself and live to find the love you are seeking. My husband and I are fine but you may find it's healthier to stay away from married women."

She rose and extended her hand thereby concluding the meeting. In a daze, he shook it, murmuring, "My sincere apologies Princess and thank-you." Without looking at Kolyn, he fled the room.

Kolyn had risen when Addie did and he stood there gazing at her, pride and admiration in his eyes. *She is more gracious and compassionate than the Pope,* he thought irreverently. *Somehow, she knows when to forgive and when to hang as in the Sanchez' case. No matter what is done to her, she still finds it in her heart to love them! And when all is said and done, she remains my sweet and loving Addie!*

"Kolyn!" she said touching his arm, "What is happening?"

"I was just thinking how amazing you are!" he said catching her in his arms.

"You were thinking a lot longer than that," she teased. "This is the second time I call your name."

"You're right – I was thinking how utterly amazing and incredible and beautiful and—

She kissed him preventing him from going on with his list.

"—and how much I love you!" he concluded triumphantly a smirk on his face.

She laughed and then on a more serious note said, "Kolyn, thank-you for finding David and bringing him here. Not many husbands would have had the courage and integrity to do that. Time and time again, you have let me make my decisions never forcing your opinions on me and I am a better person because of it. Your strength gives me strength, your love fuels my love…" she trailed off kissing him ardently.

In the middle of their kiss, someone knocked on the door. Kolyn answered it and seeing the doctor standing there with his satchel in hand, gave him a wide smile as he invited him in. The Doctor looked at him curiously, wondering if he was one of those with a morbid sense of humour. Somehow, he didn't think so but then…you just never knew…

"I've come to check up on Princess Addie," he said politely.

"Hello, Doctor," she said coming out of the kitchen area.

The poor doctor turned white as a sheet as if he had just seen a ghost. Kolyn grabbed his arm and assisted him to a chair while Addie pressed a glass of cold water in his hands. He drank in big gulps almost choking on it in his agitation. *Last night she was running a temperature of 102° F with all the symptoms of a full blown double pneumonia! And now, here she stands a walking advertisement for a health or glamour magazine!*

"Thank-you," he said handing the glass back to Addie. "I guess you have no need of my services."

Standing up, he prepared to leave but Kolyn pushed him back gently in the chair. *We can't let him leave with the wrong impression.*

"Doctor," he said, "have you ever dealt with patients who had suffered a very shocking experience but then recovered very rapidly?"

"Yes, I have seen quite a few cases like that."

"And it seemed quite miraculous?"

"Yes – but nothing close to Princess Addie," he argued.

"I understand your bewilderment. Last night at the ball, Addie suffered a great shock and she wanted to ...to die. When we found the exact cause of the upset, she snapped out of it."

Somewhat mollified, he looked at Addie a small smile appearing on his lips. "You must have a very strong constitution to recover that fast!" he said in amazement.

Smiling at him gently, she said, "I do. I have very rarely been sick and when I did, I was on my feet in no time. Plus, Kolyn knew just what to do after you gave me the antibiotics."

"I am happy to see you are doing so well. I wish my patients would all recover that fast but then – I'd be out of a job," he said with a grin.

Reassured, the Doctor left in a peaceful frame of mind, no longer thinking of magic or divine intervention. Kolyn and Addie looked at each other silently feeling they would never have been able to live this down had word gotten out of this "miraculous" recovery.

Addie started smiling as a new thought occurred to her. Kolyn smiled back, arching an eyebrow.

"We truly complement each other. I would never have thought to handle the Doctor. But you saw right away the widespread ramifications this could cause. The way I see it is that you handle things that would affect the whole group while I take care of people one on one."

He reflected on this briefly coming to the same conclusion. "I take care of the whole picture and you take care of the details!" he said, giving her a high-five which turned into an exuberant kiss.

Laughing, he decided it was time they showed themselves outside their room. "They need to know we are okay and that an errant kiss didn't destroy our marriage. Appearances need to be maintained when you're royalty!" he said his deep blue eyes twinkling with merriment and joy.

"Right! By the way I invited Danielle —

"And I invited Lucas!" he finished off for her.

"When?" they asked of each other curiously.

"I think we already know the answer to that," he said hugging her.

Hands linked, they went out to get a bite to eat. Seeing them so happy and obviously still deeply in love, people felt more tolerant toward the guy who had kissed her. The first reaction by some on witnessing the assault on the Princess had been to throw him overboard but cooler heads had prevailed. Somehow Kolyn and Addie had come to symbolize a uniting force, one that could lead and inspire them to personal greatness. They felt a certain amount of loyalty to this royal couple and as such it became their duty to protect them. That they had failed through the betrayal of one of their own was like a blow to the collective.

Prior to this, the royal couple had been like the newest celebrity to be followed and admired in the hope that some favour would come their way. Now, the most devoted "followers" had taken on the role of bodyguards thereby allowing Kolyn and Addie some breathing room. It was a refreshing change and Kolyn noticed it right away. It was not unlike how the people of the Kingdom of Cebrae treated its monarchy.

Looking over at Addie sitting there peacefully, he commented, "We seem to have been elected King and Queen of this vessel."

Startled, Addie glanced at their shipmates searching for an explanation to his comment. Seeing nothing out of the ordinary, she said, "My King, could you please clarify what you mean for the edification of your confused Queen?"

Trying to keep a straight face, her eyes were nonetheless sparkling with mischief. With great seriousness, he picked up her hand and kissed it.

"My Queen," he said his lips twitching in suppressed mirth, "you hold the fate of these people in your beautiful hands. You have but to say the word and they will do your bidding, no questions asked."

Just then a waiter approached them. "Princess, what would you like to order?"

She stared at him briefly before ducking her head in the menu, biting her lower lip in an effort to suppress the irrepressible urge to burst out laughing. She dared not look at Kolyn as she knew this would be her undoing. She was concentrating so hard on stifling her laughter that she couldn't quite read what was on the menu. She ordered the first thing that came to mind.

"The Soup du Jour, please," she finally answered flashing him a wide smile. She still couldn't look at Kolyn but she heard him stifle a guffaw and attempt to hide it as a cough.

"Certainly," said the waiter. "And for you, Sir?"

"The same," he managed to answer with a straight face although Addie was sure he was ready to burst. She took a peek at him and met his laughing eyes briefly. It was her turn to cough.

"As you wish," said the puzzled waiter looking from one to the other.

He could feel the thousand undercurrents but didn't understand what was going on.

"Your order will be right with you," he said politely and left rapidly.

They looked at each other cautiously neither one intending to break the tenuous control they had on their euphoric emotions. But as they silently gazed in each others' eyes, their hands connected across the table and the urge to laugh sublimated into a sensation of pure joy and serenity. There was so much understanding and power being generated between them at that moment that the space around their table fairly crackled with energy and then it exploded in ever expanding waves of sheer love into the room, out onto the decks and past the ship into the horizon. A strange calm settled over all aboard and from somewhere in the stratosphere, the ship seemed to sing as it danced across the ocean waves.

Puzzled, Captain Larsson halted in his footsteps and listened. The powerful engines were humming contentedly, the ship throbbing as if it had a life of its own. He was a strong and capable captain and he loved his ship but right now he experienced a kinship with it he had never felt before. The weight of commanding such a huge vessel lifted from his shoulders. With light steps, he carried on with his personal mission of finding Kolyn and Addie. *This has been the most interesting cruise I've ever captained!*

When he spotted them basking in each others' eyes, he felt the raw energy and power emanating from them. *I should have known those two had something to do with this! Together, they are extremely powerful – they could make or break a country."* Suddenly, in a dawning realization, he understood what was happening now versus the night of the ball.

When Addie "crashed", Kolyn had been overwhelmed with despair and had been in no better shape than she was. The ship had mysteriously been beset with all sorts of small emergencies – quarrels, two fist fights, the necessity to escort David to his room as a protective measure, small equipment failing to work… He had been extremely busy handling the aftermath of that fateful kiss and this was the first chance he had gotten to see them.

Becoming conscious that the Captain was standing by their table, they turned to him. Kolyn's deep blue eyes and Addie's beautiful green eyes blazed with an intense emotion. He felt himself go weak in the knees and quickly sat down.

"Captain!" they said with a dazzling smile.

"What just happened?" he blurted out in a dazed tone.

Addie looked at Kolyn and he nodded. Taking the Captain's hand, she said gently, "We are doing extremely well and I guess it just went a little beyond the two of us."

"I'll say!" he exclaimed somewhat recovered. "It was like my ship had suddenly sprouted wings. Everything got very calm as in a dream."

They looked at him silently. *What can you say to that?* The fact of the matter remained – their love *was* greater than the both of them.

"I'm happy to see you are both fine. There was a near riot aboard after that young man kissed you," he said ruefully. "It was like they had taken it as a personal affront." He paused thoughtfully and continued, "The dynamics aboard the ship changed over the course of this cruise and it was due to your influence. Usually the guests just do their own thing with some interaction and friendships springing up here and there but never like this. It's like there's an *esprit de corps*, a group spirit that has formed and you two have somehow been elected as leaders."

Addie and Kolyn glanced at each other and both burst out laughing to the immense chagrin of the Captain who had been quite serious.

"Captain," said Kolyn soothingly, "please don't be offended."

He proceeded to repeat the conversation he had just had with Addie and the waiter's choice of words.

"I'm sure she couldn't read the menu for trying to suppress her laughter plus she had it open to the desert page!"

They broke out in uproarious laughter, tears streaming down their faces. The poor waiter arrived just then with their order totally bewildered but still managing a polite smile as he placed their soup and bun on the table. "Thank-you," they both said pleasantly. He left reassured it wasn't anything he had done to cause such hilarity.

"Captain, we have thoroughly enjoyed our cruise and you may thank all of your staff for their excellent service."

"It was my pleasure to have you aboard. I hope you will have a chance to come again."

"We will make a point of it and this time we'll bring the whole family," Kolyn said looking pointedly at Addie with a wide smile.

She blushed delicately as the Captain stared at her.

"I'm sure Trinity and Jo and Mr & Mrs Dubois would love to come on such a cruise," she put in quickly knowing very well what the men were both thinking.

They chuckled not put off in the least. After Captain Lärsson left, Kolyn gave Addie a steady look and started eating his soup deep in thought. *We haven't*

257

talked about children but this isn't the time and place. Addie was also considering the same subject matter but in more practical terms. *How many children do we want? I'm sure he would like a son! We already have a daughter...*

"We should call Trinity and let her know everything is alright although I'm pretty sure she's already aware of it," she reminded Kolyn, her eyes soft with love.

"Yes, our little guardian angel," he agreed. "One day I may find out what it is that links the two of you so closely."

His deep blue eyes burned with love as he looked at her. Seeing the raw passion in his eyes, she put down her spoon and reached for his hand.

"I'm done eating," she announced, her desire for him overshadowing all other needs. "I love you," she whispered her heart beating a song in her chest.

CHAPTER TWENTY-EIGHT

Homeward Bound

Kolyn was caressing Addie's hair as she sat at his feet on a huge cushion, her head resting against his knee. Danielle was leaning peacefully against Lucas in the other settee, his arm encircling her lovingly. They were really looking forward to getting some of their questions answered regarding their new friends.

"How did you meet?" asked Addie.

"I was working in a hair salon," began Danielle. "That day had been an exceptionally bad one. Three of my regular clients had been assigned to other girls by the boss. This was not the first time he had done that and even though I had previously taken it up with him, he seemed to take a perverse pleasure in stealing from me. Anyway, to make a long story short, I was livid and I knew I had to get out of there before I did something I would later regret. I stormed out and there was this tall guy in jeans and leather jacket blocking my way. I stepped to the right and he moved in the same direction; so I went the other way and he did too!"

Lucas took over at this point. "She stood there fist clenched, rigid with anger. I didn't know if she was going to attack me or fall in a puddle of tears at my feet.

So, I bodily moved her around me and no sooner did I let go, she turns and practically steps off the curb into rushing traffic. I grabbed her jacket and pulled her to safety.

"Do you have a death wish," he asked holding her protectively.

"No! I just quit my job!" she said bristling with anger as if this justified jumping off curbs.

He looked down at this slip of a girl with her spiked hair still in the circle of his arms and knew he didn't want to let her go.

He smiled tentatively. "Do you feel up to doing one more?" he asked pointing to his head.

"It depends on what you want – Iroquois or Chinese monk?" she replied belligerently.

"Are those my only choices?" he countered with a grin.

His infectious smile won her over and despite herself, she felt her anger evaporate.

"I'm Danielle," she said extending a hand.

"Lucas."

"All right, Lucas, let's get your hair cut and I promise not to scalp you."

Danielle picked up from there. "We went out for lunch afterwards and he offered me a position as his personal assistant when he went out on archaeological digs. That was two years ago – we got married a year and a half later."

"What made you ask Danielle to work for you," asked Kolyn curiously.

"Several reasons – she seemed to be just out of a job and I needed an assistant. But mostly, it was her spitfire

attitude that I admired from the very first moment…
that and the fact that when I held her in my arms, she
didn't fight me!"

Laughing, Addie said, "Danielle, what have you to
say to that?"

"He's right! I felt safe in his arms and he was the
first and only person who had ever managed to get me
off my high horses in such a short period of time. I
knew right there and then that he was special," she
declared turning to look at him fondly.

He gave her a swift kiss and she settled more
comfortably against him, his chin resting on her spiked
head.

"What about you two? How did you meet?" asked
Lucas.

"I literally fell at his feet!" Addie chuckled going
on to describe their first encounter. "Frankly, I would
probably have fallen anyway, missed step or not – he
was so gorgeous!"

"How long ago was that?" Danielle wanted to know.

"This past Christmas," answered Kolyn. "Actually,
I saw Addie a whole of four times before I had to leave
for Cebrae. It was three months later before I got to see
her again under very different circumstances."

Danielle exchanged a puzzled look with Lucas.
"You've only known each other for five months, three
of which don't count?!" she exclaimed. Shaking her
head in disbelief, she added, "You two are like an old
couple – I mean, you do and say things that only people
who've been together for *years* finally achieve!"

Addie looked up at Kolyn, a question in her eyes. He
looked back seriously, raising an eyebrow. They smiled

as if having reached some kind of decision. Danielle and Lucas watched this silent interchange interestedly.

"We have loved each other for a very long time," Addie said cryptically.

Lucas understood right away. "You mean you've known each other before!" he said excitedly.

Shocked, they stared at him. *How did he ever come to that conclusion so fast?*

Knowing he was right, Lucas explained, "Sometimes, in my line of work you come across artefacts and other symbols that could only have been left by people who knew each other in a previous lifetime. The locations and times are often entirely different but there is this one object that links the two digs. It's quite amazing and many in my field tend to discredit the connection but I keep my own counsel on it."

Kolyn looked at him with a new measure of respect and said, "For us it was love at first sight as if we recognized each other."

"But we didn't figure it out till after I got hurt," said Addie.

"What happened?" they both asked curiously causing some of the enormity of what had just been revealed to take its rightful place as they all chuckled.

"I had to leave Addie in Edmonton because I didn't feel it was safe for her in Cebrae," he started. "Nonetheless, over brunch on our first date, she pinpointed the source of the trouble we were having." He went on to explain the sequence of events that led to her being beaten up by her father.

"This is where my five-year old daughter comes in," he said smiling at Lucas.

Pausing to organize his thoughts, Kolyn was thinking, *"This is no easier than trying to explain our own relationship! How do I convey the strong bond that exists between them? I don't even understand it myself!"*

"Trinity and Addie immediately became great friends and over the months they e-mailed regularly strengthening that bond. The night Addie was hurt, my daughter sensed something was wrong and was extremely upset."

Kolyn's eyes went dark at the memory, the anguish of that night still being felt. Addie took his hand and smiled tenderly at him. He gently caressed her face before going on.

The two listened enthralled as he revealed the rest of the story including Trinity's abduction. He omitted the role of the Guardians just saying there were others also looking out for the little princess.

"The night of the ball, Trinity called me just before you arrived. Again, she knew that Addie was in trouble despite the time and distance. We call her our little guardian angel!" he concluded smiling at Addie.

"I'm really looking forward to meeting your daughter," said Danielle.

"She is too. I told her we made some new friends and she said you'd be her friends also," said Addie brightly. "She wanted to know all about you two!"

The two couples talked late into the night gaining a new appreciation for their friendship finding more and more things in common.

"By the way, Danielle, the night of the ball when you whistled to get Lucas' attention, you nearly killed me with shock! I thought it was only Addie who called her husband that way," Kolyn kidded, his eyes twinkling as he looked at his wife.

The two girls stared at each other and burst out laughing.

Finally Addie regained some of her composure and turning her beautiful green eyes on Kolyn she said, "That whistle is actually reserved for my dog, never for my husband. I love you too much for that."

"I know, my love, but I would recognize that whistle anywhere and would still come running because it would mean you need my help!" he said tenderly.

"And I feel the same way about your special call, Danielle," said Lucas as he hugged his wife and kissed the top of her head.

They parted company shortly after, both couples elated at the thought of seeing each other again in the coming year.

Kolyn and Addie got ready for bed happy to be by themselves. The adrenaline was running high and they felt like celebrating. Kissing her passionately, he held her body close to his stroking her soft skin.

"I love you so much I have a hard time keeping my hands off of you. I want to hold you close to my heart and lips all the time," he murmured.

Drowning in his deep blue eyes, Addie felt engulfed by his love. There was only one thing that could possibly surpass this euphoric sensation.

"Kolyn, this afternoon when we were with Captain Lärsson, you hinted at *our* family," she said softly almost longingly.

He stopped breathing, the pressure in his heart unbearable. His throat tight with emotion, he told her with equal longing, "I want to have children with you, my beautiful Addie."

"And I want a family of my own so badly, sometimes it hurts thinking about it. You have no idea how lonely it has been," she said tears in her eyes. "Kolyn, it would be the most precious gift I have ever received."

An incredible joy filled his heart as he kissed her and held her fiercely.

"Deep blue eyes," she said dreamily.

"Beautiful green eyes," he said tenderly.

"Raven hair."

"Golden hair."

Feeling on top of the world, Addie kissed him deeply only stopping to come up for a breath. "I am so happy. I love you!" she declared kissing him some more.

"Addie, I'll die a happy man if you don't let me breathe," he said laughing as he rolled her over. That night was truly a celebration of love.

The next day the ship docked and after all the farewells, Kolyn announced that they would be stopping over at the Bastien's vineyard on the way home. *Do we have to? I was hoping to go home and start my new life and see Trinity and Jo and everyone else."* He saw the disappointment in her eyes and knew what she was thinking.

"My open-book Addie," he said smiling at her tenderly, "I want to go home too and make love to you in our own bed."

"You have a one-track mind," she teased but her mood lifted.

Laughing, he said, "Nothing wrong with that where it concerns you, my dear! But I promised them at the wedding we'd stop by plus there is a surprise waiting for you there."

"And you're planning to keep it so till I trip over it, right?"

"Yep!" he said giving her a hug.

She gave him a long searching look as if she could somehow pluck the data out of his mind.

"Addie, if you read my mind on this one, I'll eat my shirt," he declared laughing.

"Okay, deal! – It's just that I'm anxious to see Trinity and Jo."

He just smiled mysteriously, a strange expression in his deep blue eyes as he stared at his beautiful psychic wife.

When they arrived at M and Mme Bastien's vineyard, they were enthusiastically welcomed. Kolyn and Addie were standing there holding hands when she heard a small giggle behind her. *There's only one person that giggles like that!* She spun around.

"Trinity!" she said grabbing her daughter in her arms.

"Surprise, Mommy!" she said hugging her neck tightly. "I missed you!"

And then Jo stepped up, a huge smile on her face and hugged them both. After the initial surprise was over, Addie went and stood in front of Kolyn, hands on her hips.

She smiled sweetly and said with mock severity, "You'd better start eating! I hope you're hungry."

Everyone stared at them in amazement as Kolyn roared with laughter.

"You didn't guess," he pointed out still laughing.

"Half, then," she conceded laughing.

He pulled her into his arms and kissed her. Between chuckles, he told them about the bet and how close she had been to guessing. They all laughed in relief knowing that everything was fine between them.

Picking up his daughter, Kolyn gave her a big hug and a kiss. They all headed to the house, Jo and Addie arm in arm with The Bastiens leading the way. Kolyn dragged behind a bit and whispered to Trinity, "I love you, my sweet daughter. Again, you saved Addie but you also saved me."

"I love you, Papa. However, this time it was not just Addie's pain that I felt, it was yours too. It was very strong," she said in awe. "I also feel it when you're very happy like last night," she added squeezing his neck with her small arms.

"Yes – very happy! We are going to be a real family."

Her deep blue eyes stared into his for a moment and then she smiled, her face beaming with joy. He just nodded and hugged her once more before putting her down. She skipped alongside of him humming under her breath. He swore she was singing a variation of a previously made up tune. *I love Addie, I love Addie. She's going to have a baby!*

Supper that night was a joyous feast with their top quality wine served in honour of the royal guests. Trinity really wanted to taste it and so Kolyn gave her a very small amount in a real wine glass. She proceeded very seriously to twirl it gently like she had seen others do, to the great amusement of everyone. She went through all the motions of a wine connoisseur finally taking a small sip. Her eyes went big and round as she swallowed. Slightly shocked, she turned to look at Addie who was watching her carefully. Her deep blue eyes were filled with concern.

Addie gently took the glass from her hand and placed it on the table.

"What's wrong?" she asked softly bending closer.

Trinity moved Addie's hair away from her ear and whispered, "I don't think *you* should drink this."

Her words had the effect of a catalyst. Addie's face went pale and then a deep blush spread through her cheeks. She gaped at Trinity as the other stared back steadily, the message in her eyes quite clear. Kolyn watched them intently with an unreadable expression on his face. *What could she possibly have told her to cause that kind of reaction?!* Their hosts and Jo were equally fascinated by what was going on across the table. Silently, they watched as Addie and Trinity continued to gaze at each other, a smile slowly forming on their lips getting wider and wider till their whole expression was one of pure joy and delight. They hugged and settling back in their chairs, looked innocently at the rest of the people sitting around the table, Mona Lisa smiles on their faces. Kolyn was beside himself with curiosity but both Addie and Trinity were avoiding his gaze. Frustrated, he looked at Jo who just shrugged.

"Ma chère Addie, are you alright?" asked Mme Bastien solicitously.

"I'm fine," she answered with a dazzling smile, "but I think your excellent wine is having just as much an effect on me as it did for Trinity."

She accepted the explanation graciously while Kolyn lifted both eyebrows in disbelief. *She had wine on the ship and it didn't bother her at all!* Slowly, he raised his own glass to his lips, deep in thought as the conversation resumed around him.

Knowing she owed him some kind of explanation, Addie turned her head towards him. She smiled, her beautiful green eyes glowing with incredible joy. Thunderstruck, he abruptly set his glass down as he stared at her thoroughly confused. Her steady gaze seemed to be sending him a secret message along with a love so strong he felt himself transported into another world. He smiled, his deep blue eyes suddenly blazing with an intense emotion as their love connected above Trinity's head. You could almost feel the energy travel between the two and when their daughter took each one by the hand, the triangle was completed. The air around them shimmered and a strange calm spread into the room.

Jo was grinning from ear to ear. *I really missed those two! They make you feel so warm inside.* M and Mme Bastien had no clue what had just touched them but they smiled at each other tenderly their hands unconsciously coming together. Gone were their worries of the day, their efforts to be good hosts – nothing mattered except just being there with each other and their friends.

The feeling of peace remained even after Kolyn and Addie reluctantly broke the link. The evening carried on with tales of Addie's ability to duck badminton birdies at the exact right moment and places they had seen. It was arranged for them to take a tour of the vineyard the next day and on that note, they all retired for the night.

Snuggled under a huge goose down duvet, Kolyn smiled at Addie and asked, "Will you tell me what Trinity said?"

"She said 'I don't think you should drink this' meaning the wine," replied Addie a soft smile on her lips.

Kolyn's mind was whirling as he tried to make sense of this. He gazed at her silently as she continued to smile at him, patiently waiting for him to come to his own conclusion. She saw it coming as a rush of emotion crossed his handsome features.

"Addie..?" he questioned hesitantly not allowing himself to voice what his heart was telling him. Her smile just got wider, her eyes brighter. With a strangled moan, he crushed her against his heart.

"My beautiful Addie, how I love you!" he whispered fiercely his eyes bright with happy tears.

Ecstatic, he kissed her over and over, holding her at times tenderly only to squeeze her tightly against his chest in the next moment.

"How do you know? How does Trinity know?" he finally asked.

"I mostly know in my heart as there are no known tests that would detect it this early. As to how our little daughter knows – I have no idea!" she said with a grin.

"How she knows half the things she does is also a mystery to me," he concurred cheerfully.

"Kolyn, would you mind very much if we kept this between us for the time being?"

"My sweet Addie," he said giving her a kiss, "I think that would be a wise decision. We will talk to Trinity tomorrow although I think she already knows to be discreet."

"Yes – until we can come up with *medical* evidence, I would feel better not telling anyone. We have a hard enough time explaining some of the things we do and innately know without adding fuel to the fire."

Recalling an earlier conversation with the King, she started to chuckle. Smiling, he waited for her to tell him what she was thinking.

"When I had my audience with the King, he wanted to know why I thought our meeting wasn't a coincidence. I laughed and told him that sooner or later someone would have me incarcerated for having too much imagination!"

"You are so right! There is no point in attracting undue attention to ourselves. The world will know soon enough," he said as he softly placed his hand on her stomach. Looking at her in wonder, he added, "You are the mother of our child!"

"You are his father," she said caressing his face tenderly.

"His..?" surprise and...joy in his eyes.

"Uh-huh! A prince!" she declared with certainty.

Overwhelmed, he cradled her face between his hands and kissed her. "I love you, Addie."

"And your love is returned a hundred fold," she whispered with a beatific smile.

In complete accord, they slept dreaming of a young prince sometimes blond, sometimes dark with beautiful green eyes or deep blue eyes in turn.

The opportunity to talk to Trinity came the very next morning. Kolyn was lying under the goose-down duvet with his eyes still closed luxuriating in the warmth it provided. He could also feel the heat radiating from Addie. *She's like a little furnace*, he thought tenderly. Needing to see her, he opened his eyes and was startled to find his daughter standing across the bed watching Addie sleep. Immediately aware that her father was awake, she smiled happily and quietly went to his side of the bed. He smiled at his beloved daughter giving her a one-arm hug. Very gently, so as not to wake Addie, he helped her onto the bed. Like a kitten, she crept into the hollow formed by their bodies and snuggled there peacefully on top of the comforter, her little hand softly resting on Addie's cheek.

In a state of semi-consciousness, the latter stretched sensuously, a soft smile etched on her lips as she blindly extended a hand to caress him. When it met with an unexpected mass of long curls, her eyes popped open in surprise. There was Trinity staring at her! A delighted peal of laughter erupted from the little girl when she saw Addie's expression.

"You're not my husband!" she declared as she kissed her brow softly, simultaneously looking past Trinity's dark curls into Kolyn's deep blue eyes. The raw passion she saw there made her insides go soft as jelly.

He saw the hunger in her beautiful green eyes and shook his head regretfully eyeing the bundle between them. Addie smiled mischievously and moved her foot against his leg causing him to jump as if he'd just been electrocuted. In an unexpected move, he wriggled underneath Trinity dumping her to where he had just been and grabbed Addie in his warm arms. One squealed in protest, the other in delight. Laughing, he kissed her ardently as she tried in vain to free herself.

Unable to resist joining the game, Trinity launched herself on top of them, arms and legs spread-eagle pinning them down. Kolyn and Addie took one brief calculating look at each other and abruptly broke apart rolling to the side. As she sank in the middle, they rolled back, their arms locking above her effectively reversing the roles of captive and captured. Squirming onto her back, she smiled at them in ecstasy. She was right where she wanted to be and had both their attention – and they knew it too! The joy and happiness of being together more than made up for any scheming that might have taken place.

"Trinity," said Kolyn getting her attention, "how do you know Addie is going to have a baby?"

She looked at him seriously as if weighing something in her mind. "She is warmer and more beautiful," she finally answered with a tentative smile.

They digested this information silently as they stared at their daughter in amazement. *She's right*, reflected Kolyn. *I was just thinking she was like a little furnace and she does have a glow about her!*

"You're right," said Addie with a big smile. "And you are very perceptive, my little angel."

"We would like to keep this a secret between the three of us for now. Not everyone is as perceptive as we are and they may not understand," Kolyn explained.

"I know," she responded. The way she said that caused them to believe that she had already run into that kind of situation.

All three joined hands sealing their agreement. Then Addie said, "Trinity, know that you can always come to us and we will listen. Time and time again you have helped us with your knowledge. We trust you!"

"Thank-you, Mommy. I love you!" she said burying her face against her, her little body trembling slightly.

Addie stroked her hair gently as she exchanged a puzzled glance with Kolyn. After a short while, she rolled over to face her father and, as though to shock him, said, "I'm going to have a baby brother!"

Not fooled one bit knowing she was just testing their credibility, he told her with a grin, "Sweetheart, this time Addie beat you to the punch line! She told me so last night."

Surprised, she flipped back towards Addie and looking into her eyes, the worry and uncertainty that had been there earlier disappeared. She started to chuckle softly finally breaking into a free, liberating laugh.

They understand!

Smiling, they shooed her out of the room so they could get ready for the day.

When Mme Bastien saw them she called out cheerfully, "Bonjour mes amis. Le petit dejeuner vous attends!"

Addie's rudimentary knowledge of French was sufficient for her to understand that breakfast was waiting for them.

Giving her a wide smile, she said pleasantly, "Bonjour, Madame Bastien."

"Please call me Marguerite."

Kolyn beamed. *No one can resist her! With her charm she could probably raise the morale of a defeated army.* Then a new thought occurred to him – *What about our own people, the workers of Cebrae? They could use some help!* Deciding right there and then that she would accompany him when he next toured the island, it seemed like some of the depression that cloaked the Kingdom had suddenly lifted to a slight degree. *Together we can conquer universes*, he had said once. And he knew that to be true.

Ecstatic, he kissed the top of her head lightly. Her luminous eyes made him want to forget about breakfast. However, Mme Bastien was shepherding them to the table where Jo and Trinity were already feasting on warm croissants and homemade preserves.

With a light heart, Kolyn joined them. Looking forward into the future, his happiness knew no bounds. *Tomorrow we're going home. The Kingdom of Cebrae is going to flourish and prosper! I have found the love of my life and my family is secure... A son!*

_____

Read on for an excerpt from

The Kingdom of Cebrae

the amazing sequel to
Prince Kolyn and Princess Addie's
legendary love and power.

Coming in November 2011

Addie woke up early and quietly got out of bed not wanting to wake Kolyn who was still sleeping peacefully. She slipped on her robe and headed to the kitchen. *He said I could see the sun in the morning.* There was sufficient light in the kitchen to prevent her from stubbing a toe on something. As she looked out the window, she was astounded by the beauty of the sunrise. Enchanted, she stood there watching the sun creep up over the horizon, the morning pinks slowly fading away. Finally a ray of sunshine burst into the room. Pushing the table aside, she slowly began to twirl in the shaft of light, her arms outstretched, head tilted back with her eyes half closed.

Kolyn found her dancing in the light like a forest nymph, her long blond hair glinting as it caught the sunlight. Spellbound, he revelled in her grace and beauty, his deep blue eyes soft and tender. Noiselessly, he crossed the intervening space and wrapped his arms around her, matching her steps.

"Kolyn!" she breathed. The love in her beautiful green eyes sent his heart in his throat as he lowered his head to kiss her upturned face. Coming to a stop, he caressed her warm silken hair, his happiness knowing no bounds.

"Good morning, Princess," he said tenderly.

"Good morning, Kolyn," she responded with a dazzling smile. "You can really see the sun from here and the sunrise was spectacular!"

"Yes, my little wood nymph!" he said, once again reminded of her love for the simple and natural things in life. "Would you like to go for a walk with me before breakfast?"

"I'd love to and we could take Zeus along. I'm pretty sure he'll be ecstatic!"

"No doubt!" he agreed wryly. "All right then, let's see who can get dressed the fastest!"

Giving him an impish grin, Addie raced to the bedroom only to come to a dead halt.

"No fair," she cried out in dismay, "I don't know where my things are!"

Laughing, he teased, "Guess I win then!"

The walk-in closet was huge but she managed to find a pair of jeans and a top and was ready in a very short time. Taking in her form-fitting jeans, Kolyn gave her an enigmatic glance as he silently handed her a light windbreaker. *We're going to have to adjust her wardrobe in a few months.*

They quietly made their way out of the castle and headed to the greenhouse where Zeus slept at night. When they opened the door, he was already there waiting for them. He shot past them only to spin around and come racing back at full speed, barking in ecstasy.

"Hush, you little monster," said Addie affectionately as she gave him a hug. "You'll wake everyone up!"

He followed her in as she went to get his leash, trotting nicely at her side and sat quietly enough while she attached it, looking at her with adoring eyes. She was surprised when he heeled beautifully, not tugging on the leash in the least.

"Has someone been training him?" she asked curiously.

"Not that I know of unless Sean has. He certainly didn't behave that well yesterday when I took him out!" he disclosed with a grin.

They walked a short distance from the greenhouse and stopped in order to decide in which direction to go. Addie looked at Zeus and he promptly sat on his haunches. Puzzled by his exemplary behaviour, she turned to question Kolyn again but he was standing there his eyes wide with surprise.

"What did you just do to make him sit?" he asked in amazement.

"Nothing – I just looked at him. I was thinking he should sit though."

"You were *thinking* he should sit?" he repeated in a daze. For a moment, he stared at her and then started chuckling, his deep blue eyes twinkling with merriment.

"What's so funny?" she asked, a little put out.

"Addie," he said as he took her in his arms, "you are absolutely amazing! You either can communicate with animals or he can read your mind!"

Startled by his observation, she stood there wondering if this had ever happened before when all of a sudden she broke out in a fit of laughter. It was his turn to be put out.

With tears in her eyes, she explained, "It's a good thing I didn't try that with Nolan when I first met him on the sidewalk!"

Immediately seeing the hilarity of getting Nolan to *sit,* he burst out laughing. It was all they could do to stay upright as their imagination ran wild. Wiping the tears from their eyes, they stood facing each other, exhilarated.

"I have so much fun with you, Addie," he declared pressing a kiss on her temple. Catching her hand, he added, "Come, I will show you my favourite spot on this island. It's about a 20-minute walk from here."

The walk was mostly uphill as they crossed the airport road and entered the forest. Addie was starting to feel the heat in her legs when Kolyn suddenly announced that they were almost there. She heard the rush of a waterfall and she felt a change in the air even though they were still surrounded by tall trees with huge trunks.

"Addie, close your eyes," he requested as he moved in front of her blocking her view. "It's only a few more feet and I will guide you."

Trusting him, she held out her hand and closed her eyes. Unable to resist, Kolyn lowered his dark head and softly touched his lips to hers in a brief kiss. A sweet smile formed on her lips although she did not open her eyes.

Holding her hand securely, he led her about 3 meters and then, moving behind her, his arms securely wrapped about her waist, he whispered against her cheek, "Okay, my love, you may open your eyes."

Her beautiful green eyes opened wide in wonder as she took in the scene in front of her. "Wo-o-w!" she whispered reverently not wanting to disturb the peace of this little oasis.

The cliffs had abruptly ended and a small waterfall was delicately misting the air around them as it fell some

8-10 meters. Encircling the pool formed at the bottom of the fall were tall trees holding out long strands of vines gently swinging in the light breeze. But what took her breath away were the banks. Pale lavender and white flowers covered the bed of deep green moss that reached into the clear pool.

"This is so beautiful," she whispered in awe. "Where does the water come from?"

"That's a good question. I tried to follow it to its source once, but it didn't go very far. About 300 meters that way," he said pointing northwest, "the water comes out of the cliff face. There must be an interesting rock formation under these cliffs causing sufficient pressure to create this small waterfall."

Wanting to get an even better view, she looked back at Kolyn and asked, "Is it safe to go near the edge?"

He assured her it was rock solid and that he would often sit dangling his legs over the edge. As they took a step in that direction, Zeus, who had collapsed at her feet earlier, suddenly stood on all fours watching her warily. Another step and he was whimpering and whining in protest. Wondering what was bothering him, she glanced back at him and he let out one sharp warning bark.

"I don't think he's too happy with you going in this direction," Kolyn commented.

Smiling at the puppy's protest, they nonetheless took another step toward the cliff's edge. At that, Zeus ran to her and grabbed the heel of her running shoe in his mouth, growling furiously as he tried to pull her back.

Puzzled and slightly concerned, she asked, "What's wrong Zeus?" In response, he let go of her heel and scurried in front of her, pressing his shaking body against her legs.

Addie started backing up cautiously, dragging Kolyn with her till they were a little further back than from where they had started. Sitting down, she petted the trembling dog as she murmured, "You're trying to protect me." He licked her hand, his dark eyes liquid soft as he looked at her.

Sitting down next to her, Kolyn was very thoughtful as he pulled out an apple from his pocket. Deftly, he cut it in half with his jackknife and silently handed a piece to Addie. *I'm going to come back and check out this ledge. It's been over a year since I was here last.*

"Thanks," she said absentmindedly, biting into her piece. *Animals are very sensitive to danger. I wonder if the ledge is not as safe as it seems. He was very upset.*

"This place is really quite peaceful," she remarked, feeling better after eating her apple. "How did you find it?"

"I was nine years old. It was the summer before my last year at the boarding school. My father was mostly ignoring me; I had no one to play with and was quite miserable. I had decided to run away and find some adventure of my own so I set out through the forest with a little backpack filled with goodies I had stolen from the kitchen, my knife and a water bottle. I was lost in no time. It seemed like every tree was like every other tree," he said chuckling at the memory. "I was quite discouraged as I sat munching on my umpteenth Oreo cookie. That's when I heard the water. I ended up staying by the pool for most of the afternoon until

I realized it would be dark soon. Somehow, I found my way to the coastline by following a creek. Half the kingdom was looking for me by then. Let's just say that I was effectively grounded after that little escapade. I actually got a lot of people in trouble that time," he concluded ruefully.

Addie chuckled, "Let's hope our kids are not that miserable that they wish to run away on an island."

"You sure have a way of putting things in perspective," he said laughing. Getting up, he pulled Addie to her feet and into his arms. "I could stay here with you all day but we need to have breakfast and then there's the meeting at 10."

Coiling her arms around his neck, she kissed him tenderly and said, "Thank-you for showing me this beautiful place. I really enjoyed this time with you."

"My wonderful wife, the pleasure is all mine," he murmured against her lips. "Every day we will spend some time together, just the two of us... and maybe Zeus," he promised contentedly.

Grasping her hand firmly in his, he led the way out of the forest. They had gone only a short ways when Addie confided out of the blue, "I'm glad you didn't send Trinity to a boarding school."

"Me too – but I'm curious as to why you feel that way."

Pausing, she said, "I think it would have been very hard on her. She's very bright, for one, and that alone would have set her apart plus she's extremely sensitive to others' emotions whether good or bad. Children – and adults too, I guess – can be quite mean when they sense that someone is different." Her beautiful green eyes bore into his as she continued softly, "But the thing that would have been the most devastating for her is that she thinks the world of you and it would have broken her heart to be separated from her father."

Overwhelmed by her understanding, Kolyn mutely cradled Addie in his arms, unable to voice anything for the lump in his throat. Gently caressing her jaw with his thumb, he whispered, "Addie, every day I find more and more reasons to love you. It would also break my heart to be separated from my daughter but I think I would die if I couldn't be with you."

Cupping his handsome face in her hands, she whispered fiercely, "I don't think I could bear to be away from you," her eyes bright with emotion. "I love you so much, Kolyn!"

No matter how many times she told him, the effect was always the same. As he touched his lips to hers, his chest expanded trying to contain the love in his heart but failing, he exploded out of his head. Addie was waiting for him and as they united, a feeling of serenity and timelessness enveloped them.

A sharp yip brought them back to planet Earth. Hands linked, they peacefully continued their journey back to the castle.

"Can I tell others about this special place?" she asked.

"Yes, but not until I've checked out the safety of that ledge," he said. "I wouldn't want anyone to get hurt."

"Okay – I won't mention it until you tell me it's safe."

Knowing that checking it out wasn't without some risk, her unquestioning acceptance to his proposed endeavour surprised him.

"Aren't you going to tell me to be careful or that it's too dangerous or something?"

Laughing gently, she said, "No – I imagine you've already figured out how you're going to handle it and I trust you to keep yourself safe."

Smiling at her, he said, "You're right on both counts!"

They had almost reached the airport road when he said, "Your vote of confidence really got me thinking."

She glanced at him inquiringly.

"You see, when I give an order, it is usually followed implicitly as they all know I would never order something that would endanger someone. Also, I choose who I give my orders to knowing it is in their capacity or realm of activity to get done. But when *I* decide I want to do something a little out of the ordinary with *possibly* an element of risk or danger, I immediately get half a dozen people trying to dissuade me of the idea, pointing out the potential dangers, reminding me that I'm a prince and heir, etc. By the time they're done, I'm not interested in doing it anymore." Taking a breath, he continued, "Now, your unconditional acceptance of my actions has put me in an incredibly good mood. I feel smart, capable and above all like a MAN – not a prince, not an heir! It is so liberating!"

By the time he was done talking, he was practically prancing with joy. Hauling Addie against his lean body, he kissed her soundly declaring, "You are good for the soul!"

Laughing like kids plotting on how to get in trouble, they finally reached their destination and dropped off Zeus at the greenhouse. After making sure he had food and water, they met up with Sean who was just arriving.

"Have you been giving Zeus obedience lessons?" she asked him after the usual morning greetings.

"Not at all, princess. I wouldn't know where to start," he admitted honestly.

She glanced at Kolyn who was just grinning widely, looking extremely pleased about something. Sean looked from one to the other, puzzled.

"Why? Did he do something wrong?"

"Not in the least – in fact, he behaved extremely well for Addie this morning," Kolyn said giving her a smug smile.

Wrinkling her nose at him, she said jokingly, "Don't you dare spread rumours about me!"

He gave Sean a wink and said, "They have an *uncanine* ability to understand each other!"

At that, Addie grabbed his hand and said laughing, "Come on – let's go eat. I'm starved."

Leaving Sean staring after them, they went in for breakfast. Jo, Trinity and the Dubois were just sitting down for breakfast when they arrived. The discussion was lively and animated. Apparently, the Dubois were also attending the meeting at 10. Trinity pouted when Kolyn told her she couldn't come.

"I don't want to do my classes this morning!" she protested.

Addie winked at him thinking, "*Let me handle this.*" He smiled broadly and sat back in his chair leaving it in her capable hands. He had no doubt she wouldn't give in to his daughter's whims and he also knew that everyone would be happy with whatever compromise was arrived at.

"Trinity, are you thinking of dropping your classes because you want to spend time with us?" she asked shrewdly.

With a sad, pathetic look that would have melted anyone's heart, she nodded wordlessly. Fully understanding her desire, Addie felt empathy for her daughter. Being an only child had not been easy but her mother had always made time in her busy schedule to do things with her. Those were the most precious memories of her childhood. *Now, I'm her mother.*

Choosing her words carefully as she didn't want to make a promise she couldn't keep, she said, "This morning's schedule will remain as planned – you go to your classes and we go to our meeting but this afternoon, I'd like to spend some time with just you. Maybe you can think of something you'd like to do."

Beaming at the thought of having Addie to herself, she jumped off her chair and hugged her around the waist.

"Thank-you, Mommy! I'll think of something." Happy with the way things had turn out, she looked at her father and said seriously, "I should get ready for my classes, now."

The pride and joy in his deep blue eyes was unmistakable and it took all his willpower not to start laughing.

Giving her a bright smile, he asked, "Can I have a hug too?"

Laughing, she threw herself in his arms and hugged him fiercely. "I love you, Papa and I love Addie!" she whispered.

Dropping a kiss on the top of her head, he whispered back, "I love you too, my precious daughter."

Contented, she left the room humming a tune under her breath. Mr and Mrs Dubois smiled knowingly at each other. *That was a great solution. She is so perceptive!* Jo, on the other hand, was looking at Addie wistfully.

"Kolyn," said Addie, breaking the peaceful silence, "I don't mean to put you on the spot but I have a special request."

Raising an eyebrow, he nodded for her to continue.

She caught Jo's eye before saying, "We didn't get to finish our last few months of school and I was wondering if —."

"—you could finish it here," he concluded for her. "I was wondering when you'd bring that up!" Seeing their surprised expressions, he winked at Mr Dubois and announced smugly, "We took the liberty of contacting your school and arrangements have been made for both of you to complete your final year through correspondence. You just need to log on!"

The girls erupted in cheers. After the most suitable and appropriate thanks to Kolyn and Jo's parents, they split up to get ready for the meeting.